THE
BROKEN SWORD

A Novel of the
American War for Independence at Sea

C. D. White

FIRESIDE FICTION
2006

FIRESIDE FICTION
AN IMPRINT OF HERITAGE BOOKS, INC.

Books, CDs, and more—Worldwide

For our listing of thousands of titles see our website
at
www.HeritageBooks.com

Published 2006 by
HERITAGE BOOKS, INC.
Publishing Division
65 East Main Street
Westminster, Maryland 21157-5026

International Standard Book Number: 978-0-7884-3585-X

Author's Note

The early history of the American Navy is replete with color. The dashing exploits of men like Lambert Wickes, Gustavus Conyngham, and America's own Nelson, John Paul Jones, have occupied the fancy of many a modern armchair sailor. The tremendous odds faced, the extraordinary close-calls, and the tragic setbacks, are certainly ingredients for thrilling tales. It is fair to say that the author was most fortunate in the rich background that has served as his inspiration.

This volume is the first in a series that follows the protagonist Jack Cunningham through the bloody years of the American War for Independence. While Cunningham is fictional, the seas on which he sails are quite real. The Virginia Tidewater in the early autumn of 1775 was a turbulent and chaotic territory. Loyalties were very far from being decided. Many Virginians still entertained hopes for a peaceful reconciliation with King George III, laying most of the blame for the simmering conflict on the doorstep of England's parliament. To capture this reality I have made Jack a man marked by these deeply divided loyalties. He is not your knee-jerk patriot but rather a complex man who pledges his allegiance thoughtfully. While he may be accurately called a citizen of the world, he is ultimately wed to the land of his heart.

Since Jack is a sailor, the language he uses is sufficiently (and perhaps cryptically) technical. For the more lubberly reader I have included a brief glossary of sailing terms in the desire to make the Age of Sail mariner's world more accessible.

I would like to thank Newt Smith, Jubal Tiner, and Mary Adams for their close reading and incisive comments. Their professionalism served as a strong model for the book in its current form. And, of course, to Sarah York: for standing me ever in good stead.

C.D. White
Cullowhee, NC

1. PLAYERS UPON A STAGE

THE Virginia Governor Lord Dunmore stood musing at the taffrail of His Majesty's Sloop *King's Fisher*, squinting against the evening sun, his watery blue eyes always sensitive to sunlight reflected on the water. Very good that he had not been a sailor, he thought; all that time glaring into resplendent horizons would probably have blinded him before he was thirty. He reached into the front pocket of his bottle green frock coat, a little worse for the wear from his warring against the Shawnee the summer before, and drew out a trinket enveloped by his huge fist. Slowly, he opened his hand and gazed down at the detailed miniature of a lovely blonde woman set in a silver oval frame. Her eyes were bright but sad, a touch of undeniable weariness pulling the luster if not the frankness from her gaze. The woman was his wife, Lady Dunmore, still one of the renowned beauties of the American colonies, even after reaching middle age and claiming motherhood eleven times over.

How desperately he missed her and their children, though it had been only ten days since their departure. Still, he knew it was undoubtedly for the best to send them home to London. Twice already they had barely escaped with their lives from the angry mobs of Virginian rebels, and Lord Dunmore was loathe to give his enemies another opportunity to wound him in the one place it would truly matter. He did not doubt for a second that the insurgent rascals would seize any chance to inflict unspeakable horrors against those he loved, so blindly they had come to hate him.

Lord Dunmore paced away from the rail and crossed the wide deck, feeling far too old and ill-used. He swatted his rolled up copy of *The Virginia Gazette* against his outer thigh, fuming over what blatant sedition he had just read. He swore to himself that he would see these men and those who pulled their strings paid back for their impertinence. Of course it did not surprise him, accustomed as he was with the paper's foolish insistence on defaming his good name.

There were, of course, far greater concerns than the petty bickerings of newspaper men. If he did not move decisively very soon to end the rise of rebellious forces, all the power he still held in Virginia would be lost. And yet, how could their Lordships in parliament honestly expect him to move with authority when they had all but abandoned him to his own devices, effectively binding his hands? What counsel had he received in the past year? Only to seize and control any munitions which might be commandeered by the Virginian rebels. There were no recommendations for how to execute the plan without provoking hysteria among the colonials. When he had honored the directive on April 21st and ordered the casks of gun powder housed in the Williamsburg magazine moved to the English schooner *Magdalen* moored at Burwell's Landing on the James River, the action had touched off an outcry which surprised even Dunmore in its ferocity. Paranoia consumed the populace as rumor spread that the magazine seizure was a prelude to full-scale British invasion. Thank God that Peyton Randolph, though a cunning and generally disagreeable agitator, had stepped in and quieted the unruly mass. Otherwise they would have torn Dunmore and his family from limb to limb in their mob's fury.

Dunmore shuddered at the memory, remembering just how close he had come to ordering his staff into flight the very day Randolph had met with him in May at the Governor's Palace. That morning he had watched with silent shock as an assembly of over two hundred men and boys congregated on the mansion's front yard and swung a straw effigy of the Governor from the limb of a huge oak tree, the crowd shrieking with delight when the weak straw neck parted from the noose and the decapitated torso thudded against the ground.

Such ingratitude distressed Lord Dunmore. Was it not these very same Virginians screaming for his blood who had followed him into the western territory the summer before to war against the Shawnee Indians? Had he not led them to victory after victory, stopping the encroaching savages at every turn, opening up the western territory for strong-hearted men willing to carve a life out of the forbidding wilderness? And yet it had all gone so terribly wrong so swiftly.

His sullen thoughts were interrupted by the soft-footed approach of the captain's steward, a tall hollow-faced man with a straw hat tucked neatly under his arm.

"Pardon me, my Lord," he knuckled his forehead tentatively, apparently uncertain of the formal courtesy due the governor's civilian post. "Captain Montagu sends word that the evening meal is ready."

"Hmmm, oh yes, thank you Ringle," Lord Dunmore answered, surfacing from his abstraction. He returned the miniature to his coat pocket and followed the steward to the sloop's great cabin, trying as best as he might to push back his worries.

Lord Dunmore entered the cabin without knocking, already grown accustomed to Captain James Montagu's warm hospitality despite having kept quarters aboard the *King's Fisher* for only a few days. It had been a radical change from the treatment he had received aboard the *Mercury* at the hands of Captain John MacCartney. He despised lingering over the thought of that disreputable man's name for more than the briefest moment. MacCartney's feet-dragging and ambiguous attitudes towards the rebels were incomprehensible. Lord Dunmore had heard some of the locals considered the scoundrel MacCartney a hero to their cause when he made it publicly known he would not offer safe haven for any escaped slaves. This, of course, flew in the teeth of Lord Dunmore's decree that any disaffected Negroes seeking asylum should be offered the chance to enlist as soldiers in His Majesty's armed forces. Yet, with a few off hand remarks MacCartney had added to the public shaming of the governor and given the upstart rebels the foolish, not to mention dangerous, belief that the Royal Navy sympathized with their cause.

James Montagu, however, was a different sort of man altogether. Young and resourceful, full of English pluck and resolve, Lord Dunmore could not hope for a more able or willing officer to aid in his campaign to regain executive power. Such commendable traits obviously ran in the family. It was James Montagu's own elder brother, Captain George Montagu, who had been a stalwart supporter of the governor early on in the crisis. He and his crew of HMS *Magdalen* had faithfully served Dunmore as his eyes and ears in the lower Chesapeake Bay, responsive to whatever duty he might require of him. It had been a shame to lose the elder Montagu to the whim of Admiral Graves when he had ordered the *Magdalen* to New York. Fortunately, Lord Dunmore had been shrewd enough to seize the opportunity to put his family aboard the Captain Montagu's ship and send them back to London by presenting the officer with dispatches addressed personally to Lord North which, he claimed, included time sensitive material that was far more pressing than any orders the admiral had given. Lord Dunmore fully expected Admiral Graves to raise an indignant cry when he discovered one of his ships was on the wrong side of the Atlantic, but that was an impediment which would have to be surmounted in its own good time.

For the present, there were far more pressing issues to consider, and foremost of these was to satisfy his freshly awakened appetite. Steam wreathed Captain Montagu's elegantly set table, carrying the many splendid aromas of the evening dinner. James Montagu stood and waved diffidently to the chair at the table's head.

"Good evening, my Lord. I am pleased you are able to dine with me this evening. I hope my exclusive company will not be too boring for you. My officers are inspecting their divisions as we speak to keep the men toeing the line in case they think that riding at anchor is a justification for sloth."

Lord Dunmore nodded approvingly, grateful that James Montagu was a taut hand at discipline, a far too rare quality among naval commanders these days, he feared. "Not at all, captain. I should very much prefer a simple meal with good company. I find the social pressure to entertain with flights of discourse often contrary to the rules of healthy digestion," he finished lamely, his sorely tried strength betraying a waver in his voice.

"Are you all right, Sir?" Captain Montagu asked with concern as he resumed his seat, studying the governor's ashen face. "Are you having trouble sleeping? If your quarters are not to your liking I can see that more care is taken in your accommodations. If it is a medical problem, I could send word for the surgeon to prescribe a physic."

"No, no, captain, I am quite fine," Lord Dunmore said, anxious to put any petty concerns about his personal well-being to the side, gently raising the silver dome on a platter of roasted kidneys and scooping them liberally onto his china plate. The captain's steward was immediately at his side filling his crystal glass with a fine amber Madeira. He lifted the glass in cursory salute and drank.

"I see you have been reading the local gossip," Montagu said, indicating the broadside Lord Dunmore had absently placed beside him on the table, the dateline at its masthead reading July 21st, 1775.

"Ah, yes, that." He considered making an offhand remark disparaging the paper's main article, but preferred instead not to invite embarrassment at the dinner table or to court further aggravation, letting the subject drop. Yet while Montagu took the hint and chatted on pleasantly about inconsequential events, Lord Dunmore's mind stubbornly lingered on the content of the article which had distressed him earlier.

Perhaps the matter could not properly be called slander since the article did take its account from the governor's own words, an excerpt from a letter he had written to the British Prime Minister Lord North seven months earlier in December of 1774. The main effect of the article was that Dunmore had suggested a blockade of the Virginia Capes by a small squadron of British war ships to prevent Virginians from exporting their goods, particularly tobacco, to nations other than England. Dunmore had made the recommendation on the knowledge that the Virginia House of Burgesses had passed a resolution which would ban all exports to England as of September 10, 1775, a date now just over a month away. The Virginians self-imposed ban was their way of protesting the punitive acts leveled against the colony of Massachusetts for her involvement in the Boston Tea Rebellion. It was a variation on an old trick the colonials had used before to express their dissatisfaction with the ministerial government. In the past they had leveled boycotts on English goods, most notably to express their outrage over the Stamp Act. And because of the weak-willed parliament it had always worked, always bent the ear of the King, and always given the colonials more power than they could handle.

Lord Dunmore shoved his plate away and caught a heavy sigh, his bitter reflection overwhelming the otherwise pleasing ambience of the meal.

"Is there something wrong, my Lord?" Montagu asked, sincerely troubled by Lord Dunmore's disrupted state of mind. "If there is something else my cook could prepare more to your liking..."

"No, no, not at all, Captain, the meal is splendid," he interrupted gruffly. "I'm afraid I make for poor company this evening. Far worse than I have any right to be given the surroundings."

The cabin fell uncomfortably silent, the only sounds the gentle pings of Montagu's silverware against his china. Lord Dunmore emptied his glass and called for the steward to refill it, scraping his chair across the bare deck and pacing restlessly to the stern galley window, gazing through its gently curved frame at the busy shipping lanes of Norfolk harbor.

"How do the new marines look in your professional opinion, Captain? Enough to return the rebels to their backwoods nest," he laughed dryly, without humor.

"They are good men, my Lord. Though, as you well know, hardly enough to outfit a garrison. I do have hopes, however, that it is the first trickle in a more considerable reservoir of reinforcements. I am certain Admiral Graves understands the difficult nature of our situation."

Lord Dunmore exhaled a profanity, though he chose to discreetly refrain from any further comments regarding his view of the commanding admiral's take on the "situation." Sixty lobster backs transferred from the fort at Saint Augustine was the grand sum the admiral had ordered to deal with the crisis in Virginia and that only after months of practically begging for assistance!

"I pray that you are right, Captain Montagu. However, if you are not I am afraid I may be forced to resort to more drastic measures in terms of dealing with these rebels' abuse of my patience."

Captain Montagu visibly tensed at Lord Dunmore's words.

"You mean the slaves, my Lord?"

"Aye, I mean the slaves. Perhaps it would teach these Virginian upstarts a proper lesson if I carried through with my threats!" he retorted more harshly than he intended.

Dunmore knew that there was nothing the colonials feared more than a slave uprising. If Admiral Graves failed to supply him with a viable fighting force there was already a large and eager pool of able-bodied men who could be trained into a terrifying army. He needed only a few officers of faultless loyalty to lead them and he could soon restore Virginia to her peaceful submission to King George and his ministerial government. Yet the political implications of such a move would surely resonate, Lord Dunmore considered bitterly, his resolve diminishing. Such a plan discomfited even men as devoted to the cause as James Montagu, he could see, the young man's nervous manner impossible to conceal now that the issued had been broached.

But it *could* work, Lord Dunmore considered as he gazed on the indigo waters of the roadstead. It could be precisely the venture that would frighten the rebels into submission. If only he could find a few stout hearts to back him who might lead such an army of freed slaves against the lawless Virginians. It would have to be the Scots, the merchants who prospered from the colonial markets as they were and who had no firm roots tying them to sentimental notions of colonial independence. Men who would identify with him as a fellow Scotsman and true patriots of Britain. Only with such a loyal corps of men could he hope to brook the tide of unrest.

"You seem to be feeling better, my Lord," Captain Montagu noted Dunmore's reflective expression suddenly overspread with triumph.

"Yes, I am indeed, Captain," Lord Dunmore chuckled and clapped his hands sharply together, already beginning to lay plans for his return to the Old Dominion of Virginia...

2. A STRANGE SAIL

"PASS the word for Captain Cunningham!"

A ship's boy leapt past coils of stowed cordage on his way from the schooner's forecastle down the aft companionway. The sounds of the building seas quaked beneath the vessel's timbers as the merchant schooner listed to one side with the arrival of freshening winds. Yet little Davy Yeoman, a roguish and foolhardy lad of twelve years, did not pay heed to the fickle laws of gravity at sea. Before the boy could slow his careening gait and halt just short of the captain's great cabin door, the deck lurched mightily, slamming the child head first into the oaken portal.

A moment later Captain Cunningham swung the door open, his massive frame filling the entryway from deck to lintel post. He was a dark, wild-haired man with a deep sailor's chest and a kind, if somewhat mocking smile. He turned this smile down on the boy now, lifting the child's chin to get a closer look at his bludgeoned forehead.

"Well, Mister Yeoman, and what might be the cause of this haste? Pirates preparing to board, perhaps?" he questioned in his soft burr.

"Sir," Davy rebutted, removing his chin indignantly from Captain Cunningham's rough hand. "Mister MacDonald sends word for you on deck. The sail to windward has closed. She's come hull up. "

"Very well, I will be up directly. Please see to having that wound bandaged up. It will not answer if sawbones finds a need to amputate that particular diseased limb," Cunningham cautioned, pointing his forefinger at the boy's brow.

Davy swallowed hard and placed a hand protectively over his throat. "Aye, Captain."

Captain Cunningham turned and pulled his great coat from its peg after tossing off what remained of his porter. He struggled to swallow the bitter stuff down without wincing, knowing that he should have thought better than to buy beer off a smuggler. God only knew how old it might be, though Jack suspected the Seven Years War not an unlikely date of origin. He set the pewter tankard on the end of his desk next to the small open cask and reached into his wardrobe for his hat.

"Is there something further I can do for you, Mister Yeoman?" Cunningham asked the lingering boy, trying to keep irritation out of his voice.

The scrawny child raised his head ever so slightly as he peered around his captain. Jack shifted to one side, his gaze falling on the empty mug and the full cask next to it. He remembered his own precocious habits as a cabin boy and his tendency to always seek out whatever elusive mischief might be close at hand.

"Are you a drunkard, Mister Yeoman?" Jack asked curtly, testing his cabin boy's composure.

"W-why, no, Cap'n Cunningham, it's just that I," Davy stammered, leveling a gaze of apology.

"Here," Jack pinched the pewter rim between his fingers and flipped the tankard toward Davy, the boy's bright brown eyes fluttering with gratitude. "But if you fall from the crosstrees from being three sheets to the wind, I'll not answer to your father, understand?"

"Aye, Cap'n, aye!"

"You drink it in here with the door closed. Can't have every man jack thinking the Captain is going soft on discipline now can we?" Jack said, ushering Davy into his cabin and throwing him a conspiratorial wink.

Cunningham knew his ship well, and as he stamped forward along the berthing deck he noted a deep trembling down in the futtocks, a shuddering in the keel. The ocean had shifted and grown more powerful, showing herself to be a dangerous slumbering monster slowly coming to life. Evidently the readings of the afternoon's falling glass were bearing true. Jack could feel the change even more strongly as he climbed up the companionway and crossed to the weather side of the small quarterdeck. It was not so much that the outward signs of the weather and sea had altered in the half hour's time he had been dining in his cabin, but there was a subtle alteration in the feel of things, difficult to name yet definite. A purple twilight had begun to settle in, Venus already drawing away on her celestial trail before the waning half moon. Jack came a few steps forward and hunched over the schooner's binnacle box, squinting under the dim lantern light to study the compass card as it drifted off on a northeastern line. The coastal schooner wallowed on the heavy running sea. To the west a low smear of advancing storm clouds flashed briefly, electrically pregnant.

The building westerly winds were making all kinds of hell on the schooner's larboard quarter by beating the sea up into a contentious corkscrewing motion, causing many nervous looks among the crew. Some of the expressions belonged to well-seasoned hands, others to boys new to the maritime trade, but all betraying the unmistakable appearance of distress. They frowned and spoke to one another in mutters, sharing their reservations. Captain Cunningham ordered lifelines strung, knowing that if they came too close to the approaching storm, the sailing could become treacherous. It was also good to keep the men busy, their minds distracted from fears which he or they were powerless to prevent. Normally in such weather Cunningham would have brought the *Norfolk Gold* as close to the wind as she could sail to deflect its main force, but the rocky Virginia coast was far too close. If the wind veered or a squall bore down on them from the north, they could easily find themselves broken against a lee shore.

Cunningham glanced back over his shoulder at the white speck upon the dark waters. Having enough to contend with just now, Cunningham did not care for this mysterious pursuer or what mischief she might be intent on visiting. The strange sail had closed a remarkable distance since he had last been on deck. He lifted his telescope from the rack and laid aft to better study the unknown vessel. The small craft had stood off and on away from the starboard quarter at about a mile and a half for most of the afternoon, mirroring the *Norfolk Gold*'s course, careful never to come close enough to warrant concern. But now she had committed and appeared to have every intention of closing the schooner before making landfall.

Better always to have plenty of sea room if possible, Jack thought as he leaned his elbows to the rail and sighted through his old brass telescope. Though its lens was badly scratched and it often collapsed at impractical times, he had steadily refused to surrender the trusted piece. Ten years as a successful merchant captain had made Cunningham into a superstitious man and he was loathe to give up the tools that had so often stood him in good stead.

The image of the vessel, a single masted cutter, bobbed momentarily in Cunningham's scope before a wave broke across the quarterdeck, the frothy summer sea rising up. He held fast to the lifeline as an unexpected deluge swept over him, feeling the rope stretched taut and stressed to its limits. He wiped the slimy water away from his eyes and coughed up a mouthful of the brackish sea before again settling the scope on the ship, finding it more difficult to keep the glass fixed as the howling wind propelled a growing range of large waves that buffeted the schooner in wide arcs.

The cutter's fancy dark rubbing strake and stout mast were unfamiliar. Jack knew the lines of the local trader vessels and the Virginia Royal Governor's ships well enough to know that this cutter was not one of them. Her heavy spars were well-suited for the hard weather of an Atlantic crossing, the very reason she handled superbly in the present weather. A momentary orange bloom flashed just aft of the cutter's bowsprit and the flat hollow report of her bow chaser coughed. The ball splashed harmlessly astern, the range comfortably beyond the limits of the six pound cannon at approximately seven hundred yards. Yet her captain had made his desire for the *Norfolk Gold* to come into the wind and heave to unmistakable.

Captain Cunningham tucked the glass into the front pocket of his great coat. Studying the cutter with his naked eye, he considered how to best proceed, entertaining the idea that he might make a run for the cloudbanks to shake her. Something about the cutter disquieted him, though he could not determine exactly what it might be. The coaster might very well be part of a new English naval force sent out in the two weeks Jack had been in North Carolina loading rice. If that were so then he would be doing a very imprudent thing by ignoring her command to lie to. She could also be a new revenuer sent to keep smugglers out of the Chesapeake. It would not be the first time King George would have seen fit to place one of his deputies in the colonial backwaters to keep tabs on whom was observing the rules of commercial transit. Cunningham did not care at all for British naval interference with his comings and goings, but, as a good subject of the crown, he had nothing to fear from it either. An English ensign broke out from the cutter's flag halyards, as if to answer Cunningham's unspoken question. The alternative that he most feared was that the cutter was a warship flying false colors. He recalled some loose talk he had heard in Wilmington among his fellow merchant captains of rebel colonials sporadically raiding Loyalist commerce. Jack had not taken the rumors very seriously at the time, but the persistent chase of the strange cutter gave him reason to be wary. No man in his right mind would risk a pursuit in such foreboding waters and conditions unless the stakes were high.

Mister MacDonald appeared at the rail beside him, panting from his arduous climb up the steeply heeled deck. How the old man managed such physical demands at his advanced age remained a marvel to Cunningham. Jack had a rare affection for the old man not common among business partners. Alan MacDonald had served as the leading agent for Wallace and Associates for the better part of three decades, running the river routes of the Virginia Tidewater when Jack was still a child. The old man was not a proper seaman in any ordinary sense, charged instead with the arrangement of transporting goods to and from the trading house in Norfolk, in effect the supercargo of the schooner. However, his many years working closely with merchant captains on the shipping lanes had lent him a unique knowledge of the Chesapeake Bay and her navigable tributaries.

MacDonald sighted down on the cutter through his spyglass, biting the long whiskers curling up from beneath his bottom lip. He liked to call the gesture "tasting his salt," a practice he attended with grave ceremony.

"How far from Point Malachai do you put us?" Jack asked.

"Hard to say, Captain. One reckoning could be as good as another."

If there was enough sea room from the point, Cunningham could order the schooner on a due North course, bringing it into a line of shoals which the deeper bellied cutter would be unable to navigate. If not, the schooner could all too easily find itself trapped in a bottlenecked channel.

"What do you say to joining me for a tot in my cabin, Alan? I believe we have another half hour or more before we need to make any unavoidable decisions," Jack said with an effort of nonchalance. He suspected that Alan could read his apprehension under the mask of indifference, though, to his credit, MacDonald did not betray any undue concern.

"Aye, Captain, Old Isaac needs some time at the conn at any rate," he nodded favorably at the huge bald black man stationed at the helm. "He has to keep up his time at the wheel if he ever figures on learning the ins and outs of this old barky," he added with a stab at humor. This drew out smiles from Isaac and Jack, the men shipmates for far longer than any of them cared to remember. Jack told Isaac that he was to be summoned if anything further developed. Stepping back, he led MacDonald below deck to the great cabin.

Remembering that he had left his cabin boy in charge of the porter cask, Jack hurried to get to the door ahead of his first officer to forestall any embarrassing scene of debauchery. Thankfully, however, Mister Yeoman had exercised commendable restraint and left the pieces of Jack's living quarters reasonably in place. Jack circled around his rough hewn desk and pulled a jug of lukewarm coffee from a small pantry and poured it out into a pair of clay mugs, warming the stale drink with a thimble full of dark Jamaican rum and handing the spiked stimulant to an appreciative MacDonald. Jack sipped his coffee and crossed the small day cabin to a commode sized cabinet with blue double hanging doors to look inside at a honeycomb of rolled charts. Running his eyes carefully down a list tacked on the inside of the swinging door to reference the proper map, he located the chart of Point Malachai and flattened the parchment out on the desk before his second-in-command.

"Here is the matter, Alan, as horrible as you could ever hope to imagine it," Jack said in an apologetic tone, placing his finger on the chart at the head of a long channel circling a small but treacherous point of land. The graphed lines marking the many bisecting channels leading up to and trailing away from the point spread across the paper like spider webs. Jack traced his finger carefully down the long, narrow gut that skirted the point before it wound westward toward the Atlantic shoreline of Cape Charles. Crosshatched scribbling at the side denoted low rocky ledges flanking the primary channel, outlining a difficult passage.

MacDonald twirled the whiskers over the corners of his

mouth between his ruddy calloused fingers, a cheerful smile belying his reluctance. "Well, we can't be said to be afraid of taking chances now can we?"

"It is not preferred, but do you see any other way?" Jack returned, exasperated. Jack preferred MacDonald's consent, but regardless of having it, he felt that his counsel was indispensable.

MacDonald caught a sigh and shifted his mug of coffee to the corner of the map to weigh it down as he leaned closer to make out the charted details under the swinging lantern light. The possibility of shooting through the deadly channels obviously bore no strong appeal for the cautious old trader. "Jack, I think it might be done, but it would be touch and go even in clear weather. With this damn blow and this devil behind, it will likely be the death of us. If we run aground here," he rested his finger on the crosshatched rock shoal, "we would be lucky even to have time to get everyone into the boats before we went down, to say nothing of our cargo. If that were to happen, I'm not even certain these little boats we carry are enough to reach the shore considering this storm that's likely to catch us."

It was nothing Jack hadn't already turned over in his own mind several times, but MacDonald's repetition of his own reservations caused him deeper concern.

"At any rate, Jack, why are we so bent on outrunning this cutter? She shows every sign of being legitimate. You've never been so worried about having a revenuer aboard."

Jack met MacDonald's level gaze and nodded his agreement, but said, "It's a feeling, Alan, that's all. You already know about the privateer talk in Wilmington. These blackguards wouldn't hesitate to snatch up a prize like the *Norfolk Gold,* particularly if they made us out for Scotsmen. You, as well as I, know the rebels would relish the chance to take out their spite on their old business rivals."

MacDonald grinned, knowing quite as well as his captain of the growing colonial resentment against the increasing power of Scot merchants, particularly in Norfolk. The control the Scottish export agents wielded over local tobacco was one of many small but significant sources of irritation among the native Virginians which had led to much spirited discontent. But to think that the rebels would be so organized as to field commerce raiders in so short a time, and in the Chesapeake Bay no less, seemed to push the outside limit of credibility.

"I suppose it's possible, Jack, though I doubt the rebels would have themselves such a fine looking little cutter, and so well handled."

Jack knew that in all likelihood MacDonald was right and the cutter was simply an Englishman enforcing standard shipping checks. To insist otherwise was not reasonable, unless intuition could be figured in as a rational cause. Still, it was impossible for him to ignore a feeling that something was very wrong about the chase this cutter was giving. Everything about it invoked suspicion.

"I am probably being too cautious by half, Alan, as you suspect. There is nothing to explain why I feel it is necessary to avoid this fellow. But if he is something other than he claims..."

He did not need to complete his thought to convey the gravity of such a possibility.

MacDonald sipped his coffee, drawing back his lips tightly and savoring the lingering sting of the rum as he accepted Jack's reasoning with good-humored resignation. Jack knew MacDonald might heartily disagree with him, and were he to press him further, he did not doubt the old man could catalogue any number of cogent reasons that his opinion was the better. MacDonald, however, was not so proud as to seek to impose his influence at too high a cost to their friendship, sensing that there was a higher cause to be served by listening to and standing by his captain. Jack came forward, thumbed up the edge of the paper, and rolled the chart tightly, shipping it in the inner breast pocket of his great coat. MacDonald met Jack's firm gaze and nodded, "I will go topside and give the order to change course then, Captain."

"Thank you, Alan. I will be up in a minute."

When Jack returned to the main deck full night had blanketed the sky, the only lighting above the bay waters shed by the few faint specks of cloud-veiled constellations. Isaac had doused the schooner's deck lanterns to try as best as he could to conceal the *Norfolk Gold*'s course, the darkness making any movement along the deck very difficult. Jack was grateful that he need not worry about seeing to these finer details, a freedom which allowed him to concentrate on the larger decisions at hand. Isaac was more than any captain could desire in his boatswain, as well as a tremendous credit to his race.

The spirited chop had moderated in the last half hour, giving the schooner back some of her valuable speed and ability to maneuver. The storm, though still a potential danger, seemed to have lost some of its strength as it closed, allowing Jack to add stay sails and shake out a reef in the topsails. He hoped the added speed would not throw off his navigation, expecting to sight the breakers of Point Malachai within ten minutes. He recognized that his course was far riskier than he would have liked as he drew the chart from his great coat and consulted the channel positions once again in the failing moonlight. He grimaced as he became more aware of the narrow margin for error the close maneuver would allow, particularly at night. It was becoming far too easy to second guess at this dangerous juncture. Stopping a passing seaman, Jack sent word for his night glass. When it was brought to him he cautiously raised himself above the deck into the shrouds and began a slow climb towards the main top. The dizzying swing of the mast grew significantly more erratic as he climbed higher, hurling its weight in concentric circles. He paused as the schooner slipped into a deep trough, the mast sweeping forward. Holding on with his arms and legs entwined in the rigging, he waited for the long pole to once again point skywards before continuing his trek. As he finally reached the top and heaved himself into the crosstrees Jack took a moment to catch his breath, noting that a trip aloft was not the effortless feat it had once been.

Glimpsing forward into the foremast top hamper, Jack could just make out the faint silhouette of the lookout Edwards scanning the dark vista that lay ahead. Very good that Isaac had appointed such a trustworthy man to that task, lest they find themselves on the breakers with too little room to navigate. Jack could relax somewhat knowing that they would not sail blindly into the forbidding shoal water.

The chanting of the leadsmen drifted up, his jolly voice a pleasant anomaly in the midst of the apprehensive crew. It agreed with Jack to hear the lilting chorus of Able Bodied Seaman Gavin, another one of his tried crew who had always stood fast and firm in his duties for the several years he had served alongside his captain on the Virginia station. It was a tired phrase to say that the *Norfolk Gold* had grown into a family, but for Jack there was no better way to understand that rare feeling of *esprit*. Perhaps the tight knit ship's company owed much of its integrity to the fact that seven out of ten were Scot, every one a firebrand, rogues, never really accepted as the colony's own. The other three men were freed blacks and as set apart from the white colonials as one could ever imagine. What lives they could lead in Virginia would always be curtailed by the horrible specter of enslavement, if not for themselves then for those they loved. They, like the Scots, lived among though apart from the people of the colony, choosing not to socialize or seek mates among their race. Their choice was not due to company restriction like their white shipmates, Jack knew bitterly, but in self-defense and fear of losing their kin to the arbitrary wishes of a slave holding tobacco planter. It was a horrible truth that the colonies' prosperity was largely built on the backs of an imprisoned people. Jack had often tried to reason his way around it, but he was repelled by what he perceived as a widespread hypocrisy tainting the boundless promise of the colonies.

Jack gently drew his night glass from his breast pocket as

he braced himself against the mast and faced aft, searching the dark sea for signs of the cutter. Nothing betrayed its presence on the blackened expanse: the cutter's captain too had extinguished his deck lanterns. How Jack vainly wished for some definitive signal which would put his mind at rest regarding the stranger's intentions.

"Cap'n," the lookout Edwards in the foretop entreated urgently, "Breakers, fine on the larboard bow!"

Jack shuffled carefully around and faced forward, catching sight of a phosphorescent blemish on the sea. The livid marker cast an eerie glow on the otherwise blank waters. The rocks that lay ahead were doubtlessly those of Point Malachai, the channel opening affording Jack his chance to elude the cutter. He felt the wind on his cheek diminish slightly and back in the West. Perhaps the change would be enough to slow the schooner's approach and give her a reasonable chance of skirting the hazardous passage. He shimmied down the main back stay to quickly recover the deck, approaching the wheel to give his order. Jack shared his plan with Isaac, pointing out the channel he intended to follow, making certain that he understood in detail the course he should steer. Nodding confidently, the big shouldered boatswain guided the schooner closer to the outcropping. Jack ordered a team of men aloft once more to take in a reef on the topsails as men on deck furled the driving stay sails, allowing Isaac to bring the schooner in under easy power.

MacDonald came aft and crossed to the weather side of the quarterdeck, his stark white head and cream colored waist coat easily discernible in the moonlight from the many darkling shapes of the common seamen.

"Well, Jack, we shall see how committed our pursuing friend is now, eh?" MacDonald laughed grimly, a narrow crescent of bright dentures flashing.

Jack nodded absently, suddenly consumed with a desire to take Alan aside and question him once again for his advice outside the earshot of the others. He put the idea immediately aside, knowing that a last minute change of plan would never work. To put the question to MacDonald now would only undermine what resolve Jack had gathered. He searched the old man's half concealed face in the dim light, hopeful of catching some flicker of reassurance. Alan's steady gaze met him and, as if reading Jack's thoughts, he nodded shortly and said, "A right steady run it should be, Captain Jack."

Jack placed an appreciative hand on the old man's sleeve and turned back toward Isaac, committing his full attention to the schooner's handling.

"Ease a spoke to starboard if you please, Isaac."

"A spoke to starboard, aye, Captain."

The steady slide of the water grew choppy as the *Norfolk Gold* neared the breakers, batting the hull rhythmically. Jack snapped open the chart to reference their current heading against the leadsmen's soundings. They currently sailed across an underwater plain at three and a half fathoms, roughly twenty-one feet, eleven feet clear of the schooner's keel. The channel he was searching for opened up to four fathoms, though it would be flanked by a rocky shoal at just under two fathoms, a depth he was uncertain they could clear. The navigation would be particularly tricky because two channels ran very close together, their openings appearing almost identical on the chart. One, the closest to the breakers, wound tightly around the point and led to a deep bottom of six fathoms which lasted as far as Cape Charles. Its twin sister ran straight into a hidden reef which allowed no possibility of steering out once entered.

As they drew nearer to the deadly spit of rock, Seaman Gavin's lead chants grew increasingly urgent as the water shoaled gradually to three fathoms, then to two and a half, only five feet clear from keel to the ocean's bottom. The sweating mariner rapidly drew the long weighted line up fist over fist after each successive reading, before flinging it out again into the churning water, intent on keeping his soundings as timely as possible.

"Steady as she goes, helm," Jack assured, pressing his lips together tensely. The break water's crash grew steadily louder as they approached the channel opening. Jack forced his hands together, interlacing his fingers to keep from betraying his tested nerves. Time hovered in Jack's mind, the seconds dragging by as he waited for each new sounding.

"By the mark, four!" Gavin shouted triumphantly; a few reserved smiles lit momentarily and back slaps were quietly exchanged. MacDonald wasted no time in conveying his congratulations, approaching Jack with an unaffected expression of delight.

"It appears you've found your elusive little notch after all, my bonnie captain!"

"Deep Six!" Gavin enthusiastically confirmed their passage.

Jack could not repress a boyish grin, allowing for a genuine if unorthodox display of emotion on his quarterdeck. He had just opened his mouth to rejoin MacDonald's bawdy allusion when the sharp report of cannon fire punctured the steady hiss of the sea. Jack spun round and searched the sea off the starboard quarter for signs of the not so distant peal. Less than a minute later a rolling fire pattered bright splotches of color against the gloom, casting a brief outline of the cutter. They tensed, waiting for the storm of iron. Nothing.

"Has he lost his mind?" MacDonald growled. "What sort of man would fire a full broadside unprovoked on a merchantman?"

"I am not sure he is firing at us, Alan," Jack said as he passed the night glass to his close friend, gesturing for him to take a look off the larboard quarter. MacDonald dubiously handled the telescope, though skepticism quickly faded once he glimpsed through the scope at the cutter.

"Damn my eyes, Jack! Another schooner's come to blows with her."

"And giving them a warm time of it from what I can make out," Jack replied, repossessing the glass and leveling it in meticulous study. "I suppose you would think me a fool for wanting to get a closer look?"

MacDonald visibly paled at the suggestion, a tried expression pinching his troubled face. "Well, Jack, it would be mutiny to call you a fool. Let us say, though, that a wise businessman always prefers a shrewd solution. I would terribly regret not landing our cargo safely on the docks before embarking on, *adventures*," he put in with grave finality.

Jack smiled humorlessly, the weight of the conundrum on his shoulders. "Alan, my friend, I am not bent on adventures. But look here, this fellow has come to grips with an unseen foe. And, from what I can judge it appears to be a common one."

The scene lit anew with another withering cannonade from the long deck of the attacking schooner, revealing the silhouettes of a great mass of men swarming over her bulwarks as they boarded the cutter. Just brief, dark shapes scurrying against the distant blur of two unidentified ships' hulls, but the character of the attack seemed to suggest so much... Jack steadied himself and faced MacDonald's set countenance, bellowing his orders forward, "Isaac, prepare to tack, if you please, making new course South by Southeast. I should like to come up on their quarter at a safe distance."

"South by Southeast, aye, aye, Captain!" In a peremptory tone Isaac shouted the preparatory commands to the seamen and the main deck thumped to life with the unseen stampede of men rushing to their sail trimming stations. Jack's stomach knotted with apprehension as he placed his hand to the backstay to steady himself as the *Norfolk Gold* came about and settled on her new tack. He caught his breath, hoping he had timed the order to tack accurately, knowing that the shoal water left little room for error. As the *Gold* settled on her course and filled with the wind fine on the beam, he knew that he had made close but good work of the maneuver. However, this course of action would not sit well with any of the members of the crew, nor with the agents of the trading house were they to become wise to it. To give succor to an embattled British warship was madness and Jack well knew it. The sudden and violent appearance of the schooner with her superior numbers had swayed his decision. Surely it must be the privateer Jack had mistakenly feared the cutter to be. It would explain why the cutter would have been so desperate in her pursuit, effectively playing the part of the shepherd by trying to bring the *Norfolk Gold* safely under her lee.

Jack set his face stolidly, pushing aside doubts of the perhaps deadly risk he was about to take. He could not simply abandon a man who had tried to warn him of imminent danger. The rules of the sea and the laws of his conscience forbid it. However, what he precisely hoped to do once he closed on the entwined ships was not clear. The *Norfolk Gold*s armament was limited to eight half pound swivel guns, pieces maintained primarily for repelling pirate attacks. In small arms she carried a small chest of rusty cutlasses, half a dozen pistols of dubious quality, and a pair of ancient blunderbusses. His men were not fighters, many of them either too sensible or too old to cast themselves into the smoky breach of close combat. His only advantages were in the *Norfolk Gold*s stealth and the element of surprise. Jack ordered the men to fit the swivel guns on their mounts and had them load the small cannons with musket balls and langrage, small bits of miscellaneous rubble. He sent Davy Yeoman to retrieve the blunderbusses from his cabin with shot and powder from his possibles bag. Once Davy returned with the two short hand cannons, Jack lay one flat on the deck and leaned the other, wide muzzle up, against the inside of his thigh, gently pouring in a measure of black powder from a silver powder horn. MacDonald, unable to suppress his curiosity any longer, approached and lifted the other blunderbuss from the deck, eyeing it and his friend skeptically.

"Jack, lad, do you seriously mean to get us caught up in

this fight?" his voice was weary, touched with a strange sadness. For a moment Jack paused loading the weapon and met Alan's pleading gaze, moved by the sincerity of his expression but unable to spare him more than a quick assent and a few words of encouragement. After he had taken the other blunderbuss from Alan and treble shotted it with heavy musket balls, Jack stowed the weapons just forward of the main mast in an empty coop; he doffed and stuffed his great coat in a shapeless ball beneath the twin pieces, freeing his arms to come at the coming situation unencumbered. He did not mind the wet chill which soon plucked at him, preferring to have every nerve as tightly stretched as possible. He turned his gaze aloft and studied the set of his sails, losing himself in a technical abstraction of how best to steer in order to maximize her present plan of canvas. His studies became so preoccupying that he was unaware of MacDonald's approach at his side until the old man had been at his shoulder for a full two minutes. Alan's presence, though silent, was weighted with insistent protest, and Jack felt the need to try to put his friend's fears to rest.

"Don't worry yourself too much, Alan, I haven't gone completely mad. I don't intend to come directly to arms with these rascals. Just get close enough to see if there is anything we might be able to do to help our English friends."

"And why are you now so sure that they are English?" Alan rejoined hotly. "Not half an hour ago you insisted that they might well be the privateer's men you now believe this schooner to be. If I may say, Jack, I'm not sure you rightly know what to make of this spectacle yourself!"

Jack shrugged, clapping down on his tongue, not trusting his words once his long reserve of patience had been exhausted. As the schooner's captain, he had never before had his plan of action questioned so boldly. That the challenge should come from his trusted friend made the affront painfully more shocking. It must be redressed, he resolved, though now was not the time. He fixed the ships in his night glass again, but the great guns had fallen silent.

Occasionally a pistol or musket cracked, a quick spurt of flame flashing, but nothing which might light up the scene of battle. The fighting must have become very difficult, the men struggling against one another in the terrifying darkness, killing one another with clubs, knives, or whatever else might be at hand. He shuddered, remembering a night nearly sixteen years ago when as a petrified cabin boy he had cowered in his captain's cabin while a similar scenario had transpired. The sounds of steel hacking into flesh and bone and the heavy thud of his captain's lifeless body as it fell on the deck above him suddenly returned, the memory's intensity undiminished across the many forgotten years since.

Jack shook off the morbid train of thought and passed the order for the men to stand to their small cannons. He could feel his apprehension slowly beginning to unravel, a smooth exhilaration taking over as the moment swiftly came on him. Fewer than five minutes now before they would arrive off the interlocked ships' sterns. Isaac steered a close but safely distant course, giving Jack sufficient room to order a tactical retreat should the need arise. The cracking of pistol shots began to grow more regular as the *Norfolk Gold* approached, the snapping reports occasionally offset by a long hiss of sword blades gliding together. Remembering the blunderbusses, Jack retrieved the powerful short range weapons from the coop and set them at the half cock. He paced the line behind his men as they stood to their swivel guns, sensing their uneasiness rise as the *Norfolk Gold* neared the embattled ships.

"Steady, lads. I don't mean to lay aboard her, just have a closer look."

His voice, quiet but insistent, appeared to have its desired effect on the crew, easing the tension. The growing outlines of the ships loomed out in a wraith of smoke, the sounds of stamping feet on the decks now audible in the eerie calm which had succeeded the storm's passing. Jack stood to the bulwark, searching for men aboard the cutter to signal.

"Isaac, man, steer us in closer!" Jack hoarsely whispered. The boatswain's eyes rolled with incredulity as he glimpsed the scant fifty feet separating the *Norfolk Gold's* larboard bow and the cutter's quarterdeck. However, with a technician's precision, Isaac spun the wheel as crisply as a roulette wheel with one strong hand before checking it a moment later with the other. The *Norfolk Gold* swung obediently onto her new course, headed to skim the length of the cutter at fewer than a dozen feet.

A sudden, well organized volley of musketry rumbled from the break of the cutter's quarterdeck. Jack strained his eyesight to make out the identity of the shooters through the rolling bank of gun smoke. So much remained hidden by the gloom that he could not be certain of the soldiers' number, uniform, or on whom they were firing. Then he saw the rank of men kneel as a second line stepped into place, the scarlet regimental coats of the English marines plain despite the smoke and night as they lifted their firelocks to their shoulders. This time Jack was careful to follow the line of their fire as another rippling volley zipped down the length of the cutter and sliced into a swarm of ragged men gathered in its fo'c'sle. A rabble of uniformless men continued to advance against the thin line of marines, their swords and tomahawks bared as they prepared a frontal assault. Jack summoned his resolve, filled his lungs, and cried shrilly, "Marines, clear away, we have them!"

The English officer glanced over in a daze at the closing bulk of the *Norfolk Gold*. For a long moment Jack feared the man did not register his meaning before his weary eyes lit with recognition and he yelled to his marines to lie flat on the deck. Readily, they obeyed and Jack screamed for his crew to open fire.

The swivel guns barked in a stuttering but wicked rhythm, spewing the iron shot and assorted debris into the shocked crowd of rebels at a distance of less than twenty feet; the blast cleaved great rows through their gathered numbers. Their bodies fell back under the force of the unexpected cannonade as their screams of pain came in terrible cacophony. Jack, seized by the success of the moment, pointed one of his blunderbusses into the crowd of retreating rebels and jerked the trigger. The short barreled gun punched his shoulder, rocking him back on his heels as it spat its deadly charge into the backs of the privateersmen, felling three of their company. He placed the other blunderbuss to his shoulder but, before he could fire, his shot was screened by the cutter's main shrouds as the *Norfolk Gold* slipped past the halted vessel.

"Brings us back around if you please, Isaac," Jack ordered breathlessly.

"Aye, aye, Captain," the boatswain acknowledged, his worried expression now considerably relieved knowing that the *Norfolk Gold*'s standing and running rigging had weathered the encounter undamaged.

As the *Norfolk Gold* swung across the ships' bows and came up on the privateer schooner's larboard main chains Jack could see that the cutter's marines had reformed and exploited the advantage of the *Gold*'s surprise attack. The red coats, along with their navy shipmates, quickly chased down and corralled the few privateer blackguards who survived. Jack ordered the canvas furled down to bare poles and double anchors set to keep the *Norfolk Gold* from drifting too close to the shoals. The swivel guns he had the men reload, albeit clumsily and slowly, as a precaution against any rebel retaliation. The measure proved to be little more than ritual, as the cutter's crew soon sent along a strong boarding party to capture and take control of the privateer schooner. With both vessels now decisively under British control, a small troop of English sailors charged toward the privateer schooner's near bulwarks, cheering and raising their cutlasses in salute to their merchant allies. Jack's crew answered back with great howls of celebration, their voices thundering across the water like jubilant cannon fire.

"I suppose we gambled wisely, eh, Alan?" Jack said, his

spirits soaring with victory, his previous bitterness against his friend forgotten in the moment.

Yet the ill feelings swiftly returned as MacDonald regarded him icily and said, "I hope you will note in your log, Captain, that I protest this action. You will understand, I must in the nature of my position as ship's supercargo, always advise the best course in terms of ensuring our cargo safely delivered. It is only business."

How little his tone seemed like business, seething as it was with injured feelings, Jack noted. He had no choice but to accept Alan's request and said his dissension would be appropriately annotated in his log. MacDonald turned and paced away, a sense of profound disdain lingering. Jack returned the loaded blunderbuss to the empty coop and donned his heavy great coat. He pulled the wool material snugly about him, a chilliness far more penetrating than the weather causing him to shudder.

3. IN DUBIOUS ALLEGIANCE

JACK turned a razor one last time over the few stubborn whiskers just beneath his ears and tapped the blade's edge against the small china bowl basin, the resonant ring reminding him faintly of church bells. Though hardly a religious man, the suggestive note agreed with his idea of a serene morning, giving rise to the hope that the accidental music might bode well for the day. As he crossed to his cot to brush out his best burgundy coat, Davy Yeoman rapped on the cabin door and pushed it open. The boy hovered at the threshold, his wide eyes soaking in the finery hung upon Captain Cunningham in place of his normal sailing attire.

Jack broke the silent appraisal with, "Am I to take it that the English captain has sent across a boat, Mister Yeoman?" He knew there was little other reason for his cabin boy to be disturbing him so early in the morning, at six bells in the morning watch, 7 a.m.

"Yes, Captain. A Mister Fitzwilliam, a midshipman, has come aboard sending his captain's compliments and wanting you aboard for breakfast."

"Very well, light along. I will be up," Jack said shortly, not liking the boy's foolish gawking. Davy shuffled awkwardly, letting his eyes roam over the long, bejeweled sword and scabbard slung rakishly from Jack's hip. Jack shot him a cold glare as he lifted his stocking foot to the door's edge and swung it shut with a swift kick. A full minute passed before he heard Davy's retreating footsteps. Jack shook his head, fearing he had shown too many favors for the boy's own good. He regretted the agreement he had made with Davy's father to take the twelve year old on board to teach him the sea trade. The slow-witted child was fast becoming a nuisance and, despite the debts he owed Farlin Yeoman, Jack had half a mind to send the urchin home to Plymouth on the first available packet. However, it was time honored tradition among men of the sea to show kindness and patience to its youngest apprentices. Perhaps in time Mister Yeoman might make a sailor out of himself, though Jack suspected he might make landsmen of his shipmates in the meantime.

Jack whisked the brush down the outspread coat sleeves before drawing the tailored frock carefully onto his long arms. Shrugging his shoulders, he tugged gingerly at the cuffs to bring the wrinkles into a smooth line down his shoulders and back, always conscious of the diplomatic effect of being well-dressed. Jack had expected the Englishman's invitation as soon order was restored aboard the cutter, and he was not disappointed to have spent the early morning primping. He turned and studied the fit of his clothes in a tall mirror hung on the inner door of his wardrobe, running his flattened hand between his hard belly and the waistband of his satin gray breeches. Somehow they fit more snugly than he remembered, collapsing much of his excitement over the approaching meal. He had always tended to add weight when in port for more than a day or two. The layover in Wilmington had been nothing short of entrapment with so many cordial dinner invitations, rich society, and richer dishes.

Jack tested the closeness of his shave with the back of his hand, his calloused fingertips useless for such delicate work. It appeared to be a passable job, only a few resistant dark whorls visible in his deeply tanned cheekbones. Normally he went unshaven when at sea but he seemed to remember hearing that navy captains frowned on such casual grooming standards. He disliked the idea of coming off like a

Frenchman in his fancy clothes and scraped face. Deciding it was best just to get on with the introductions, he donned his hat and was out.

An adolescent midshipman greeted Jack amidships, a tallish, awkward looking boy with a bad complexion. His blue officer's coat seemed rather thinly spun and less than adequately fitted. His canvas breeches were likewise of rough craftsmanship, undoubtedly issued from the cutter's slop chest, and hung loosely over a pair of scuffed hobnailed boots. Not a young man with many prospects for advancement in His Majesty's Navy, so ill-shod and apparently unconnected. Yet, he was decidedly affable and friendly, Jack thought, as the lad cheerily stepped forward, smiling hugely and wringing his hand in introduction.

"You must be Captain Cunningham, Sir. Pleased to meet you at last. I am Midshipman Fitzwilliam of His Majesty's Cutter *Boxer.*"

"Pleased to meet you Mister Fitzwilliam," Jack returned warmly, encouraged by Fitzwilliam's unfeigned expression of delight. "And to have a chance to see your fine looking cutter so trim and ready after last evening's troubles," he motioned across the water to the *Boxer* bobbing lively on the surf.

Mention of his ship brought a sense of officialdom back to the midshipman and he straightened up purposefully to deliver his captain's invitation to dine aboard the *Boxer*. Jack accepted with the appropriate pleasantries and followed Fitzwilliam into the launch, seating himself alongside his new friend in the stern sheets. The bowman pushed off and the oarsmen laid into their work, pulling across the easy sweep of fair seas. The journey was not protracted; even though the *Norfolk Gold* had dragged its anchors more than a hundred yards when a freak squall bore down after midnight, the distance to the *Boxer* was no more than a quarter mile. It did give time, however, for Jack to get a good feel for the vessel he was about to board by talking with the convivial midshipman. He learned that the cutter had come by way of Halifax, Nova Scotia via New

York as part of a reinforcement for Lord Dunmore in the Chesapeake Bay. Apparently Admiral Graves had been reluctant to let her go from his squadron, since Fitzwilliam said the *Boxer* had served as the flag ship's tender for most of the summer. Eventually, through some invisible echelon of influence, the *Boxer* had been ordered with all possible speed to serve as part of the deposed Virginia Governor's forces. She had made landfall only five days earlier and since that time her captain had aggressively pursued any suspicious shipping traffic moving in or out of the Chesapeake capes.

Fitzwilliam's easy manner suggested a healthy morale aboard the cutter. Perhaps it was a nervous carryover from the action of the evening before, though Jack suspected the young man's elevated spirits were shared by his shipmates. Certainly they seemed to be common to the men of the boat's company, all of whom bent to their oars with active strength, not one of them dipping his stroke shallowly or otherwise shunning his part. Jack was eager to meet the man who could inspire such a seemingly loyal and happy band of men.

As the launch neared the *Boxer* Jack could see that the repairs the English crew had made were only superficial. Her wounds were far more grievous than Fitzwilliam had admitted. The cutter's single mast had been braced up with supporting spars where a great chunk of wood was missing, apparently chopped away when the privateer schooner fired round shot into her. Her nettings were likewise shredded, and much of her top hamper had been so freshly spliced that the new rope showed starkly white against the black webs of tarred rigging. The oarsmen tossed oars as the boat glided to the *Boxer*'s larboard bulwarks and the bowman hooked onto the main chains. Fitzwilliam stood and ushered Jack forward, his friendly banter rising up again as he boasted the talents of the Captain's cook. Jack listened politely though his mind had begun to wander regarding the condition of the captured privateer schooner, since she was nowhere to be seen. Distracted thus, he swung himself easily up the accommodation ladder to the *Boxer*'s main deck. A crash of arms and stamping boots startled him as he set foot on deck, a small party of marines doing full honors as they presented their firelocks in salute. He looked round bewildered, uncertain if the courtesy was indeed intended for him. One look at a mischievously smiling Fitzwilliam confirmed that it was. Jack faced the gathered marines and bowed his acknowledgement, sending a rippling through the ranks as the marines cut the salute and returned their muskets to their sides at order arms.

"Welcome aboard the *Boxer*, Sir," Fitzwilliam said as he came up alongside Jack. "Captain Amis thought you should receive the full rites of any naval captain coming aboard in light of your brave conduct last evening. Of course, I shouldn't speak for him. I'm certain he's eager to tell you as much himself. If you will please follow me..."

Jack nodded, uncomfortable with the unexpected attention of the *Boxer*'s crew. It was remarkable to think that the British captain had thought so highly of a simple merchant skipper to have arranged the military salute, a gesture typically reserved for commanding officers and esteemed dignitaries. He tucked his arms behind his back, affecting a casual stroll and inclining his head amiably to the men he passed as he trailed his escort below deck to the captain's cabin.

He was led to a small but elegant cabin of dark wood shot through with resplendent shafts of sunlight lancing in from the open skylights above. The sudden brightness took Jack by surprise, temporarily blinding him, his eyes having just become accustomed to the dimness of the 'tween decks. So it was a voice, rather than a person, he first met as a shadowy figure moved from behind a large, square desk and wrung his hand.

"Welcome aboard, Sir. I am Captain Amis, commander of His Majesty's Cutter *Boxer*, of ten guns."

Jack gave his name and said he was honored to be aboard. Gradually his eyes adjusted and he saw standing before him a round faced gentleman of about forty wearing a periwig and the uniform of a Lieutenant in the Royal Navy. He was generally unremarkable in appearance, his countenance and body sharing a softness that bespoke an abundant if not necessarily easy lifestyle. There was nothing about Captain Amis's manner that might suggest noble birth, though he was undoubtedly well off in terms of wealth. The few pieces of furniture in his cabin and the overlapping Persian rugs carpeting the deck of his day quarters, lent a sense of luxuriance. Jack doubted he had been in the navy for very long. Amis had a far too relaxed and self-assured air for someone of his mature years in charge of such a junior command. Any officer his age would typically have served at sea from the time his was fifteen or younger and should by all rights be a very senior Post Captain assigned command of a Ship of the Line, not paddling around the colonial coast in a seventy foot cutter.

Amis's steward took Jack's hat and showed him to a plush high backed chair across from his captain's desk. No sooner was Cunningham seated than Amis handed him a steaming cup of black coffee, making apologies that the breakfast was not ready yet due to some misfortune with the galley fires.

"It has been something of a mad house since last evening," Amis explained, sipping cautiously from his own mug of scalding brew. "Normally I wouldn't tolerate such a delay when it comes to breaking my fast, but the good fellow who cooks for me lost his helper in the fight with the rebels. He is coming at the thing fairly single-handed. I hope your crew was not hurt terribly in the exchange?"

Jack bowed his head soberly, more aware now how fortunate he and the men under his command had been to escape unscathed.

"No, we did not take on any fire. Your marines pursued the rebels as soon as we fired our swivel guns. I don't believe that we were the rebels' main concern after that."

Amis grinned, pleased at the compliment for his lobster backs.

"I will have to pass on your kindness to Lieutenant Porter. He was certainly grateful for your courage. He is the marine officer who led the party against the brigands. I am sorry to say that our surgeon had to amputate his arm in the night. A devilish shame to have that happen to such a good, young officer. He suffered a cutlass wound which nearly did the sawbones' work for him as it was. Still, he led his men on, despite his personal injuries. His spirit is what in many ways saved us, in great compliment to the singular courage you displayed yourself, Captain Cunningham," Amis concluded significantly.

Jack shifted uncomfortably under the praise, aware of his inadequate role in the night fight as well as the terrible sacrifice the gallant marine had made. The marine side party, a corps of men who were known as lions in war, had done him a great honor with their salute, doubly poignant considering that their own brave officer was lying below in a blood stained sick berth. He vowed to himself not to forget their gratitude.

Jack eased his coffee to his lips, involuntarily wincing as he tasted the drink, such strong flavor previously unknown to him. Captain Amis smiled, though not mockingly, at his reaction.

"It is African," Amis said, as if that was sufficient to explain the properties of the concoction. When Jack made no rejoinder the British captain went on, "I have become addicted to it since my days as a trader along the Slave Coast. Are you familiar with the Dark Continent, Captain Cunningham?"

Jack said that he was not, though he had heard many interesting reports about the land's interior, some men claiming to have sailed a great distance into the mysterious region of the Niger. He could see that Amis was eager to share his experiences in the foreign land, so he inclined his head attentively forward and drank from his cup of coffee as he listened.

"It is a fabulous country of ancient Princes, far larger

than any man has right to claim as his own. Its people roam the continent with extraordinary ease, like children of the Sun. There is more jungle there than all the forests anywhere in the world, as well as vast deserts, and open grasslands. I regret that my experience there was so *mercenary.* You see, I have been a slaver for most of my years at sea. Came to it naturally having been raised in Liverpool and inherited the profession from my father. It is terrible to think what a profit can be made in the dealing of human flesh..."

Captain Amis seemed to sink into the hidden depths of his own voice, as if a deluge of unspeakable memories had unexpectedly washed over him. His red rimmed eyes turned liquid as he buried his face into the steam wreathed coffee and drank deeply. The somber moment was interrupted by the entry of the captain's steward, bearing a heaping platter of jam, bacon, and biscuits. Captain Amis waved his man in with a distracted air and dismissed him as soon as the table was properly set. He and Jack moved to their new chairs accordingly and fell into a few minutes of light conversation, inquiring after one another's previous commands, as well as their respective family situations. Jack told Amis of his wife Rebecca and their small child, a daughter Jack had not once seen in the two years since she had been born.

"It is amazing for me to think," Amis said, spooning a liberal dollop of marmalade onto a thin wafer, "that a young married man like you should choose to serve so far from kith and kin. Surely it must lead to certain temptations? Forgive me if I speak too boldly, Captain Cunningham, but I hear these colonial women are nothing short of succubae when it comes to their rustic charms."

Jack smiled noncommittally. "I am sure I wouldn't know anything about that, Captain Amis. You seem particularly interested. Could it be that you are you in the market for female companionship yourself?"

Amis shrugged as he bit into his biscuit.

"A man of my years can never be said to shun the

attention of the fairer sex. I have been happy at sea for many years, but that is not to say that I don't sometimes suffer from the pangs of loneliness. The sort of woman who might see fit to trail after me at my whim would not be unwelcome, though she would have to be most pretty of face and figure. I cannot abide an ugly woman! But I suppose that would be expecting a great deal, seeing that I am something less than an Adonis myself. I understand that the factors in your trading companies here are prevented from marrying colonial women. Is that true?"

Jack nodded. "We sign a contract before we cross over which stipulates we are not to make any ties with the colonials that might interfere with interests of the company. It allows the company to keep things simple. There are fewer complaints from the junior factors when they are reassigned new trading routes."

"Still, it must be a very hard thing to keep your men's morale up, so long deprived of female company in the permanent sense. Still harder on you, seeing your wife and home so infrequently?"

Jack paused before answering, a wave of complications subverting his prepared answer. The memories of England were not all welcoming; far too many old debts and strained relations kept him from embracing a homecoming. Few people understood his reasons for keeping away, particularly those closest to him. An old mistress in Surrey could not be put off if he were to come back now flaunting his comfort and wealth. Another in Kent might very well raise a holy scandal if she quit the company of her aristocratic husband. It was one thing to expect Rebecca to tolerate these affairs when separated by an ocean, but quite another to put up with intrigues on her own doorstep. The very least he could do for her sake was to remain discreet. The distant colonies were just remote enough to allow adequate room for Jack's reckless sexual temperament, and for that reason he was none to eager to quit his American habitation. Of course, publicly he would never admit this. Whether Amis was keen to this deception, Jack could not tell, though the Englishman did not betray any sense of recognition. Little that it mattered, reflected Jack. The cutter's captain had far too many concerns to bother himself over adulterous gossip.

"I have been meaning to ask you, Captain Amis," Jack said as he reclined in his chair and pushed his half-eaten meal to the side of the capacious dining table. "I noticed the rebel schooner has already gotten under way. I presume you wasted no time in sending her into Norfolk as a prize?"

"Yes, indeed. My first Lieutenant, Mister Warren, took charge of her in the first watch. I sent him in the event that you had yourself weighed anchor during the night. I instructed that he was to make contact with you in the harbor so that I might have a word. I expected you may well have lingered here, but I did not want to risk missing your departure. You are inbound with cargo I take it?"

There was a sudden though careful shift in Amis's tone as he casually posed the question. No doubt the Englishman was shrewd at his work, even now putting his circumspect inquiry with skilled and light-handed diplomacy. Jack was uncertain as to why Amis was so careful with the words he chose, though he was slowly becoming aware that he had underestimated the Englishman's acumen. He decided to string him along with as few details as he could in order to buy time with which he might gain a better sense of the man sitting across the table.

"Yes, the routine run," Jack answered dryly.

"This routine, if you don't mind my asking, what would that be?"

"Rice, other assorted dry goods. Brought up from Carolina," Jack said, a tone of testiness deliberately evident in his voice.

"I suppose that would be through the trading port of Wilmington, is that right?"

Jack grinned to hide a flicker of annoyance. He was beginning to see that nearly every sentence Amis uttered ended with an interrogative. Perhaps this cordial invitation to dine aboard the *Boxer* had not so much to do with gratitude as it did with investigating some vague suspicion on the English captain's part. Jack emptied his mug of coffee and clapped it down on the table.

"If there is something directly you wish to know, Captain Amis, I would prefer you ask it openly. I am not eloquent enough to twist my tongue around the truth, unlike so many of my fellow captains these days."

Amis leaned back in his chair, his hands crossed over his curved epicurean belly, smiling. Jack was grateful at least that the Englishman was not patronizing enough to deny that there was anything out of order in his line of questioning. Grateful, but wary as well of a man so cautious as to avoid an obvious deception.

"Please, don't take offense, Captain Cunningham. You must pardon my *thoroughness,* but I am charged with a rather difficult task, you know. If it is not too much to ask, I really would prefer having a chance to review your bills of lading. Just to put any doubts aside as to the exact nature of your cargo."

"Do you seriously suspect that if I were smuggling that I would turn my ship around and risk my life to try to help you?"

Amis shrugged his shoulders. "You must admit, such a maneuver would go a long way to dispel my natural suspicion of a vessel's captain that had done his best to evade me, going so far as to risk his ship through a forbidding shoal passage, would it not? If I were such a man it would be exactly what I would do."

"And why then," Jack made no effort to conceal his rising indignation, "would I go to the trouble of such an elaborate ruse if I had already successfully rid myself of you? If I had already outsailed your cutter, what reason would I have to convince you of my friendly intentions?"

Amis smiled, conveying a sense of disappointment in Jack's logic. "Well, Captain Cunningham, it certainly would not be a difficult matter for us to identify your ship inside the capes. Chances were nine out of ten that you were bound for Norfolk to discharge what cargo you were carrying."

"Which is why you were so quick to send the captured schooner in ahead, to track my movements," Jack said, realizing the extent of the Englishman's contingency plans.

Captain Amis motioned to his steward at the cabin's threshold to bring in another pot of coffee. The man bowed submissively as he poured both mugs to the brim. Jack watched Amis closely to gage the degree of satisfaction present in the Englishman's eyes.

"Please do not be offended, Captain Cunningham. I have no intention of commandeering anything that you carry which is legal. Once I have sent an officer across to review your records I will be content to let you sail to your intended destination, provided you allow us to escort you in safely to the Hampton Roads. You will be very eager to get your cargo in and upload tobacco bound for England with the export deadline coming up so soon, I'll wager. What is it, September 10th, I believe, and the Virginia Rebels have vowed to stop any tobacco exports to England. Running too close to that deadline could do terrible harm to your profit margin, I imagine, particularly if you were to find yourself with a hold full of the weed but unable to clear the docks for a swarm of rebel gun boats."

Jack could see that Captain Amis was anything but uninformed. For a man who had been assigned to patrol the Virginia Capes for less than a week, he seemed well briefed on the political nuances of the region. The looming deadline for exports to England was indeed a pressing matter, both for himself and the trading company, one Jack had hoped to avoid at such a close call. There was no doubt that he was in the Englishman's thrall; best to acquiesce to his demands and hope to ingratiate himself. No vulgar wit or insolence would bring him any closer to accomplishing his goal of making a final and very profitable run back to England before the colonial rebellion deteriorated any further. Once, an old river hand hauling tobacco on a private barge down the Rappahannock had given Jack well-intended advice regarding the best way to wriggle into a man's good graces. "You canna fear taking a bit of the great man's boot 'pon yer back. It may smart and dirty ya', but no gentleman ever hates a piece of rug. Makin' yerself into something' less than a man can save yer neck!" the old bargeman had said. Those words returned to Jack more pertinently now than ever.

***

Returning aboard the *Norfolk Gold,* Jack was accompanied by the well-meaning Midshipman Fitzwilliam. The boy had been given the task to verify all official paperwork pertaining to the merchant schooner's cargo. He proved to be bumbling and ineffectual in this capacity, taking until the noon meal to conclude his minute studies. Jack did not fault the young man for his assiduous attention to duty, gathering his hatred for the English captain instead. As soon as Fitzwilliam was done and put off in his boat, Jack ordered the anchor hove short and weighed and as much sail laid on as the poles could carry in order to make Norfolk before sunset. They sailed in company with the *Boxer* under a hazy, overcast sky on a moderate sea, making their westing at just over seven knots. Once clear of the shoal water Jack turned the con over to Isaac and went below to his cabin.

Slamming the door behind him, Jack unbuckled his belt and unceremoniously flung the fancy German rapier onto his swinging cot. The breeches and clean shirt he dispatched with similar enmity. The costume of a dandy, he thought bitterly. Suited perhaps for the effete dealings with the likes of Captain Amis, but offensive to the duties of an honest sea dog. What he had mistaken for gratitude on the part of the English had been in fact a clever way of lulling him into compliance. His mind rioted at the false humility he had been forced to show, the nauseating deference...He shifted into canvas seaman's trousers and stuffed his stout legs into well worn black boots which came to the middle of his calves. Over his head he pulled a shirt checkered blue like that of a common fisherman, comfortably cut allowing for unrestricted movement in the arms and shoulders. He seated himself on the edge of the cot, resting his head in his hands, trying to coax a sense of familiarity by placing himself in the midst of recognizable surroundings. He was not accustomed to feeling exploited, out of control, and the sensation had shaken him.

A sharp knock at the door broke his concentration. "Come in," Jack answered brusquely.

In stepped MacDonald, bareheaded, reddened by sun and drink. From his side hung his red baize basket guard broadsword sheathed in a copper scabbard. He glimpsed at Jack's slumped shoulders and glum countenance, grinning cynically.

"I know you must be rattled if you have forgotten our daily exercise," MacDonald gently mocked his captain's low spirits. "Surely, a trip across to our good ship *Boxer* dinna leave you completely out of sorts. Don't take it as all of that, my bonnie Captain. If you are not up to dealing with a pitiful little old man like me, then I'll just leave you alone in here to stew..." MacDonald said, pretending to withdraw.

"Not so quick as that," Jack said, planting his hands at his sides and pushing himself to his feet. He crossed to the stern wall and plucked a naval issue hanger slung from a small hook. He drew the curved sword swiftly from its homely black scabbard and swung its fine, evenly balanced blade in a crisp down stroke. The weight of the weapon felt smooth and reassuring. An unexpected awakening of delight creased the corners of his mouth.

"You're sure now, my lad, that you're comfortable handling a man's weapon," Alan teased. "We could always have a go with those fancy rapiers of yours if you're feeling a mite squeamish."

Jack's answer was a silent point of the blade toward the door.

"Well, all right. But remember I gave ya a choice!"

Jack followed the waddling shape of his unpredictable friend through the darkened ventricles of the 'tween decks, the sharp smells of tar and hemp contesting with a denser atmosphere of unvented body odor. Perhaps nothing in comparison to the tight living quarters aboard an English Man-of-War, but an offensive stench nonetheless, one that Jack's peculiarly sensitive nose had never grown accustomed to despite his many years at sea. As he crossed through the dim but familiar space Jack's mind wandered back to his conflict on the quarterdeck with MacDonald the night before. In retrospect it seemed amazing that such a bold challenge had been laid down, doubly so since Alan had so easily and curiously resumed friendly feelings. Jack was puzzled by the sudden change in attitude and felt there was some element in his friend's erratic behavior which was not accounted for. Perhaps Jack had been too hard in his judgments, too rash in his decisions. Certainly the meeting with Captain Amis had confirmed Alan's reservations about rushing to the Englishman's aid. But to flatly insult him on his own quarterdeck at such a crucial moment under the eyes of the men was simply intolerable. Jack gripped the hanger tightly as he stepped onto the main deck, hoping the upcoming physical exercise might relieve him of this fruitless aggravation.

The idling men were gathered in a large circle amidships, apparently as anxious to look on the gladiatorial spectacle as the two swordsmen were to participate in it. In their cruises aboard the *Norfolk Gold* the crew had come to look forward to the daily ritual of benign combat between their captain and his supercargo. Jack looked round at the gathered company, seeing them discreetly exchanging bets and wrangling over whether it was their captain's strength and youth which might prevail or MacDonald's steady precision and skill which would best his captain. Drawing himself up straight to salute his friend, Jack studied the old highlander's misleading appearance: stoop shouldered with a short and round torso, but joined with unusually long legs, like a man spliced from two separate bodies, one a giant and the other a dwarf, altogether awkward and grandfatherly in his looks. But Jack knew better. The sword the old man carried was the same he had wielded nearly thirty years earlier at a small place just outside of Inverness called Culloden. The steel in his gray eyes was the same that had stared down the open mouths of English field pieces spewing grape shot into his clan's fatal charge. MacDonald crisply returned the salute and assumed the *en garde* position. Jack likewise protected himself as he circled to the right, carefully placing his footing against the gentle roll of the deck.

Alan crashed in with a savage flurry of high attacks, using his heavier sword to quick advantage and immediately putting Jack on the defensive. The sudden aggression caught Jack by surprise, accustomed to his friend's preference for testing his opponent's defenses before committing his strength to a full attack. Now the game was something more than the normal play of technique; there was spirit in the contest, and the crew, recognizing this, began to whoop and chant encouragement.

"Lay into 'em, Captain, he's all bluff!"

"Come on, MacDonald, spit the lad for Bonny Prince Charlie's sake!"

Alan feinted low and to the inside to try to draw Jack in for the shoulder thrust but the cagey skipper would have none of it, dancing away with a curt snap of the hanger's *forte.* The light navy sword might lack the heft and cleaving power of the Scottish heavy sword, but in the hands of a skilled fencer it answered well. He keenly felt the advantage of it now, still easily balanced in his hand as he held it in a straight line for Alan's sweating and creased forehead. The broadsword rose to swat the accusatory blade away, but Jack repeatedly edged the point closer, teasing Alan with its dangerous closeness, drawing further strength from him with each parry. He paused with the blade leveled at a high angle, then surged into his adversary, firing his front leg forward, the blades singing together in a high pitch as the steel glided toward Alan's chest. Alan abruptly wrenched low and to the side with surprising swiftness while keeping his blade firmly pressed against the attacking hanger. With his weight fully committed and the lunge completely sprung, Jack was unable to correct the angle of the thrust, and his sword shot past his intended target. He felt the sharp prick of the broadsword catch on his midriff, the blade arrested. Gazing down, he caught sight of Alan's grin and reluctantly lifted his free hand in acknowledgement.

The crew erupted into a combination of cheers and catcalls at the score's recognition. One point only, Jack told himself, though if the stroke had been real it would have been a damned lethal one. He returned to his position, swinging the hanger about him in wide concentric circles, as if to rid himself of specters of self-doubt before returning once again to the *en garde* stance.

This time Jack assumed the aggressor's role, striking with a series of high chops intended to wear down Alan's apparently faltering stamina. Each collision of steel forced a grunt from between the old man's clenched jaw, proving to the spectators that their captain was sparing no regard for his opponent's age. The moves were not haphazard despite their strength, each cut forcing Alan into an off-balance block. As the seas steepened the deck grew more erratic in its pitch and yaw, forcing each of the swordsmen to step in time to the living play of the forces underfoot. Here Jack felt his youth gaining on his old friend, his superior agility adapting at once to the shifting gravity. He attacked lightly at a low angle and to the outside of Alan's relaxed guard before flicking the point swiftly toward MacDonald's unprotected chest. The hanger lingered in place like a picador's lance. It was Alan's turn to raise his hand and as he did the crew fluttered in a commotion of applause and profane oaths.

Jack tried to conceal a grin as he felt a growing confidence in his strength. Never a pure technician in the employment of a sword, he had a rare instinct for sensing his opponent's weakness and ruthlessly exploiting it. He gazed across at Alan, now not the insubordinate agitator of the night before but a winded and outmatched old man. Jack sprang forward in another attack, using the false edge of the blade to beat the heavier broadsword up while working in close with a combination of inside slices. Alan retreated, tentatively dragging his feet across the gyrating deck, off-balance, his ability to recover swiftly waning. Jack stepped away from the relentless attack, prowling around his enemy in a tight circle, his blade leveled severely. The rush of blood pounded in his ears, shutting out the imploring shouts of the men, as he continued to circle his target with the precision of a born predator. With a high feint, he dove in with a powerful blow at Alan's midsection. The old man staggered back, bringing his broadsword into a misplaced block. Jack's hanger smashed against the sword and deftly wrapped a tight circle around it, giving the youthful skipper crucial leverage as he shoved the highlander's sword up above his head. Without hesitation, Jack shoved into Alan's exposed torso, knocking him to the deck. Alan's broadsword clattered across the planks, flung nearly to the scuppers. Jack leaned over his friend, the point of his hanger pricking the old man's Adam's apple. His eyes were not so defiant now, Jack thought as he gently leaned on the hanger's pommel, drawing a small trickle of bright blood from his fallen adversary. Not so proud...

"You've won, Captain!" Isaac shouted, his voice peremptory. Jack looked round at the bosun coming directly on him, his muscled arms akimbo as he stepped from the staring circle of the crew. He glanced back at his prostrate friend and lifted the hanger from Alan's throat, looking to the bent faces of the men he commanded. He shoved his way below decks, his dark face reddening, anxious to be out of their sight.

Once he was alone in his cabin he closed his eyes and

leaned against the steady oak of the bulwarks, feeling the living rhythm of the schooner as she plowed through the sea. Shame overtook him and then a rising anger. He gripped the exposed blade of the naval hanger until the steel bit into his calloused flesh, watering the sword with his own dark blood and bringing the sharp pain. Grimacing, he hurled the hanger at the blind bulwark where it clattered and rang. The sound it made was nothing at all like the peals of church bells.

4. MOORINGS

THE offices of Wallace and Associates: a high walled, lightless affair with windows set not far below the cornice so that even at noon the copyists labored by the shivering illumination of candlelight. These copyists were a pallid and cheerless species, arrayed in threadbare frock coats and bent over their repetitive work with creased foreheads and ink stained fingertips. The more careless and shabby even blotted their weak chins and sagging cheeks with spots of the ubiquitous ink as they absent mindedly scratched their faces between documents. Jack sometimes fancied that the ink blots were a disease common to such bureaucrats, a kind of pox on a life of mindless drudgery. To think that this existence was at the other end of successful trade troubled him. He could think of nothing more removed from the wild spirit and risk of the open sea; yet this lifeless occupation was just as necessary to ensure that the rich tobacco was properly routed and documented. He passed the gauntlet of menial laborers and came upon the short bald man sitting behind a mahogany desk at the base of the stairs.

"Well, about time you saw fit to present yourself. We were beginning to believe you had absconded with the company's wealth," the man said cheerfully, hoisting his eyebrow in mock reproach.

Jack dropped his captain's log on the desk with a heavy thud.

"You may find it interesting reading, Mister Bairn.

Something less than routine. And it should sufficiently answer any questions regarding my alleged waywardness."

Bairn picked up the log, weighing it purposefully in his palm then put it aside, peering back at Jack over the flat edge of his spectacles.

"Why don't you tell me instead? I've had enough trouble making out illegible handwriting for one day," he said, waving a thin hand over his many stacks of lading bills, receipts, and inventories.

"Can't do that, Old Stick. You know as well as I the man sitting at the top of the stairs would have us both stripped and flailed if I were to make you privy to the details of a cruise before he's had his chance to damn my eyes," Jack said, grinning as he tucked the log back under his arm. "Shall I go on up or would you prefer to announce me?"

Bairn grimaced, shaking his head and laying his hand on Jack's sleeve, bringing him closer to share a confidence.

"You won't be able to see him this morning, Jack. He's in a foul temper the likes of which even I haven't seen. Factors from all the stations have been coming and going since before breakfast. Some come in looking furious and others apologetic as they walk in the door, but they all leave looking the same, like they've just been scolded by the tongue of their Maker. I haven't heard anything straight from the old man's mouth as to why what appears to be all hell is breaking loose."

Jack suspected Bairn was being arch in his warnings but, after a closer look at the chief bureaucrat's besotted but honest face, he became convinced of his sincerity. To have a troupe of the company's trading agents inexplicably descend on the home office was strange business. Some bad political weather must be on the brew. Jack knew, however, that a nosy old sot like Bairn would have heard something in the taverns, some gossip with a foundation of truth behind it to account for the odd happenings.

"Come on, Old Stick," Jack teased, "surely you must have some notion of a reason behind what's going on, or I don't know my Senior Clerk all that well?"

Bairn grinned with feigned reluctance before leaning forward. "Well...I have heard a few things. Nothing straight from the Old Man mind you, but interesting developments, if they are true. Last evening a factor who dined with me at The Raleigh claimed that he had spoken with members of the Rebel Virginia Committee for Safety two days ago and they told him that all exports to England were hereby banned immediately. Apparently, this Rebel rascal then went on to say that any company ship choosing to ignore this order would be intercepted by Rebel gunboats, boarded, and burned to the waterline."

"That sounds a bit like my eye and Betty Martin, pure bollocks!" Jack answered quickly, "The ban on trade is not supposed to take effect for another two weeks. That is what the House of Burgesses agreed to nearly a year ago. They can't simply go back on their word, their law."

Bairn shrugged. "I'm not exactly certain a Rebel gentleman's word means all that much, Jack. As it is right now, if what the man told me is true, any factor that is upriver in the tidewater might very well be bottled up with whatever cargo he has loaded and is ready to transport. It wouldn't be very hard for the Rebels to put a few sailing barges along key points of the river with enough cannon to keep them from passing. Could be a right mess."

Jack turned the information over inside his head as he gazed up the tall stair, his eyes roaming over the small parapet guarding the company's senior merchant, Stanislaus Fraser, from sight. He recognized that he needed more time to mull this information over before coming directly into the mouth of the lion.

"Very well, Old Stick. Let Mister Fraser know that I was here and will pay a return call in the morning. I will be at my room at The Raleigh should he need to contact me in the meantime."

"I will, Jack. And I would take my time if I were you. I might be stuck inside this infernal cell but I do have a weather eye for that man's foul airs!"

Jack gratefully stepped back into the balmy morning air as he turned up Gloucester Street, the breeze humid but nonetheless a refreshing change from the gloomy chamber of the company office. Kicking his heels around town did not sit well with him, particularly with a full cargo hold waiting to be unloaded. He tried not to think about what Bairn had said regarding the changed deadline on exports. If the clerk was right then the trip to Wilmington and the tons of rice Jack had shipped to the Chesapeake would be worthless. The rice was apportioned as a ready commodity to exchange with the tobacco plantations that thrived throughout the Virginia Tidewater. The wild weed of tobacco was the liquid currency in the colonies and a rich prize to bring home to the British Isles. If the Rebels had begun to enforce their shipping ban it could be disastrous in terms of the money and manpower he had invested in the latest haul. It would be hard to explain to a crew of men already anxious and ready to be paid off for their labors.

Turning up an alley of abandoned tenements Jack passed a file of British soldiers marching towards the waterfront. There were fewer than a dozen men in their detachment, led by a Lieutenant who was little more than a pink cheeked stripling. Jack slowly shook his head as they passed, reflecting on how lackluster an impression the English army now made in comparison to the time when he was a child. When he was cabin boy aboard the *Vicious* of 36 guns, the marines and soldiers had looked in their scarlet jackets like fusiliers spat from the depths of hell, ready to march through the vast Canadian wilderness to fight the French and their heathen Indian allies. Now the soldiers of the mighty British Empire were a few children playing in the ill-fitting costumes of their elder brothers, cast arbitrarily into a political and social quagmire they didn't understand; though, they did march with pride, strutting with swagger and beauty wherever they arrogantly walked upon the Earth. Damn foolish, Jack nearly remarked aloud.

He came to a brick edifice at the end of the blind alley and rapped brusquely on the door's frame. The thin eye slot shot open as the bolt was snapped to the side, a pair of keen green eyes fixing him with suspicion.

"What's your business?" a strident falsetto demanded.

"Open up, you shrimp! I've come to see the moneylender."

"And who might you be, Sir, and what makes you think he is in?" the cracking voice answered, unswayed by Jack's bluff manner.

Jack put his mouth close to the aperture as if preparing to whisper some secret information, but as the doorkeeper's ear turned to receive a quiet word Jack bellowed with manly gusto, "Parkinson, you swindler, let me in or I'll have every cent due me before I see your drunken hide in the King's courts!"

From within he heard a scuffle as a piece of furniture was overturned with a splintering crash and the doorman yelped as he was dragged aside. The heavy oak door was unbolted and swung open, expelling a blast of heat that nearly knocked Jack over as he stepped across the threshold. Inside the cavernous house a bright fire burned in the grate, casting the only light present in any of the rooms but for a few oil lamps burning dimly in the far corners. It was an awful place, rank with the smells of neglectful bachelor housekeeping. His host, a gaunt man with a wooden face and coal smudged eyes, shaped his empty mouth in mimicry of a smile and said, "Captain Cunningham, a right pleasure to see you back. I was not expecting you back from the Carolinas for another week."

Jack knew that Parkinson was lying, although he recognized the lie was uttered more from habit than from a need to deceive. He did not care for the false pleasantries, summarily brushing them aside.

"Come, Parkinson. I don't believe for a second that you're happy to see a man you owe money. I'm not coming for a full reparation. I simply need a little to tide my crew over until I get this cargo straightened out."

Jack saw relief spread across the moneylender's face. Parkinson truly was an inferior species, always scurrying from one investor to another, covering investments, spending lavishly, and then covering again. Still, there were advantages to keeping close relations with men who put their hands into the pockets of influential men. Parkinson's son scuttled from the shadows, a bare-chested, filthy lad of about thirteen years with an undernourished and skeletal frame, regarding Jack with great curiosity.

"You must be the brave gatekeeper," Jack said, moved to speak with the boy, a sense of compassion for the child's isolation driving him. The boy flashed a dingy smile, nodding his head vigorously. Jack wondered how long it had been since the boy had last eaten a proper meal. The life as the son of a scoundrel must be a difficult cross to bear, he thought grimly.

"So, Captain Cunningham, how much will you presently be needing to meet the needs of your crew? I can't promise that I have much available immediately, but I will do my best."

Parkinson was careful picking his words, feeling Jack out for the minimal amount of money to placate the moody merchant skipper. He noticed Jack's lingering gaze on the boy, and, mistaking it for something lurid, laid his attenuated hand on his sleeve, pulling Jack gently aside. "Perhaps some further recompense can be extended, something off the books? If you value him, it can be arranged," he stated plainly. Recognizing the vile proposition, Jack glared into the man's lifeless eyes, struggling to master a surging hatred for the moneylender. Turning his empathic gaze back on the hunched boy, he appraised his potential strength as a seaman, and though he found it woefully lacking, his conscience bade that he accept the proposal before he let the poor soul live under such parental cruelty.

"I have a counter proposal. What if I bought the lad outright for my own permanent uses?" Turning to the boy,

Jack asked in a friendly way, "What do you have to say lad, would you fare well with a change of scenery and learning the ropes aboard ship? A ration of grog like any full grown man?"

The young Parkinson glowed at the suggestion, his mouthed appreciation coming in a growl of delight. His father grinned momentarily with relief before realizing his reaction did not suit the role of bereaved parent. Straightening himself purposefully and clearing his throat like a mechanical thing he claimed how difficult it would be losing his boy to the fortunes of the sea, hinting that it was a price far greater than any he could properly name. Jack was no dullard and seeing what the moneylender was hinting at, he said to take a reasonable sum off the account to pay for the boy, while warning Parkinson not to exaggerate the amount absurdly. Bending to the counting ledge, Jack worked a few numbers out on a scratch piece of paper. He figured up the amount of hard currency he would need to pay the crew in their appropriate shares while leaving enough for himself to get about town until some more solid arrangements with the cargo was made. The moneylender's eyebrows shot up with alarm as he looked over the figure, but seeing that Jack was in no mood to be trifled with, he bit his tongue and disappeared into the back room to retrieve the strong box.

"What is your name?" Jack asked, fixing his attention once again on the boy.

"Peter, Sir," the youngster returned shrilly.

"Well, Pete, you won't get by with this skylarking. Get whatever dunnage you need and get ready to ship out."

"Dunnage, Sir?"

"Clothes, man. Any personal effects you can fit into a sea kit."

Pete scratched his head in confusion.

"Never mind. Get a shirt and your shoes at least."

The youth sprang towards the back of the house. Jack brought a handkerchief from his pocket and mopped his beaded forehead. Why the moneylender insisted on keeping a fire in the height of the Virginian summer entirely escaped him. As he toyed with the idea of dumping a bucket of water on the flames Parkinson returned with a canvas bag loaded with coins, flinging it carelessly onto the counter. Jack pinched the bag open with his fingers, pocketed what he needed for his personal use, and then secured the bundle with a short length of rope, double knotting it. Pete returned in a shirt that came nearly to his knees and a pair of tattered pumps which looked as though they predated Queen Anne's War.

"Well, Pete, say goodbye to your father like a good lad," Jack said without much feeling. The boy crossed the room with his eyes on the floor, halting a few feet shy of the man who had sold him into a life of uncertain future and likely peril. Parkinson inflated his chest with false pride as he expelled a sentimental oration on the demands of fatherhood, explaining that despite the emotional damage Pete's absence would cause him, the opportunities it would bring the boy could not be ignored. It was better for the lad not to be raised by a bachelor after all, he claimed. Concluding the lament with a few insincere tears, Parkinson turned his back, saying that he hoped to see Pete sometime again before he died, though he was firm in his wish that the youngster never look back, pining uselessly on the lost comforts of hearth and home.

As Jack and his newest crew member stepped back into the alleyway, Pete seemed already to be making good on his promise of not looking on leaving home with regret. The boy strode beside his captain with a jaunty step, his grimy face lit with excitement. We will see how long that lasts the first time he wretches his heart out in a ten foot swell, Jack thought with amusement. Deciding to make the best use of his time, he pulled the boy aside where the alley met the main avenue to give him his first assignment as a hand aboard the *Norfolk Gold*.

"Look here, Pete. This bag is headed for the *Gold*, that's

your ship, you understand? It's warped alongside the wharf. It's the only black hulled schooner tied up right now. You think you can find that on your own?"

Perhaps it was giving the youth too much responsibility too quickly, but Jack sensed Pete was good for it and would not risk any naughtiness that might cost him his berth on the schooner. Certainly it would be a far better life than remaining under the nominal supervision of his father. Such an example of trust could be a good thing for the lad to see from the beginning.

"Oh, yes, Mister Cunningham. I'm right clever at figgerin' out as such."

"Good. Take this to Mister MacDonald. Tell him to pay it out accordingly to every man aboard and then let them loose on the town. Also tell him to keep three men aboard to watch the cargo. One of these men is going to be you. Let him know he needs to work you into the watch bill and issue you a proper seaman's rig from the slop chest. Think you can remember that?"

"Yes, Sir!" Pete said, eagerly knuckling his forehead.

Jack smiled. "This isn't the navy so you don't need to salute. Just remember to ask permission to do something if you don't know whether you're allowed to do it or not and say "aye, aye, Sir" whenever somebody else on the schooner gives an order."

"Aye, aye, Sir!" Pete returned punctually.

Jack handed the money bag over to the boy and watched as he danced away through the throngs of street traffic, past the high elbows of teamsters and pimps, bumping against the low shouldered cart horses with plunging necks, headed in a dizzy zig-zag toward the general direction of the waterfront. Well, another charity case added to the roster, Jack observed wryly. He only hoped it proved to be a sound investment in due time.

As he picked his way through the massed pedestrians Jack suddenly became aware of a gnawing hunger. Errands were a necessary but famishing part of his chores as ship's captain, and as he quickened his step he resolved to allow himself an extravagant dinner when he reached The Raleigh.

Stepping into the familiar front room of the inn, Jack was immediately greeted by the soliciting tones of Mrs. Cambrey, her red, round face assuming its carefully practiced diffidence. She inquired after his recent trip, hoping that it had gone well and that he remained in good health. Though generally a kind woman, Mrs. Cambrey was not a sharp wit and in a few minutes Jack had tired of her clumsy flattery. Peering past her into the large room of the inn's dining wing, he could see that there were a number of familiar faces which he presently preferred to avoid. Claiming to feel ill and weary—a fiction not far from the truth—and averse to socializing, he asked Mrs. Cambrey if she could see to it that a few leftovers could be sent up to his room with a bottle of wine. Upon hearing her assurance that she could do better and have a fine meal especially prepared to his liking, he dropped a couple of coins into her chubby hand and mounted the stairs.

Jack's room was a small triangular space in the inn's attic. Its single window was set in a dormer that added a little height above the area where he kept a shoddy clerk's desk. His bed was pushed against the room's inner wall to make room enough to pass between a single rocking chair and the plain wooden commode with chamber pot. The ceiling was low and steeply pitched, even at its greatest height allowing just over seven feet of head room, so that as Jack stepped in and crossed to the room's corners he was forced to stoop. Accustomed to the tight quarters aboard ship, the confining dimensions did not bother him unduly, though he was sometimes prone to swear violently if upon awakening in the middle of the evening to make water and forgetting the ceiling's proximity, he would crash his head against the unyielding wood. The room, however, was cheap and the only one in The Raleigh that Mrs. Cambrey would let for more than a month at a time. Besides, the window looked just over the top of the bank opposite of the inn, allowing a splendid view of the waterfront and the nearest arm of the harbor. Jack could even make out the spiky quills of the masts of the merchantmen warped alongside the wharves. He narrowed his eyes, trying to see if he could distinguish those of the *Norfolk Gold* from the others, but the distance was too great.

He settled back onto the mattress, kicking off his boots and stretching to his full length. It was good to be back in The Raleigh, a place where he could shuck off his worries like some men could shift their clothes. He closed his eyes, letting the warm sunlight from the open window play over him as it rode in on a fluttering breeze, allowing his mind to turn serene and reflective. Was it always like this, coming back to his secluded piece of the world, alone and without responsibility, embraced by solitude? It was hard sometimes to feel like a man could find a place to fill out his own skin apart from the constant demands of others. Certainly it was never possible aboard ship where every crew member depended on the captain's all-knowing and all-powerful Word. He laughed quietly to himself, thinking of what certitude the men faithfully placed in his knowledge and abilities, wondering if any of them truly suspected the depth of self-doubt which permeated his every decision. Of course, he was never permitted to show that weakness, give the men any hint that he too suffered from human flaws. Any such suggestion of vulnerability would be the first slippery step toward lost religion for those who risked their very lives by believing in Him.

A soft knock at the door retrieved him to the present. The lure of fresh vittles Mrs. Cambrey might have concocted quickly overthrew his abstractions. As he approached the door and pulled it open a new hunger stirred within him. A young woman wearing a thin gray dress that gathered in narrow folds across her bust stood bearing a tray topped with medallions of fried pork, a silver coffee pot, and a small stack of flat bread. She wore a mob cap that unsuccessfully struggled to contain her mass of light blonde hair, the fragrant twists escaping in random patterns down the long slope of her neck, carelessly fanning across her pronounced collarbone. The dress pulled across her ample, inviting lines, the lines of a fine schooner, Jack thought, his gaze lingering on her intriguing shape...

"I hope this means I am a good surprise?" she said, smiling.

"How did you know I had returned?" Jack answered, unable to be articulate just now, an animal force surging within him.

The young woman shrugged, laying a hand on his shoulder and leaning forward to kiss his cheek. She placed the tray on top of his desk and began to set places for both of them to dine. Before she accomplished this undertaking, Jack seized her by the waist and pulled her to him, clutching the long hour glass of her midriff as her hips angled gently to meet him. In a controlled fall to the bed, they clawed at each other's bodies, articles of clothing discarded anxiously. As her mob cap was removed the full wildness of her hair splayed down the long hollow of her back. Jack lifted the hair from her shoulders and bit lightly into the nape of her neck, causing her to lurch unexpectedly and utter a soft moan. Urged on, he repeated the love play down the length of her back, kissing and setting his teeth lightly into her soft skin, lingering purposefully in the sensitive places which caused her to twist in pleasure. Turning her gently over, Jack was drawn instinctively closer by the strong smell of her sex.

***

Late into the afternoon they lay unclothed beneath the warm currents of an offshore breeze, talking quietly and listening to the sounds from the street below.

"So you will still try to find out what the company wants you to do? Surely they won't forget about one of their best captains?"

Jack managed a slight shrug. "I suppose so, Charlotte. You would be in a far better position to know how your father tracks his shipping than I. The Fraser clan has never been one to let any surplus of currency slip away if they could help it, judging from my experience. I wonder if our liaisons are not some ingenious plan on the part of your father to assure I don't embezzle any profits. You wouldn't happen to be a spy would you, Miss Fraser?"

Charlotte's fine eyebrow arched teasingly as she rolled onto Jack's chest. "Why on earth would you think that? Do I not cut the perfect picture of innocence?"

It was Jack's turn to assume a wry expression.

"Somehow, I think my answer would get me into dangerous waters. I will say that you are certainly more than initially meets the eye, though what *does* meet the eye is in no way wanting."

She smirked with curious satisfaction, placing her long fingers on Jack's chest, lightly drawing a circle over his weathered, scarred skin. He caught his breath sharply and drew her onto him, kissing her with renewed spirit. Giggling half-heartedly, she pushed him away.

"My poor, Jack. I've been simply horrible to you, haven't I? All this time and I haven't allowed you a moment to eat. You must be starving and now the food has gone all cold. Come sit with me at least. I must make up for this neglect."

She rolled deftly away from his grasp and drew the dress over her head, her blue eyes laughing with thinly veiled mischief as Jack regarded her with a reproachful air. She was right, however, in that he was close to fainting from lack of nourishment. Flinging the sheets off haphazardly, he searched for his missing articles of clothing, finding a stray boot and his fisherman's shirt pooled in the room's far corner. The remaining pieces stubbornly remained hidden somewhere in the cyclone of twirled bedding. Giving his trousers up as temporarily lost, Jack scratched his chin pensively before deciding to array himself in the bed's top sheet, hanging it on his tall frame like a toga.

After a short meal of clammy pork medallions and lukewarm coffee, he was feeling decidedly better, his full range of animal appetites now sated. Well, perhaps temporarily at least, he thought, beginning to feel the first renewed hint of sexual stirrings as he gazed across at the shallow rise and fall of the beautiful girl's deeply shaded bosom...

"It really is getting late," she said, inclining her head to watch the late afternoon foot traffic plunge down Raleigh Street. "Wouldn't want to upset my father with an unaccounted absence. That wouldn't do for either one of us, would it, Jack?"

Certainly it would not. Jack knew full well he was engaging in a dangerous game by indulging in this distraction with Charlotte Fraser. Knowing that it was a risky affair, to both business and body, did little to dissuade his desire, unfortunately. Though only nineteen, Charlotte had the natural and confident manner of a woman several years her senior. It made her disturbing in many respects, suggesting depths to her person that put Jack on his guard. She was a vague twist of lovely smoke: pleasant danger. Undeniably, it added an element of excitement to the already exhilarating sport of their coupling.

Jack answered, "I'm sure you've planned some excuse if I know you at all, Charlotte. I believe you can manage to linger until I've finished my coffee, surely?"

Charlotte bit her lip in meditation, one of her more recently adopted coquettish gestures, before nodding slowly and placing her cup demurely to her lips. Jack lost his train of thought as she swallowed, the long current of gently moving flesh shivering down the length of her lifted neck.

"You would be well told to keep clear of father today, Jack, he is not happy with the news of the export deadline being changed. It means a great deal of money lost, money he was counting on."

"So the rumors are true, the rebels have gone back on

their word?"

"Yes, of course they shunned their word. Look at the amount of rich cargoes they have trapped. Have your enemy gather all of his resources in a mad dash to beat the shipping deadline and then, just when he has amassed as much as he can, slam the door shut and scoop up everything he has. It's perfect really."

Jack grimaced. "You seem to be enjoying this too much by half. I would like to believe you aren't so contrary."

"It is rather funny seeing father so tangled up in knots. He hasn't been this bereaved since his old Major Domo absconded with all of the silverware and sold it for a passage to the West Indies. Come, Jack, I don't scandalize you too much, do I? It's not that I don't understand how important it is, but I can't linger on these boring things for too very long without becoming sick of it all. Tell me, now: why does all this business worry you so much? You are a rich man, more rosy than a plucked goose. Why does it matter? You could sail home on the first tide and leave this political rondette to the bloody fools that are too stupid to settle the thing civilly, and be as free as a lark. What do you have to gain by keeping a hand in this troubled business?"

"You have a rare talent for lecture, Miss Fraser. As to why—well, it's more complicated than—at any rate, why are you berating me like a mongrel dog? Aren't you supposed to be happy and courteous when your man comes away from the sea? You are cutting a very poor figure for the lovelorn."

"My man," she blew out the words with a curt edge. "Don't play the hurt hero. Your face is all wrong for it. Besides, I am sure neither one of us would be hard put to find a supplement in the bed. It is part of a sailor's life, isn't it? Or perhaps I have been lied to all my life."

"Please don't be difficult. You have an unfair advantage in that you are a woman." Jack was about to continue, but taking in the rising tempest in Charlotte's eyes with a quick glance, he softened his words. "And I am too tired to offend my Dear One. Forgive my bad manners; I am only worried about how I should cover my debts. Business is money and business has spoiled and so too has my mood. I am not at all myself."

Considering his retreat severely, Charlotte granted him pardon with a slight, brisk nod as she carefully tucked her abundant hair into the mob cap. "I will forget your rudeness, Captain Cunningham, only because you are too stupid to know when you have injured your most faithful friends."

"We are still friends, then, I take it?"

Again, she studied him through long, slanted eyes. "Only due to my own sense of Christian forgiveness and my love for Scotland."

It was not the first time he had heard her say as much. Sweeping her into an embrace, he pressed her strong body against his. Her sweet ideas of patriotism were traits that recommended the dear girl very much indeed.

Soon after Charlotte left, Jack set the room back to rights and pulled out a sheaf of papers to write a letter. He had a bottle of Marsala sent up with a fresh pot of coffee, allowing both equal precedence as he drank one sip from the long stemmed glass and one from the tiny china cup, as he lingered over the blank page, wrestling with the elusive composition. Soon, he found himself turning to the wine with growing frequency. Thus buoyed, he hurled the words out in fits and starts. Once finished, he studied the correspondence with a critical eye, belching softly with satisfaction.

The letter was for his wife, Rebecca, explaining the reason for the prolonged delay in his return home. It was liberally sprinkled with soothing flatteries and vague sentiments of affection, just the thing she would require, he thought with a touch of smugness. Jack was the first to admit that his wife was a damned beautiful woman, but the long time apart from her had confirmed his suspicion that they were simply too different to ever be permanently happy in one another's company. Jack was not naïve enough to believe that marriage guaranteed a man happiness, but he was keenly aware of a particular kind of lack with Rebecca, an unspoken indifference. For a long time he had felt guilty over his aversion, but time had allowed him to grow accustomed to his feelings. Now the only lingering regret was for the little time he allowed to spend with his daughter. He salved that bit of his conscience with the fact that he knew many good women whose fathers were rarely present during their rearing. The mother was far more important in a child's life, Jack had to admit, and he was consoled with the confident knowledge of Rebecca's impeccable maternal character.

But her skill as a wife, that was another matter. While most men he knew took very little consideration of their wives' opinions concerning whether to buy a new carriage, move an invalid cousin into the guest quarters, or any other small but significant event of routine domestic drama, Jack was always solicitous of his new bride, making sure that what decisions he made would not unnecessarily put her out. Rebecca, however, stubbornly refused matrimonial content. He wondered if he had unwittingly given offense by some thoughtless remark to have turned her so decidedly against his advances, but wracking his mind as thoroughly as he could, he never turned up a satisfactory result. Eventually, the pain of denied pleasures became excruciating for a man of Jack's rambunctious appetites. Rebecca's distant manner was pointedly unkind because of her conspicuous gift of *Eros*. Her face was the model of classical beauty, her body the inspiration for pornographic pamphlets. Never could Jack have imagined a woman more physically desirable nor one more sharply aloof when it came to sharing her sexual charms. The husband and wife's rare unions were brief flopping affairs of mute antipathy, punctuated by the few desperate clutches—entirely on Jack's part—during the penultimate carnal release. A year of this treatment began wearing heavily on Jack's nerves, and when he was offered a chance to return to the colonies and the company, he had not given it a second thought.

He folded the letter and sealed it, putting it aside for the post first thing in the morning. As he stood, he felt a sudden rush of blood to his head. Blinking back his dizziness, he gave one last glimpse at the street below, lightly trafficked now as the street beacons were being lighted by the constables. Flinging himself on the bed and turning his head to the wall, he wondered why he felt so very low.

5. DEN OF INTRIGUE

NOT many of the *Norfolk Gold*s crew had returned from their night of shore-going revelry by the time Jack came to collect Mister MacDonald shortly before 9 a.m. Those who had were in a sorry state of affairs, two of whom were passed out in the scuppers face down, an unnatural shade of green. One, seaman Gavin, was accompanied by an orange haired doxy nearly as big around as the schooner's capstan, her copious frame overstretching his, her mouth gaped skywards, snoring with prodigious volume. The only man on the main deck who appeared about his wits at all was the young Pete Parkinson, newly togged out in canvas slop trousers and a clean shirt.

"Well, Pete, looks like you've found a way to cut a rhumb line, after all," Jack greeted the boy.

Pete struggled to decipher if his captain was indeed paying him a compliment, his narrow face contorted with thought, before he finally decided from Jack's tone that a "rhumb line" was indeed a good thing. Pulling himself up smartly, he reported the deck all secure and stated that the only sober man aboard, other than himself, was Mister MacDonald.

"MacDonald is in my cabin, I take it?"

"Yes, Captain. He is up to his elbows with some sort of papers. Said I wasn't to disturb him unless it was an emergency."

"Very good. Light along and fetch a swab to clean up the

deck. If Mister Gavin and his trollop haven't roused themselves in five minutes, dump a bucket of salt water on them, understand?"

The boy's eyes flickered with devilry. "Aye, aye, Captain!"

As he entered the great cabin, Jack could see that Alan was in no mood for banter. True to young Parkinson's description, the first mate was covered up with a small flotilla of labeled papers placed about the cabin's space in an elaborate pattern that exceeded even Jack's algebraic imagination. Casting his gaze across the deck, he suddenly remembered why he hated the dreary repetition of lading bills. Keeping a straight account of the men's pay was bad enough for him, but the precise figuring required by cargo discharge entailed an unthinkable hell.

"Would you be upset if I told you that all of this was likely done in vain?" Jack asked dryly.

Alan continued to shuffle through the nearest stack of documents. "And good morning to you too, Jack. I trust you had a pleasant evening's rest."

Grinning wryly at the implied criticism, Jack swept the tails of his coat to the side as he settled his bulk on a small chair across from his first mate. He noted that the wound on the old man's neck from the dueling practice, a slight puckered stripe of dried blood, was not bandaged. Alan's set countenance was as solid as a sea chest, frowning and intent. Coming to the end of the inventory, he laid the list aside and turned a bland expression on his captain.

"What did you mean by all in vain, Jack?"

Explaining as briefly but comprehensively as he could, Jack detailed the changing of the export deadline and what it boded both for the company at large as well as the personal fortunes for the captain and crew of the *Norfolk Gold.* Alan was naturally discomfited by the news, shifting in his chair and making petulant sounds in the back of his throat when he heard further details. Once Jack had laid it all out, Alan slammed his flattened palm against the edge of the desk with such force that a nearby stack of papers fluttered to the deck in long, erratic circles.

"Damn my eyes! I should have known this would happen. There was every sign of it before we left for Wilmington, but I thought—well, that doesn't matter. What does Fraser say?"

Jack shrugged. "I am going to see him this morning. Yesterday he was covered up with every other company ship's captain and supercargo who wanted their own problems sorted out. Perhaps with a day to respond he might be better disposed to helping us. How is the neck?"

Alan touched his fingertips briefly to the open sore. "Merely a scratch. You were more game the other day than I credited, Jack."

"About that, Alan, truly I apologize. I was in a terrible way after my meeting with the English captain and I took out my spite on you. Please understand I was not myself. I felt devilish bad about it afterwards."

Alan laughed richly, leaning back in his chair, sighting his friend down the length of his aquiline nose. "All just so much stuff, laddie. I can't fault an opponent for his desire to win a bout. Wouldn't be worth this old man's time otherwise. As it is, I think I may have had it coming to me after that nonsense on the quarterdeck when we were coming through the shoals. I should be the one to apologize to you. No right and certainly no sense in what I said. Please withdraw my note of protest; I had my mind somewhere else."

Jack smiled, feeling a general easing of his conscience and a wealth of affection burgeon for his old friend. "I'm uncommonly grateful, Alan, for your kindness. But I fear that your protest seems to signify more clearly than I thought at the time. I dinna like that damned Englishman's way of treating me, all condescension and dirty looks. He reminds me too much of a lordly vulture. To be boarded and searched is one thing, but to be shepherded all the way to our home anchorage to make sure we weren't clever smugglers is another world entirely!"

Alan nodded. "Yes, I noticed that silly midshipman walking the waterfront this morning at first light pretending to take an interest in everything in the harbor except us. At least the Englishman's foolish enough to use that popinjay to see to our business. If he continues along that line we shall avoid any problems."

A sudden earsplitting keening sounded from the deck above, the voice of a female demon spurred to rancorous activity. It was followed by a low octave guttural howl and a tremor of stamping footsteps. Alan lifted an eyebrow inquiringly.

"Our new recruit's first official duty," Jack explained, "Waking the ship's drunkards after a night of imprudent consumption."

"Ah, I see. Capital idea, though I'm not sure I'll answer for our young lubber's safety if Mister Gavin ever clasps onto him. I pray that he is nimble."

"I think it is safe to say that Mr. Parkinson has no small experience with eluding the hands of punishment. I dinna mean to cast him on you like I did, without any kind of formal notice, but there were a few things I had to settle at The Raleigh before I returned."

Alan was quite sure Jack had settled an account with a tasty strumpet, if he knew his young intemperate friend at all, but rather than giving voice to this conjecture, he merely shrugged and said, "I'll never say no to a willing hand, though I have to cut a straight line with you, Jack, you are a far more trusting soul than I to have sent a guttersnipe bearing a month's pay for a shipload of men. I'm amazed he didn't disappear on the first packet for Barbados."

"It was an uncommon risk looking back on it. You could not credit how badly he had it where I found him, Alan, his own father willing to pimp the child out for any lecher's buggery. I knew he would be as loyal as a spaniel if I showed a little kindness; I would say that it answered well."

"Hard to argue, Jack, even if your methods appear half-baked, your results are better than burgoo. That reminds me; I caught Mister Yeoman hording cheese in his sea kit last night. Had nearly two pounds of the stuff disguised with his dirty trousers. I'm not certain that I know what the wretch had in mind for that much of the moldy rubbish, but I've told him he's not permitted another tot of grog until you've seen to him."

Jack placed his fingertips to his temples, wondering briefly if a proper application of pressure there might drive out his worries concerning the habitually diabolical nature of his cabin boy. After a moment, he opened his eyes and stated wearily, "I fear we have shipped Beelzebub himself. Does he understand how serious the theft of ship's stores is?"

"I'm uncertain he understands much beyond his own name presently. He turned up on deck this morning god awful sick, nearly retching his heart onto the deck. Only reason I found his stash was because he was passed out drunk when I went to look for him last evening to paint the forward bulwarks."

Jack caught a sigh and shook his head disconsolately. He felt no small part of the blame for his cabin boy's delinquency, fearing that he may have allowed Davy far too many liberties for his immature years. Some lads were able to adapt to the change of the regimented life of living aboard ship, stow away their childish natures and weak, cloying thoughts of home. Others, however, would be fully grown men before becoming capable of shaking off the shackles of a simple heart.

"I leave him to your discretion, Alan. I will substitute young Pete as my steward. Perhaps life among the foremast jacks might help poor Davey see the error of his ways."

"Or harden his criminal soul," Alan noted with a smile of irony.

"A possibility, but he will lose his lubberliness at least. For now, however, we have greater concerns. Namely, seeing what the company has in store for us and the tons of rice uselessly stuffing our guts. I would admire your company this morning, Alan, when I pay a call on that villain Fraser. I collect it would not be too much of an imposition?"

"I would be honored to add whatever weight I can. I will see Mister Gavin to take charge of the ship."

After a few minutes to ensure the irate and heavy-handed Gavin was not intent on the extermination of the hereto nimble footed Pete Parkinson, Jack and Alan hired a cab to carry them across Norfolk Square to the main trading office of Wallace and Associates. As they rode over Jack lapsed into a quiet solitude, considering the possibility that Fraser might very well be as helpless to suggest a solution to the problem of their destinationless cargo as he. Jack hoped the old miser would at least offer them a modest, if somewhat depreciated, advance on the goods his schooner carried. If not, he would be stuck in an unenviable position, desperately calling in any old favors with local farmers and merchants to turn the cargo over at a bad loss. The crumbling state of affairs within the colony would make such hasty arrangements nearly impossible and might very well bankrupt him. It could become necessary to sell the *Norfolk Gold,* stranding himself ashore without prospects for any immediate future employment. His brains were rattled thus as the coach creaked to a stop before the company office and he piled into the street...

"There's no right way of saying this, Alan, but I would admire if you saw fit not to mention our scrape with the Rebel pirates. It doesn't do us credit in the Old Man's eyes."

"For certain, Jack. You can count me even."

Reassured, Jack led the way through the shadowy threshold and past the rank and file arrangement of the copyists at their desks. Pulling up short of the gatekeeper Bairn, he received a cursory nod and the words, "He's been expecting you for this past hour." Drawing up his resolve, Jack mounted the long stair with Alan following closely behind. Cresting the parapet of Fraser's upper chambers, he was immediately fixed by the Senior Merchant's bleary, colorless eye.

"Cunningham, you whoreson, sit down. We have a mountain of hell to summon up. You too, MacDonald. It concerns you as well."

Jack and Alan warily pulled a pair of hard stools from the far corner of the merchant's office and dragged them across from Fraser's document heaped desk. Fraser was an enormous man, copper haired with a pocked, sallow complexion. His girth was not constituted purely of fat but rather of a prodigious gathering of hard tissue beneath an outer layer of softness. Jack suspected that an ancient longshoreman's physique lurked somewhere underneath the pasty outer shell, slowly gone to ruin from the many years of bureaucratic labor. Nothing about the ill-looking man suggested that he could sire the likes of one Charlotte Fraser, a girl remarkable in her physical beauty, and Jack idly wondered if the late Mrs. Fraser had not been rather liberal in her affections.

"Look here, Cunningham," Fraser's grating, ill-tempered voice jarred Jack's speculations, "I know why you are here as well as every other ship's master in the Chesapeake. Just as I know you were here yesterday and thought better of bothering me with your problems when you learned what I was dealing with. Now, the fact that you were enough about your senses to give me time to sort these dealings out is the only reason I will help you."

Jack caught a surprised glance of congratulations from Alan but chose to discreetly ignore him, containing his relief over finding himself for once in Fraser's good graces.

Fraser continued in his surly way, "Now, I know the *Norfolk Gold* is stuffed to the gills from your latest rice run. I'm sorry to say that the situation being what it presently is, I'm unable to pay you off to any advantage. However, I have been made aware of a possible opportunity for you that may provide a means of discharging your cargo, though it involves bringing a third party into the exchange." Fraser cleared his throat to call attention to the significance of the enterprise he was about to propose. Wise to the cue, Jack leaned forward attentively. "You will have heard perhaps that Lord Dunmore is seeking loyal captains in order to supplement his naval forces within the Chesapeake?"

"I have heard rumors of as much for the past month. Though I don't credit how that should affect us. The *Norfolk Gold* is far too lightly armed and undermanned for such duties. She could be little more than a tender," Jack explained, a trifle defensively.

Fraser arranged his round, red hands across his inflated belly, making a poor effort to contain his tried patience. "You will then kindly observe the details, Cunningham. Indeed, as you point out, the *Norfolk Gold* is too lightly armed and manned for war fighting. However, Lord Dunmore has seen fit to let the company know that he has arranged for an exchange of commodities that would go far toward bringing a merchant vessel up to fighting trim. The specifics of this are not important for the sake of discussion, but it is sufficient to say that ship's cannons may be acquired in exchange for food provisions, namely the very rice you are carrying." Fraser again paused, allowing time for the import of his words to sink in. "After such an exchange was finalized, a fast ship like the *Norfolk Gold* might bring great credit upon her name as a vessel in the King's service, perhaps earning a significant sum in the number of prizes she would secure."

"You suggest we turn privateer then?"

"No, nothing so romantic. Lord Dunmore wants to have a close hand in the deployment of his ships. He would be willing to hire your ship for a handsome fee, placing an officer of the Royal Navy aboard her in temporary command. With him the officer would bring a small number of experienced navy seamen to supplement the schooner's numbers. Of course, you would be expected to stay aboard serving in an advisory capacity, providing the officer with your knowledge of the local area. In many ways you would retain control of the *Norfolk Gold,* with the important exception of when you might be engaged in action against the rebels. It is a rare chance for someone in your position, Cunningham, and I, for one, believe that it is much better than you deserve."

Jack was unable to decide whether Fraser was sincere in his advice. There were several problems with the proposal, foremost of which was surrendering sole command of the schooner to some English officer whom Jack had never met. It had been several years since he had served as a subordinate to another captain's wishes and he well knew there was nothing more difficult for a proud man than to serve as a tyrannical commander's toady. It would also mean that his crew would be carried on the books as seamen of the navy, making them subject to the infamous harsh discipline of the service. They might resist the strictness, causing problems to the schooner's smooth functioning; they could also resent Jack for his complicity in the change of command, breaking old loyalties that would not easily be re-forged. And yet, what other real options did he have? If he was unable to find some means of employment very soon then the crew would be without work and available for conscription by the English anyhow. For the black men it could be much worse if they chose to seek a livelihood in the colony and were captured by the rebels, condemning them to the bottomless tortures of slavery. No, he must make the decision that would give the majority of his men a fighting chance, even if only a slim one, to continue to ply their trade as free, self-determined men.

"I am grateful for this opportunity, Mister Fraser. Who do I need to see to say that I will accept this offer?"

Fraser grunted with gruff approval. "Very good, you aren't as foolish as I believed. You shall not have to concern yourself with these details. I took the liberty of passing along your name to Lord Dunmore yesterday. He will send his officer to you sometime this afternoon, I expect. Any decisions you arrive at after that are between you and the navy. Now, if you will please be moving along, gentlemen, I have a small crisis to deal with before the noon meal, and no more time to waste on the likes of you."

Driven unceremoniously from their seats, Jack and Alan

collected their effects as they began to leave. "Oh, Cunningham," Fraser's booming voice chased them down as Jack placed his neatly buffed shoe to the first step down. "I would advise you to be more careful in future merchant excursions. It may suit you very well to give chase to rebel pirates when you are sailing in the King's navy, but it was a stupid adventure to undertake when you were carrying cargo. If you had caught me in a bad humor I should have fired you and your crew on the spot for such recklessness, regardless of whether or not the cargo made it safely into port. I have my spies, Cunningham," Fraser explained. "Fortunately it appears someone with your rash spirit might do well as a private man of war. Do try to not to get yourself sunk. I can replace ship captains, but the ships themselves are another matter altogether. If all goes well perhaps this rebellion can be stamped out before the year is out and I can find a place for the *Norfolk Gold* on the company list sometime in the near future."

Jack nodded curtly at his dismissal and clattered swiftly down the steps.

Turning out into the street, Alan soon fell behind the hurried stride of his youthful captain. Catching up with an awkward rheumatic pumping of his limbs, he grasped Jack's sleeve, entreating a more humane pace.

"Sorry, Alan. I'm damn well out of my wits. Somehow I feel like I've been tricked into a tight spot. Did you see that old devil's scowling and condescension? There's no accounting for such impertinence. But what choice do I have? Let the rice rot and tell every man jack to fend for himself as best as he can?"

"Aye, there's a bad rub to it. I would damn well like to know who saw fit to tell him of our run in with the pirates. It wasn't none of our men, I'll vow."

"No, I believe you're right. I'll warrant it was that blackballing Englishman Amis. He has the cut of a man not unwilling to gab to everyone's discredit. Who told Fraser is not important now, however. I don't presume to think you will want to stay on since I know how you feel about this rebel fighting, but I would be damned sorry to see you go."

"It's true, laddie, that I'm not given to these wartime antics lightly, but you'd be mistaken to think I wouldn't still be pleased to sail with you, Jack. When it comes to turning arms on Virginians I can't promise I will be happy in my duties, but I don't believe you're likely to have a better pilot aboard."

"I would be a fool to dispute that. And I welcome you as a friend, which I could certainly use right now."

After picking their way down to The Raleigh, Jack and Alan found an unoccupied corner in the tap room and sent the pot boy off to fetch a backgammon set and a couple of tankards of porter. By the time he returned with the requested items the chamber had begun to fill up with the usual midday crowd of sailors, shopkeepers, and tradesmen. Jack nodded politely to a few old acquaintances while he talked quietly with Alan. Putting the backgammon set aside after a couple of games, both of which fell in Alan's favor in two solid gammons, Jack sent the pot boy off for another round of porter. As he did so his eye happened to fall on a dark-faced man casting about for a place to sit in the crowded room; he knew the fellow well enough to motion him over to share their table. As the man pulled a chair up to the table the pot boy returned with their drinks only to be sent off again to serve the latest addition to their party. The boy sneered disapprovingly at the newest customer, but went obediently on his way just the same.

"Captain Cunningham, it has been an age," the man said with an easy, confident voice that threaded through rather than boomed over the general din of the crowded tap room. His thinning black hair was pulled back tightly in a queue; he wore side whiskers that tapered unfashionably down to the middle of his jaw, framing his gaunt face. However, his forbidding appearance belied a warm, amicable manner which immediately became apparent by the uncommon grace he exhibited in his person. His carriage was natural yet attentive, apparently traits of a well-bred gentleman. His dress was likewise fine and tastefully simple, limited to a tailored gray frock and matching waist coat with a pair of white cotton breeches; a man attired so that nothing at all suggested him to be a smuggler.

"Good day, Captain Greene. Any gossip from the free-trade?"

Greene smiled noncommittally as he drew a cigar from his inner coat pocket and lit it by a candle flame. "There are of course ups and downs, like any business, as I am sure both of you gentlemen well know. However, it is fair to say that I have no problems keeping myself in hearth and home. What of the *Norfolk Gold?* I hear she has timed her return to Norfolk in an unpropitious manner. Some dreadful stories have it that she has a full cargo with no ready buyer because of the export regulations. Surely my two old friends would not be so clumsy as to let a few *legal* restrictions keep them from turning a profit?"

Jack nodded, fixing the gentleman smuggler with a glum look. "Your insight is as good as your company, Daniel. We've struck a deal to hire the *Norfolk Gold* out to Lord Dunmore. Perhaps that way we can recover our losses until this rebellion is straightened out."

"A bold stroke," Greene said, taking his tankard of porter from the exasperated pot boy. "Though not necessarily a wise one, if you will excuse my directness. What is it, Jack, that makes you believe this rebellion will end anytime soon? For God's sake, it hasn't yet truly begun."

"You seem particularly ardent for a disinterested moonraker," Alan cut in gravely. "Or am *I* being too bold?"

Greene shrugged. "I will not say that I don't have an interest in seeing Virginia free of British revenuers. Having the Royal Navy occupied with enemies other than a few harmless men of private enterprise would certainly allow me to breathe more easily. I am not opposed to the quieter living one could have if the English were terrified to sail into the Virginia capes."

"That would only occur if Virginia had her own navy," Jack stated flatly. "And there aren't enough shipyards between here and Baltimore with the men or the desire to build a fleet worthy of sailing into action against what the English already have anchored at Hampton Roads. The English are here to stay, and they will sell any losses at a very dear price."

"Perhaps, but that is assuming the Virginians would choose to fight the Royal Navy on its own terms. We are far too clever for that when we have all the secret coves and anchorages of the Chesapeake at our disposal. It is absolutely the ideal place for a hornet's nest of privateers! I should think a steady loss on the King's books of his colonial shipping would make him think twice about whether this fight is worth it."

"You seem suspiciously at ease in allying yourself with these rebels, Daniel. You know as well as I do that pilfering on the scale you mention would not be recognized as the lawful looting of a privateer. You would be hung as a pirate. Surely you are not thinking of such a course yourself?"

Greene narrowed his reptilian eyes in speculation before managing an answer. "Well, Jack, I would be lying if I said the idea had not occurred to me, but I think too well of my own skin to get directly involved in such intrigues. Particularly knowing that you're intent on augmenting Lord Dunmore's forces. I would hate to find myself up against such a shrewd enemy, especially in light of what I heard you did to those privateersmen a couple of nights ago. What was the name of that new British cutter, the *Bouncer*?"

"The *Boxer*," Jack corrected. "And how, exactly, are you so well informed in the matter, Daniel? Your gossip seems to outsail even the best coaster."

"It sails faster on a Wednesday, I think, when the old harbor hands have nothing better to do than frighten each other with their hysterics. You would not credit this, but the word is about that Dunmore means to land troops within the week, take the colony back under his control by force of arms. Has many folks uncommonly worried. I would be careful who I let know I was hiring my ship out to the English. Norfolk is quick becoming a tough spot for a Tory."

"I've never had any part of calling myself a Virginian. No man here would ever fault me as a liar."

"All the more reason to be careful, Jack. As a friend I'm trying to let you know the best point of sailing, if you can reckon my drift. There are many ears in Norfolk that pass along what they hear with no sense of consequences. The rebels are gaining ground in the west and they mean to come here before long. When they get closer you might not find The Raleigh such a friendly place."

Jack accepted the advice without further challenge, emptying his second round of porter but declining a third, feeling a vague need to keep his wits keen. Greene drank off the rest of his beer coolly, turning the majority of his attention on MacDonald, whom he found far more receptive to pleasant conversation. Jack faded back into himself as he mulled over the possibility that he had involved the crew of the *Norfolk Gold* in a far more dangerous game than he first realized. Greene would not have been so forthright in his warnings if he did not have solid reasons to back up his conviction. No man was more likely than a smuggler to come by such furtive intelligence. Besides, Greene was not the kind of man to spread bad word for the sake of having something to say; he was rather reluctant to speak of politics, the military, or anything that did not pertain directly to the successful conduct of his smuggling business. If it was true that the rebels had already deployed spies in anticipation of an attack on Norfolk, Jack had to devise a way of keeping his plans concealed. Greene he could trust as a fellow captain and a relatively honest man. The same was true of Alan. What worried him most were the hands aboard the schooner, eight men who had no real choosing in the matter of allegiance and who might well prefer to sail against the king's navy rather than support it. How far could he trust them to keep their sailing orders secret the first time they put into port?

"What is it, Jack? You look like you've just sprung a mast," Greene interrupted his thoughts.

Jack smiled in an effort to disguise his sour humor. "Too much to drink on an empty stomach perhaps. I believe I will go up to my room and rest. I am expecting someone after all."

Alan nodded and emptied the remaining contents of his tankard. "I'll be off as well. Plenty of work to see to once the crew staggers back on board."

"I feel as though I have broken up the party. My apologies to you both," Greene said quickly coming to his feet. Jack laid his hand on the gentleman's shoulder to keep him in his seat.

"Don't be silly, Daniel. We are loitering here too long by half. Keep the table and drink the next round on me." Jack motioned the pot boy over and offered a handsome sum to keep his friend well into his cups for the rest of the afternoon. "And don't say another complaining word, Daniel. I may soon need to call on you for favors."

"I would be happy for it," Greene confirmed, enthusiastically wringing Jack's hand in farewell.

Alan followed Jack through the squirming throng of the midday dining clientele until they could hold more discreet conference at the base of the stairs. Leaning close into Jack's face, Alan spoke in a hurried undertone. "Do you take any account of what Greene says? Do you believe there might already be rebel spies in Norfolk?"

"I would be damned hard pressed to say it was not possible and we would be terrible fools not to act accordingly. Once you reach the schooner make sure the crew understands we have to be ready to sail at a moment's notice. No man is allowed to go ashore under any circumstances. Once I meet the English officer here I will come aboard and sling my hammock in the great cabin for as long as we remain in port. By the time I see you next I hope to have a better idea of what folly I have committed us to."

Alan smiled wryly as he struck Jack on the shoulder to bolster his spirits. "I will see to it, Captain, and perhaps see to a bottle of claret in case you find yourself particularly thirsty."

"Make it syllabub if you can, Alan. I have had a craving for the stuff since you last made a batch at Christmas time. It would go well into bringing a festive atmosphere to this cruise."

"Very well, Jack. Until tonight."

"Until tonight, my friend."

Jack had not been alone in his room for more than five minutes when he heard a sharp, official knocking on the door. Sitting at his desk as he rolled up a shaving kit into a small white towel, he called for the stranger to enter. With his back to his visitor, Jack placed the shaving kit beside a knotted canvas bag of personal effects he had gathered to take on board the *Norfolk Gold*. Still without turning around he said, "I take it you are the fellow who means to captain my ship, is that right?"

The man cleared his throat diffidently and spoke in a quiet but assured voice.

"That is your decision of course, Captain Cunningham. But I am here to see if we might be able to come to some agreement. Permit me to introduce myself, Lieutenant Thomas Warren of His Majesty's Cutter *Boxer.*" The man crossed the creaking floorboards.

Jack swiveled round in his seat and shook the Lieutenant's hand, gesturing for him to take a seat on the bed and asking if he could offer him a short tot of rum. Warren declined as he removed his hat and placed it on his knee. Jack made a quick study of the man's features: a long and thin but not unhandsome face, perhaps a year or two past thirty, roughly his own age, blighted with a rather bad scar stretching from the bottom of his right ear to the corner of his compressed mouth. He wore his seagoing rig: a faded coat of blue and canvas trousers tucked into a pair of dripping sea boots. His civil manner suggested he was not coarse by nature but a peculiar blend of the gentrified warrior, equal parts of sound ability and good breeding. He held an envelope between his long, pliant fingers—the hands of a musician or perhaps a painter, Jack thought briefly, his eyes naturally falling on the piece of paper as he wondered what significance it might hold.

"The *Boxer* you say," Jack remarked pensively. "I am somewhat confused. I have been aboard that ship and met with her captain. Why were we not introduced?"

"I was away the night before as prize master of the *Tornado*, the rebel schooner that you fired into in our defense. I was upset to learn I had to bring the schooner in before I had a chance to personally congratulate you on a fine piece of fighting seamanship. It was a very neatly done thing, if I may say."

Jack inclined his head civilly in acceptance of the compliment, wary of succumbing to flattery. "I remember Captain Amis mentioning you were gone on such an errand when he had me come aboard. You have served with him some extended period of time, no doubt?"

Warren shook his head. Reconsidering the offer of rum, he asked for a short tot of the spirit, very short if he may, drinking it off in a gulp. He smiled somewhat shamefacedly and asked for another not so short helping. Jack noted the silent longing within the cold eyes and pinched face, the insuppressible craving. As he leaned forward to pass a full clay mug over to the officer he caught a strong odor of drinking done earlier that morning. The man must drink a gallon ration a day, Jack thought, amazed that he had not detected the habits of an addict sooner. Warren leaned back and swept the mug to his mouth in a swift, smooth motion, tossing the neat rum down his throat, his Adam's apple bobbing twice and no more. He set the mug on a short end table and returned to the conversation.

"What was your question, Sir? Oh, yes, the time I have served under Captain Amis. No, I have not served with him long at all. I am in point of truth not a proper member of the

Boxer's compliment. I sailed with her in Halifax earlier this summer in order to join Admiral Graves's squadron in New York. However, finding no ready position there as a ship's Lieutenant, I was ordered to accompany the *Boxer* to the Chesapeake to see if there were opportunities to succor Lord Dunmore's forces here."

"And if you will pardon my curiosity, Lieutenant Warren, how is it that you found yourself ashore in Halifax when there is a war on? Surely the navy must be eager to put as many ships to see as she can. I would not expect it difficult for a man of your obvious experience to find a place to swing your hammock."

Warren stiffened perceptibly at Jack's pointed line of questioning, but recovered his cool manner before replying tersely, "I was the subject of a court-martial, Sir, in which my former captain accused me of negligence. I was exonerated fully. I have the papers from the Halifax port admiral here if you care to review them." He thrust the sealed envelope to the end of the bed. When he saw that Jack had no intention of reading the report, he stuffed it back into his pocket, sighing softly. Jack was cautious in his next step, aware that naval officers were touchy about matters of honor, not wanting to provoke a duel over a misspoken word. After a minute, he passed Warren another drink.

"I am sorry, Mister Cunningham. I am sure I appear absurdly quick tempered, but you must understand how a reputation can damage an officer's career. The service is another world entirely, I'm afraid, from the joys of private enterprise."

Jack considered telling Warren that he understood all to well the particular demands of the service as one who had served before the mast, as one of the common powder monkeys, in the Royal Navy, but he bit his tongue, not wanting to give the officer the advantage of knowing too much about his personal background.

"Please, Lieutenant, don't mistake my questions as

accusatory. I am apprehensive about handing my ship over to another man's handling. Surely as a sailor you can understand that? Also, I am not sure why the *Norfolk Gold* would suit your purposes. Wouldn't the captured rebel schooner—what was her name—the *Tornado*, better answer what Lord Dunmore has in mind?"

"At first appearances, I would be inclined to agree. She has the advantage of already being armed with cannon. However, during the fight she was holed at the waterline rather badly. I had the pumps manned continually to keep her from sinking. Also her cannons are only shabby little two pounders. Their shots did nothing to the hull of the *Boxer* though they did wreak havoc with her rigging. At any rate she is pretty footsore at this point and her timbers are not long for this world. According to what I have heard from Captain Amis and Midshipman Fitzwilliam, however, the *Norfolk Gold* is in her prime, a trim coaster. Additionally, whereas I would have trouble making up a full compliment for *Tornado,* your schooner is already manned up to merchant needs. We would need only a few navy seamen and a small band of marines to bring her up to the compliment of one of His Majesty's fighting schooners."

"And then I am supposed to hand my cargo over in exchange for these weak two pound guns? That doesn't seem to be a trade very much to my advantage."

Warren shook his head. "The cannons that we would ship are not here in Norfolk. Lord Dunmore has passed along intelligence of a cannon warehouse on the Rappahannock River. It has already fallen under rebel control but he suggested we might arrange a parley with the rebel leaders in order to exchange your rice for six pound cannons with shot and powder."

Jack whistled. "The good Governor certainly expects us to turn a neat little trick, doesn't he? What makes him think they won't unload our cargo and blow us to kingdom come with their warehouse full of powder and shot? Sounds like a damned suicidal business to me."

Warren nodded in accordance with Jack's protests. This mission apparently held no great allure for him either. The cannon seizure was the sort of task that would be horribly dangerous yet bring no professional credit. Perhaps that was exactly why it was given to a washed out Lieutenant with a tarnished record, Jack thought grimly. He sized up Warren with a new awareness of a pervasive desperation in the navy lieutenant's awkward movements: the obsessive drumming of his fingertips, the measured, soft tapping of his boot. He could be a terrible risk to the safety of Jack's ship and crew. At the same time, Jack felt an instinctive liking for Warren, a sense of his fundamental trustworthiness and ability as a seaman. He also seemed to be a fair man, one who understood the need to govern his crew cautiously and who was slow to punish with the cat of nine tails. Such qualities would be a must with Jack's merchant crew.

"Mister Warren, despite my reservations, I must admit I am not in a position to discriminate in my course of action. While I might prefer to sell my cargo and be safely away, I will consent to this action with the condition that I am to remain aboard the *Norfolk Gold*, not only as her owner, but as her unofficial second-in-command."

"I would not have dreamt it otherwise, Mister Cunningham."

"And I further understand that in addition to a fair distribution of any prize money which might fall my way, Lord Dunmore has agreed to hire my ship for these services at a fair rate. This has to be squared away immediately."

At this point Jack and Lieutenant Warren fell into detailed negotiations of the fees that would have to be secured to confirm the deal. After both men were satisfied with a copious accounting that filled both the front and back of a foolscap, they shook hands and made plans for the change of command to take place on the following day at two bells in the afternoon watch. Warren promised a dozen seamen picked from the best of the fleet and another ten marines with a sergeant in command to join him. Jack wrote down the figures and made a note to have Alan take on provisions sufficient to last for three weeks at sea. Warren parted in good spirits, promising a quick and successful mission, before clattering quickly down the stairs.

Jack came around to the window to watch Warren leave The Raleigh and turn up the street. After swinging past a detachment of marching English fusiliers, the Lieutenant's blue coat merged into the colorless mob of fishmongers crowding the provisioning wharf. Warren was certainly not to be found wanting in industry or initiative, Jack realized, but whether or not he was equal to the upcoming task was yet to be determined. Pushing back these concerns, Jack collected his shaving kit and stuffed it into his sea bag. It was better to leave without causing notice if Daniel Greene's warnings about rebel informants had been correct. Jack had chosen a side in this fight now, for better or for worse, and he needed to conduct himself accordingly. Casting one farewell glance at his lonesome home ashore, Jack gathered his resolve and left without looking back.

As he cleared the inn's anteroom and stepped into the cobbled street, a strong sea breeze suddenly caught his tricorne and plucked it neatly from his head. With superb reflexes, he swung around and snatched it out of the air in one brisk motion. As he did so he saw from the corner of his eye a man in a black frock coat and round hat abruptly change directions and hobble off with the aid of his walking cane, heading in the general direction of the banking district. Immediately, Jack's suspicion was aroused. Stuffing his hat firmly back over his wild head of dark hair, he stamped after the strange man at a discreet distance. The stranger jabbed his cane into the ground before him, his white hair waving frantically over the collar of his shabby coat. Twice the man glanced back over his shoulder, dispelling any doubts Jack had of whether or not the man had been following him. Pausing behind a halted coach, Jack peered through the carriage window, watching as the white haired man turned past a weaver's market, and propelled up a steep side street. Stepping from cover and circling the team of mud splattered horses, Jack felt the first hard drops of a summer shower thump down on him, the rain shockingly cold. As he crossed the main road and turned up the hill the sky simply opened, the water coming down in solid banks, the violent rending of thunder a veritable assault upon the ears. Soon the flooding streets of the waterfront district were hurriedly emptied, with the exceptions of the white haired man and his determined pursuer.

Due to the downpour's severity, Jack was forced to keep closer to the old man than he would have liked, lest he lose him in one of the upper side alleys. He moves damned fast for someone with a limp, Jack remarked to himself, panting at the prolonged exertion of climbing the steep road. It was not unusual for Jack to demonstrate extraordinary physical prowess aboard ship, whether it was lying out along a yard in a stiff gale or heaving on the braces alongside the common foremast jacks. Covering long distances overland, however, was not at all a kind test of his pulmonary health. As he crested the top of the hill, the white haired man again abruptly changed directions, swinging toward the alcove of a grog shop called The Nine Lives. As he did so Jack could swear that the limp had vanished and the cane was now tucked under the gentleman's arm as neatly as a parade baton. Just then the fellow glimpsed in Jack's direction and suddenly broke into a sprint. Jack gave chase without a second thought, lumbering down a mud washed intersection, very nearly careening into a stack of open crates as he struggled to keep up with the nimble character. It did not take him long to realize that he was fairly beaten. The white haired gentlemen swerved through a clustered aggregation of fruit carts, hurdling a barrier of spilled and split watermelons as he disappeared into the commercial district, choked even in the downpour, with throngs of farmers. Jack swore uselessly as he watched the imposter slip away. Without any further recourse, he slung his sea bag over his shoulder, flicked his hand in mock salute to his departed adversary, and trudged back toward his schooner in the pouring rain.

6. A SCHOONER OF WAR

EVEN after toweling off, shifting to a change of dry clothes, and eating a fine evening meal of roasted lamb with jelly and a glass of syllabub, Jack remained in a terrible funk. Alan offered to leave him alone in the cabin if he preferred, but Jack insisted that his gloomy mood would only worsen with the multiplying factor of isolation. Instead, they played a rather passive round of backgammon in which Jack suffered a horrible streak of bad luck with the dice, allowing Alan to once again gammon him miserably. However, the occupation of the game distracted Jack from his previous string of somber musings. His brains had been tangled up with the matter of the white haired gentleman and what significance it boded for the *Norfolk Gold*'s first cruise as a British warship. As he raked the playing pieces into the inner table and latched the two halves of the game board together, these fears about the future came smashing back down on him.

"Aye, it's a right strange business for certain, Jack. But saying this man following you means what we plan with the navy has gone sour is taking it a bit far, don't you think? And even if it has, that shouldn't affect our chance of success that much as I understand it. If we hope to make the exchange with the rebels it could only help us if they know we are coming in good faith. They might be less inclined to think the parley is some kind of trick. Maybe we should be telling them every move we intend to take. It might very well save our skins."

Jack frowned. "Somehow I doubt Lieutenant, or rather, Captain Warren will see it with such a practical eye. He is a military man after all."

"Perhaps you shouldn't say anything then."

"Perhaps, though I know keeping matters of intelligence secret from a ship's captain might rightly be interpreted as insubordination. More to immediate concerns—how long will it take to bring aboard stores? I would like us to be ready to sail on tomorrow evening's tide if it can be managed."

"I believe that can be arranged. Everyone in Norfolk is fighting one another for the chance to hawk their goods. The panic of the rumored English invasion has them all as clucky as hens in a foxhouse. All we will need can be had cheaply and quickly."

"Very good. I'll leave you to take care of that first thing in the morning. Perhaps you can see to buying a few more pistols and cutlasses, as well. What we have right now is ancient. However, what concerns me more is the crew. I don't like bringing so many unfamiliar men aboard all at once. Do any of our boys have an idea of what we're about?"

Alan shook his head as he lit his after dinner pipe by a long tallow and shut the little grimy lantern door. "Only gossip. They mostly suspect we will run the gauntlet of rebel river boats to sell the rice for tobacco."

Jack nodded, satisfied to let the misinformation set for the time being. "We will muster after breakfast and I will tell them of the change of command, give them a chance to jump ship if they want. No need to alarm them tonight, though."

"That's particularly kind of you, Jack, especially considering we will probably need as many hands as we can gather," Alan said reproachfully.

"I know we are hard pressed as it is. However, we can't afford to sail into action with reluctant men either. God knows what dregs Warren will bring along with him. If I cannot keep a few loyal men close by I fear we could be headed for disaster."

After a sound night of rest Jack rose at 6 a.m. for a shave and early breakfast. He was not very hungry but knowing his day would be overfilled with activity, he ate the cool porridge. He wanted to tour the deck one last time before the men turned up for their morning duties, and to have a moment alone with his ship. As he gained the deck by the aft companionway he saw a fog lying heavy over the inner harbor, hiding anything beyond twenty feet. The weighted silence added to the solitude Jack expected this morning. It would be hard handing the *Norfolk Gold* over to another man's command. He knew every inch of her seventy foot length and hundred and ten tons, knew her strengths as well as her flaws. She had made his fortune, served him far better than he deserved; now she would be subject to a far more perilous service. The very least he could do was see her turned over to the best captain and crew he could find, staying aboard as an advisor to lend his own expertise when it might matter. He placed his hand to the rail, feeling a tactile pride ride through his body as he remembered the many close calls and lee shores the schooner had weathered under his hand.

His silent reverie was broken by the soft footed approach of the anchor watchman making his rounds. It was the bosun Isaac, nodding good morning and reporting the deck all secure. Jack thanked him and asked how long before he was due to be relieved, only to find that Isaac had just now come on duty until all hands were rousted out. Jack wondered if he might accompany Isaac on his rounds to share the foggy morning, a proposal the bosun gratefully accepted, saying he would be pleased by the captain's company any time.

"Have all the men been accounted for?"

"Aye, Captain. All men are in their hammocks, though a few have cudgel lumps on their heads. I reckon there was some trouble at the grog shops, but none of 'em look like they'll try to malinger."

Jack smiled. He would never begrudge his men spirited recreation as long as they were able to answer duty's calls the following morning. Far better for the men to expel their pent frustrations on fellow jack tars within the walls of public houses than to bottle up their rebellious tempers for the duration of a cruise. Repressed spirits never boded well for a happy ship.

"Look Isaac, I have been meaning to tell you something. I will address the crew at large at two bells in the forenoon about a matter that calls for a vote."

"A vote, Captain? I've never known as how we've done business like that aboard the *Gold.*"

Jack nodded, clasping his hands behind his back as they turned up along the larboard gangplank and circled the double lashed boats. The fog was slowly beginning to dissipate, stripped off by a steady breeze. A noisy gull waddled down the main yard and abruptly fluttered off in a seaward direction as Jack and Isaac passed beneath the bird. The pallid slush of the rising sun peeked over the eastern horizon.

"Normally I would agree, Isaac. However, the matter is not the typical decision of a ship's captain. It is too far reaching to leave only in the hands of one man. As it is, I will only take volunteers on our upcoming cruise. Any man who has reservations will not be thought wanting in loyalty, but those who stay must be willing to follow orders without question." Jack spoke the words with quiet emphasis. He stopped pacing and gazed at the lifting fog, sensing with a sailor's mystic certitude that a strong blow would come on that afternoon.

"I figure you can't tell me exactly what it is that makes this cruise different?" Isaac asked, tapping the clogged waist of the watch glass.

Jack shook his head and resumed his march. "I cannot say where we are going and for what purposes. However, the *Gold* will be under the command of an English navy officer and as such all those who choose to remain aboard her will be subject to the Royal Navy's Articles of War, myself included."

Isaac swallowed the humid air with a sharp intake of breath. "That will scare the men," Isaac admitted. "They ain't navy jacks at heart, Captain. Most of 'em are too old for that kind of business."

"I know, that is why I am giving them the chance to get off before the change of command takes place. I will be honest with you, Isaac, for the Negroes it may be damned hard going. I cannot guarantee the navy is much better than the Virginian's slavery. I will do my best of course, but no promises."

Isaac nodded gravely, taking his captain's words into account.

"I will finish your watch, Isaac. Go below and spread the word of what I mean to talk to the men about after breakfast. Give them time to gab it over and come to a decision. They will have to cast their lot one way or another by noon."

"Aye, Captain."

Once the crew was mustered, Jack could read the tension on the faces of the men as plainly as if they had openly spoken their fears. They stood in loose, muttering groups as Jack stepped up to his small quarterdeck and faced forward. He let the moment linger as they hushed in expectation of his address, the ambient sounds of the inner harbor making a familiar and reassuring undercurrent of music for a sailor's ear.

"I know you've heard what we're facing," Jack began in a low but firm quarterdeck voice. "And the time has come for each man to decide what course is best for him. At noon today an English officer will read himself in as captain of this schooner. When that occurs the *Norfolk Gold* will no longer be a merchant coaster but become one of His Majesty's ships of war. Everyone who remains on board her will be entered in to the ship's books as seamen of the King's navy, including me," he paused to let the men take in at a glance one another's reactions. "Beyond that, I am not able to share the nature of our mission.

"I have sailed with some of you for many years. In that time I have come to know your strengths and abilities as surely as I have come to known the *Gold* herself. Over time I have come to know her weaknesses as well, as surely as I have yours, and as surely as I have my own. I know that the last thing you want is to fight. You have lived too long without a place to call home to believe in any of the high causes that normally lead men to war. For the Scots, you have lived in the colonies for most of your life and yet you are branded by these Virginians as foreigners, outsiders. For the Negroes, you have only to look as far as the tobacco fields to see what these bloody colonials mean for you, a life without possibility of future or fortune. If you agree to sail with me, I cannot promise an easy life, but I can assure you that I will show an even hand and look to your welfare as best as I can. We sail not simply for England, but for the right to call ourselves free men!"

Jack's exhortation hovered into silence as the men regarded him with set faces. The awkward remains of his words withered into stillness. Feeling his face reddening in embarrassment, Jack was on the point of seeking the sanctuary of his cabin when Isaac stepped forward, shaking his powerful fist and exclaiming, "Three cheers for Captain Cunningham!"

"*Huzzah, huzzah, huzzah!*"

The chorus of strong voices froze Jack in mid-stride. The sincerity behind the faces struck him further, driving home the conviction that the men supported him as their leader; they would sail wherever he sailed. Caught off guard by the outpouring of feeling, Jack shuffled awkwardly under their salute before touching his fingers to his hat in acknowledgment. The cheers grew in volume at this gesture, a remarkable force of sound for only a dozen men to make. Alan seized Jack suddenly by the bicep and shouted above the noisome praise, "They're with you, lad, to a man!"

Jack pressed Alan's hand and moved on, aware of a light headedness coming over him. As the crew quieted he ordered a double tot of rum issued to every man who chose to remain aboard. The cheers erupted once again, the whooping following him below even as he quit the main deck to repair to his cabin.

The effects of the applause quickly subsided, however, as he considered the consequences of the miracle he had wrought with a few glib words. He may very well have been successful in his aim of inspiring the men to action, but to what end? He knew that despite their single-minded support and desire to carry out his orders, the men's age might prove to be far more restrictive than their devotion. The Norfolk Golds were either children or elders. With Isaac, Gavin, and the two boys excepted, there was not a man younger than fifty. Could they really be expected to answer the rigorous demands of naval duty and discipline?

Jack was still sunk in these mixed emotions some hours later when Pete rapped smartly on the great cabin door and informed him that a procession of seamen led by a naval officer was approaching the gangplank.

"Very well, Pete. Please send Mister MacDonald my compliments and have him muster a side party to receive Captain Warren."

As Pete exploded out of the cabin on his way to the main deck Jack donned his coat, a forest green garment which he fancied was suitably military for the occasion. Checking himself briefly in his dressing mirror, he settled his three cornered hat neatly over his unbound hair and swung out to see his new captain properly welcomed aboard. What he witnessed, however, was distressingly less than adequate. The side party, a dubious description of the begrimed assembly, stood in their working ducks, some picking tars from their fingernails, others scratching their faces idly, as Isaac piped Captain Warren aboard. Jack grimaced, hoping the considerate man he had met in The Raleigh yesterday would be a forgiving one as well. Strangely, or perhaps graciously, Warren ignored the lackluster greeting, nodding briefly in Jack's direction and stepping aside to allow the rest of his party to board. They stamped in line ahead: a file of skinny, sallow faced sailors, no doubt the cast offs and sea lawyers from their ships' companies they were picked. At a distance another group of men tentatively advanced: Negroes dressed in the wild sundry garments of field slaves. Under their arms they carried cloth parcels clamped tightly to their breasts. As they boarded, their eyes turned aloft in mute wonderment at the intricate rigging shooting skywards, a sight strange to their inland eyes. Jack nodded to Isaac to have them stand in a semblance of ranks in order to hear Captain Warren read his commission.

Reading himself in as the *Norfolk Gold*'s temporary commander with brisk indifference, Warren ordered the ship's company dismissed from parade while the new men were properly worked into the watch bill, a task Jack entrusted to MacDonald. Warren then asked Jack the state of the stores on board, all of which had been properly stowed away just moments before his arrival. Satisfied with this state of affairs, he invited Jack to give him a thorough tour of the ship from keelson to masthead. Completing this perfunctory evolution in detail, they concluded the inspection in the great cabin. Jack showed him to his quarters. He apologized for having to screen the area with a partition of canvas, but because of the added ship's company and the limited amount of space aboard the schooner, Jack would have to share the cabin with him if that was acceptable.

"No apologies, Mr. Cunningham. I wouldn't dream of depriving you of your cabin. Nor would I want you very far from me. I trust you will not begrudge your nurse-maiding touch when it concerns the handling of the *Norfolk Gold*," Warren smiled.

Jack noticed the pinched, pale expression in the young commander's face. Another bout of addiction no doubt. He must be trying to slowly wean himself off, Jack realized grimly, and having a beastly awful time of it. As if by unspoken communion with Jack's speculation, Warren sat down heavily in the desk chair and asked if he might have a small sampling from the spirits locker. Bowing his head and affecting not to notice Warren's sudden attack of nerves, he poured a glass of Madeira. Smiling wanly, Warren asked if he might have some of the neat rum instead to quell his headache.

"Thank you, Mr. Cunningham," he said, clapping the drained mug on the desk and shifting it out of his reach. Some of his color began to return, suffusing an illusion of health across his weary face. He took in Jack's look of concern with a short glance. "Perhaps now you have a better idea of why the admiralty has such problems finding a place for me aboard one of His Majesty's frigates," he laughed mirthlessly. "Spirits are a hard damn devil to shake; you can have my word on that."

"I have seen it many times before, Captain Warren," Jack answered tonelessly, unsure how to take the officer's confession.

"Of course, you are a sailor after all. It has always been a weakness of mine. Can't very well expect a boy to grow up on grog rations from the time he is twelve and not develop a powerful thirst for the stuff by the time he passes for Lieutenant. Yet, the weakness is entirely of my own contrivance, I'm afraid. Well, I feel better now at any rate. Now, to things more worth our professional concern. From our tour I must say I'm very happy with the state of the schooner. She's holding together well for a ship of her years, good caulking, no hogging on the deck ends of any notice, a hobnailed bottom well cleaned from what I can see. She is enough to make up for the rather shoddy look of her crew."

"About that, Captain Warren, I am truly sorry for the bad shape of the side party..."

Warren cut Jack's apology short with a dismissing wave of his hand. "The gesture was more than adequate. I did not come aboard with the illusion that I was stepping aboard a Man of War. The *Norfolk Gold* has been a merchantman up until today. I would be suspicious if she was too ready to adhere to the regulations of the King's navy. What worries me is the men's age; I didn't realize how many old men you shipped. They may be well suited to keeping a merchantman up to trim, but how well they can fight the ship is just as important if we are to succeed in our mission. That could be more of a problem than I initially counted on. If we are expected to carry out regular patrolling it is likely we will come across rebel privateers not willing to be boarded quietly. I am afraid I haven't brought much to the table myself. The men I was able to cull from the Hampton Roads fleet are puny blackguards to a man, the runts of the litter. The 'marines' I was promised are in fact those ignorant Negroes freed from slavery this past week who quit their tobacco fields when they heard Lord Dunmore's promise to enlist them to fight against their former owners. No sergeant to command them or the arms and ammunition to train them, again as I was promised, only the parcels which hold winter uniforms. Winter uniforms in this ghastly heat! If they wear them in the sun they will be dead after a five minute review." Warren shook his head, pausing to soothe his exasperation. "I suppose there is no room for complaint. I should be happy for anything at this point."

"If I might propose a suggestion, Captain Warren," Jack began quietly, still awkward and unused to showing deference on his own ship. "I may be able to draw on an account with a local gunsmith. He would surely have adequate shot and powder. As for uniforms, we can have the men mend their own trousers from spare canvas. Instead of regimentals they can wear red kerchiefs to denote their unit over their cotton shirts. Might not please an admiral's inspection, but given that they're not rightly marines to begin with, I don't believe anyone would complain."

Warren touched his fingers to his chin in contemplation, a bemused smile slowly creasing his face. "Mr. Cunningham, your value as my right hand is already apparent. Please see to these contingencies at your earliest convenience. I gather that it would be absurd to sail on this evening's tide. However, if it is at all possible I should like to be away from this damn harbor on the morning's ebb."

"Aye, Captain," Jack said bowing as he took his leave.

Not trusting the job to his subordinates, and seeing Alan and Isaac already tied up with the difficult task of squaring the newly joined Norfolk Golds away, Jack decided to pay a visit to the gunsmith himself. He was greeted rather gruffly by the gunsmith's wife, a small gap toothed woman who looked on Jack's curiously clean garments with suspicion, as if they were not quite canny. Reluctantly, she admitted him to the back room of the shop where the smith stood over a pair of German dueling pistols, replacing the hammer springs on each finely milled piece. After a half hour of wrangling over past accounts and promises of an advance on potential prize money, Jack secured the smith's permission to select a dozen muskets with shot and powder. These he had carted off to the schooner before the smith had a chance to second guess the deal. The kerchiefs to serve as the Negroes brand of distinction he acquired from a company water clerk, paying for them out of his own pocket. By the time he returned to the *Norfolk Gold* he was pleased to find that the watch bill had been worked out to general satisfaction and the new joins had already made their respective mess numbers. There had been some slight dispute as to where the marines slung their hammocks, a few of the new men complaining that they shouldn't be forced to berth alongside a "passel of darkeys, and lubbers at that." However, the problem was solved by moving the marines aft on the gun deck so that they might be just outside the captain's cabin and immediately at hand in case of emergency.

On the morning tide the *Norfolk Gold* slipped her moorings and came around by the head wearing jibs and topsails. A steady blow had come on in the middle watch and as the schooner gathered way a dimpled plane of lively water spread out before her. Jack paced the quarterdeck with parental fastidiousness, checking each stay and shroud for tautness, keeping a critical eye on her handling, though he knew the men who sailed the schooner, experienced hands that they were, could have carried out the harbor maneuvers without a single word from him. As the main sail was sheeted home with a squealing of the blocks, the *Norfolk Gold* dug into the sea, the wind on her port beam. Jack strode up the inclined deck to grasp the larboard shrouds, a crackling rush of whitewater chugging out from the schooner's wake; from forward the spindrift was cast as high as the flying jib. Within a few minutes of the vigorous motion the black marines burst through the hatches, desperately clawing past one another to empty their troubled guts at the lee rail. Jack noted with a touch of amusement that they had all been conscientious about wearing their proper uniforms, tying their red kerchiefs around their necks before swarming up to the main deck to purge foul waters. He would give them the rest of the afternoon to become adjusted to the contrary movements of the schooner under sail. Then they would have much work to do with damned little time to do it.

After sighting Cape Charles on the starboard bow Captain Warren ordered the schooner to tack in close to the western shore, giving him a chance to glass some of the smuggler's coves above Hampton that were reputed to hide rebel shipping. He made extensive notes to himself on a scratch piece of paper, pointing out suspicious locations to Jack, soliciting his advice whenever he was unsure about the soundings of an area. Once this cursory reconnaissance was completed, Warren gave the helmsman a course to bring the *Norfolk Gold* safely away from the shoal water and out to the center of the bay to make the remainder of her northing toward the Rappahannock River. Sailing at an easy six knots, Jack felt it was time to give his marines a chance to practice their manual of arms. Receiving Warren's permission to execute this training, Jack called Isaac over to act as his supernumerary. After explaining what he intended, Jack charged his bosun with issuing arms and ammunition and told Gavin to load three empty casks into the jolly boat, stringing them out evenly on a towline. Once this was done he had the boat lowered over the side and rowed parallel to the *Norfolk Gold* at a distance of approximately sixty yards. After this was accomplished and Jack was satisfied with the sight of three identical barrels bobbing from astern the boat, he crossed over to where his ten marines stood in line abreast. They handled the muskets awkwardly with looks of thinly veiled horror; apparently the former slaves were slowly beginning to realize that these crazy white men were serious in their intent of making them fight. Jack nodded to Isaac. The bosun filled his lungs with wrath and howled a string of demeaning epithets to get the marines' attention. The men shook in consternation, some afraid of doing so much as much as blinking while Jack addressed them.

As he stepped forward Jack lifted a musket from the trembling hands of the marine nearest him and drew a paper cartridge from the man's possibles bag. As he tore the cartridge tab with his teeth and primed, he spoke the firing orders aloud, remembering them through the many clouded years since he had last witnessed musketry drill. He was no amateur with the handling of a musket, but the service had a pattern and language all its own, for good reason he knew. If the marines were to be expected to favorably exchange volleys with the enemy then they must function according to these regularly repeated orders. It was the only way to establish fighting efficiency amidst the turmoil of battle. Now to give them a good example to set them headed in the right direction. He tamped the charge home then drew the rod swiftly out and sent it clattering back into its cradle. Drawing a full breath, he raised the butt to his right shoulder pocket, resting the full stock on his flattened palm. Balancing against the heave of the deck, Jack expelled half of his caught breath and fixed his aim on the lead cask. As he slipped his index finger inside the trigger guard and gently applied pressure, he blew out the remainder of his breath, emptying his lungs to still his body at the moment of firing. The hammer snapped forward and ignited the charge. The stock punched sharply into his shoulder and a bank of black smoke whirled up, obscuring his sight.

"A foot short and half a foot wide," Alan called from off to the side, spotting the shot with his spyglass.

Jack nodded with satisfaction as he handed the musket back to the marine. Good enough at that distance in choppy seas. Now to see how trainable these 'marines' were.

"Gentlemen, you can see that a musket even at this range and in this weather is capable of hitting an area target. You are not riflemen hunting game, and I do not expect miracles, but as a concentrated volley a few should be fortunate enough to strike the cask. Some should fly high and others low. What is important, however, is that you place your shots on time and in the proper area. Now, ground your muskets and make ready."

Jack paced a few feet behind the marines, giving them just enough breathing room to allay their nerves. By now the idle sailors had gathered at a respectful distance to watch the musketry spectacle. Some muttered in undertones and were answered by smothered guffaws. As Jack turned his head over his shoulder the mockery fell silent.

"Marines, support arms!"

The men drew the long pieces up in a vertical line and folded their left arms across their torsos, cradling the muskets under the stock. Jack checked them to see that they all made the movement correctly. A few marines had enthusiastically brought their weapons too high, clamping the stock below the trigger housing and losing the point of balance, the muzzle waving drunkenly in the air as the holder struggled against the awkward position. Jack came forward and loosened the men's hold on their muskets, sliding the weapon back to its proper location.

"Thank you, suh," the marine who had given up his musket for Jack's demonstration said quietly. His intelligent eyes were fixed on Jack with a pleading expression. He was uncommonly small of stature, perhaps only an inch over five feet. With a shock Jack realized he could not be older than fifteen. Damn young blood to spill, he thought gravely.

"What's your name?" he asked.

"Pliny, Suh."

"Mister Pliny, please do not talk in ranks."

The boy's face clouded over at the gentle rebuke. It would take a careful hand to bring these men into their roles aboard a fighting ship, Jack remembered. Before moving on he pressed the youth on the shoulder and whispered, "Doing fine, lad. Keep a sharp eye!" Mister Pliny nodded stiffly, fixing his gaze resolutely ahead.

"Handle cartridge!" Jack bellowed.

The marines unfolded their bent arms, allowing their muskets to drop to approximately thirty degrees, while with their free hands they drew the paper cartridge out of their possibles bags, tearing the casing open with their teeth. One poor fellow had gotten carried away in a dramatic flourish and bitten in too deeply to his cartridge, getting an acrid mouthful of gun powder. His priming charge thus wasted, his fellow marines waited for the next order with burgeoning smirks while he fished out a second cartridge and took a more discriminating bite.

Shaking his head, Jack gave the next order, "Prime!"

Each man successfully emptied the priming charge into the pan without incident.

"Load and draw ramrod!"

Buoyed by the uniform success of the priming, the marines grounded their firelocks and stuffed the cartridge into the weapons' muzzles. In a ragged line, ramrods were drawn; one hasty marine began to drive the cartridge home before being frozen in place by a cautionary growl from Isaac.

"Remember, gentlemen," Jack said, taking the

opportunity to deliver an extemporaneous lesson. "We must function as a unit. If one man is ahead of the rest he is wasting his shot. Now, ram cartridge!"

The men thrust the ramrods down, a whoosh escaping the barrels from the sudden compression of air. Their faces were set, their confidence growing with each movement. Jack marveled at the quickness these men learned the drill. Perhaps their inexperience was not a detriment but an opportunity to craft them along the lines the schooner would require.

"Return ramrods and make ready!"

To a man, the muskets were brought to a crisp vertical angle and the hammers cocked. By now the men had become accustomed to the pitch and roll of the deck, their legs wide apart and adjusting to the continuous motion underfoot. They stared fixedly ahead at the string of casks.

"Present, and fire!"

At the moment the order was given a freak cat's paw of wind beat down on the *Norfolk Gold* beam heeling her over a strake. At that unfortunate moment all but one of the marines pulled their triggers, peppering the sea twenty yards short of the intended target. The one who had held his fire for the coming uproll discharged his musket a few seconds later, striking the barrel just above the waterline, sending a great sodden chunk of wood flying into the air. The lone marksman was Mister Pliny, and he was smiling.

"Well done, Mister Pliny!" Jack congratulated. "A handsome piece of work and an important one for us to remember as marksmen at sea. Always wait for the uproll. Now, again, and this time with spirit damn you! Handle cartridge!"

Jack worked the marines through the firing evolution an additional two dozen times, pushing them for quickness rather than accuracy. If it came to a ship to ship exchange he knew the rate of reload would prove more telling than their ability to group their shots at long distances. The only further mishap occurred toward the final few volleys when, in the excitement of the moment, one of the marines had failed to return his ramrod to its cradle before presenting arms and firing. The odd warbling report and the unmistakable sight of a three foot dart springing over the waves betrayed the culprit immediately. He received no upbraiding for his error other than an incredulous exclamation from Isaac and the undisguised scowls of his fellow marines. Despite this, Jack was generally pleased with the men's progress and dismissed them at one bell before the evening meal.

When he joined Captain Warren in the great cabin Jack received congratulations for his ability as an officer of marines. He bore the praise uncomfortably, aware that the role he had played had been only an approximation of proper military training. Still, the assurance that the navy officer approved went far in shoring up his confidence. Alan joined them in a few minutes, bearing the revised watch bill for Captain Warren's perusal. Dismissing the business out of hand, Warren said that he trusted Mister MacDonald's abilities in the matter and invited him to sit down for a glass of claret brought over from his personal stores. The old Scotsman said he was pleased to share the present company, drawing a chair up alongside Jack, and nodding his thanks as he was passed a glass of the wine.

"I must be honest, Mister MacDonald, I would like you to be present for more than the pleasure of company," Warren began. "I was just on the point of discussing the plan of action with Mister Cunningham. Best if you get the venom straight from the viper's mouth, I say. Both of you will have to be apprised of the specifics in order to pull the thing off." He spread a chart of the lower Rappahannock on the desk, weighing down the corners with a pair of Warren's personal dueling pistols. "I have told you the basics of acquiring guns for the *Norfolk Gold*; now it is time to exorcize the devil in the details. First, you will have heard that we are to parley with rebels. This is true only in part. The arrangements for the exchange have already been made by agents for Lord

Dunmore. These rebels appear to have already signed an unofficial pact allowing the transfer of guns for rice. How Lord Dunmore secured this agreement is at present a mystery to me; however, I have been assured that no resistance is anticipated. Therefore, if all goes according to plan, we should be expected by the men who currently posses the guns and the exchange should be carried out without further incident." Warren paused, tracing his finger down the long hook of the lower Rappahannock. "On the other hand, experience tells me that surreptitious deals have a tendency to miscarry, and I am not counting on the full cooperation of these arms dealers. The business smacks more of piracy in my eyes, and I seriously doubt whether we can take these men at their word. For that reason I believe it is prudent to lay a contingency plan. This will involve you specifically, Mister Cunningham, and you to a lesser extent Mister MacDonald."

Jack and Alan exchanged a silent look. Neither had anticipated any specialized duties on this first mission, and they visibly chaffed at the implications. Warren, sensitive to their discomfort, explained more than he would have normally liked to assuage their reluctance.

"In the main, I wouldn't ask men who are essentially civilians to do the King's dirty work, but after your outing with the marines on deck this afternoon, Mister Cunningham, I knew I had to have you placed in command of them. According to the information that has been passed to me, the rebels will be expecting us sometime tomorrow afternoon. Since it is only a three hour sail in fair weather upriver to the warehouse, we will drop anchor tonight somewhere near the mouth of the York and cover the rest of the distance after first light. I expect even if Lord Dunmore's alliance with these rascals is good they will still be suspicious if we arrive unduly early. Once we arrive here," Warren placed his finger on a small inland curve of the river bank, barely perceptible. "We will drop anchor. We must not go further upstream than this because it will bring us into range of a rebel earthworks that may house enfiladed field pieces. I will go ashore a few hundred yards upstream to meet with the rebel representatives. I will be bearing a personal dispatch signed by Lord Dunmore positively identifying me as the appointed agent for the transaction. Since the boat will be moving upstream I will require a crew of our strongest rowers. Perhaps if the wind is favorable we might be able to fly a lugsail as well. While I am in conference with the rebels I want you, Mister MacDonald, to load the gig with as much rice as she can carry. When you have received my signal, a bonfire lit at the river bank, you will send the boat out to me. While it is being unloaded I will send my boat back to the *Norfolk Gold* so that it too can be loaded with rice. We will keep this rotation up until all of our cargo has been discharged. At this point we shall begin loading the cannons and ferry them back to the schooner."

MacDonald cleared his throat to put a word in. "If you'll forgive my asking, Captain Warren, that's putting us in a tight spot isn't it, giving up all our cargo before we get the first gun? Why can't we have the gig designated for the rice and at the same time start bringing aboard the six pounders in the jolly boat?"

Warren nodded. "I would have preferred that, but these are the terms of the deal made by Lord Dunmore. The rebels will be put off by any change in the plans once the thing has been sealed. However, you have touched on the very thing that has me worried, and that is where you are concerned, Mister Cunningham."

Jack shifted in his seat and placed his glass of wine on the desk, committing his attention sharply.

"Before we reach the anchorage I will put you ashore with your marines somewhere around here," Warren indicated a rim of flat woodlands roughly two miles downstream from the warehouse. "You will march them upstream while endeavoring to keep yourselves concealed. From what I gather, that shouldn't be difficult since I understand the riverbanks to be thickly forested. Likely your greatest challenge will be in covering the ground in good time. Once you have traversed the distance you will take up a position that allows you a good view of the warehouse's wharf but which also flanks the rebel earthworks. You will not reveal your positions unless it becomes absolutely necessary. If the exchange goes as planned, all I expect you and your marines to do is squat on your heels and watch. It is my hope that we will then return to the *Norfolk Gold* and pick you up where you were landed, leaving the rebels none the wiser to your presence, and you and your marines having done nothing more than take an invigorating walk through the woods."

"But if the rebels back out?"

Warren sighed heavily and removed the pistol end weights, rolling up the chart crisply and returning it to the locker. "Confidentially, gentlemen, I believe Lord Dunmore's assurances about these blackguards about as much as I do that Christ is an Englishman. The rebels are backstabbing devils by nature. If something goes wrong, whatever that might be, I want the marines to storm the earthworks and secure any guns that might be in place there. Once that has been accomplished the *Norfolk Gold* may safely proceed upstream to the wharf to land reinforcements if it becomes necessary. However, under no circumstances are you to weigh anchor until the earthworks have been captured, Mister MacDonald, regardless of what happens."

"Aye, Captain," Alan acknowledged mechanically.

"Very well. A glass then, gentlemen, to the *Norfolk Gold,* her crew, and expectations of success!"

Jack was on watch when the *Norfolk Gold* dropped anchor in the shoal water at the mouth of the York River, the summer twilight lingering late into evening before gradually succumbing to darkness. The moon would not be up until early in the morning and an overcast sky blocked out much of the ambient starlight. Jack was grateful for the darkness and the solitude, the assurance that the men were below and sleeping, a heavy silence pervading the schooner: a chance to walk the decks and think without the jarring interruptions of routine duties. Since dinner with Warren he had been occupied with a host of conflicting feelings, thoughts too intimate to share even with his dear friend Alan. He hated the idea of leading the marines into action, not merely because of the natural apprehension one might expect with the possibility of action; he had after all killed men before, river pirates along the Carolina coast as well as the rebel privateersmen just a few days earlier. He was not a complete stranger to taking a man's life when it meant saving his own. But this idea of leading men to slaughter Virginians unawares was entirely different. It resembled the business of mercenaries, cutthroats. It caused him to question the allegiance that up until now he had so easily assumed. True, he was a Britisher, but what stake did he truly have in asserting the colonies obedience to the empire? His one deeply held conviction had hinged on the idea that he would lose business with the establishment of an independent Virginia, but he began to wonder if that was actually the case. Wouldn't it be logical to assume that the traders and farmers would always need a means of shipping their goods, whatever the state of their government? Perhaps that was what Daniel Greene had been alluding to when he had seen Jack in The Raleigh. Why serve the masters with the price of war when there was plenty of profit in peace? And yet here he was, committed to killing men if they refused to comply with English law. As a Scot he knew a hereditary loathing for the Englishman's pomposity. True, there were many good men who were English by birth, Warren included, but the nation's character was on the whole revolting. He thought of Captain Amis, a fitting avatar for English impudence: the false gentility, the suspicion, the slippery diplomacy, the hunger for power.

Conversely, the Virginians had their own problems in legion, some of which Jack found nearly impossible to reconcile. They were a closed society, prone to damaging gossip and violent conquest. They were never satisfied with the square of land they owned, always looking westward to the Blue Ridge Mountains, the demarcation between civilization and wilderness, the gates that led to the Indian nations. The Virginians were children, bickering over land disputes with neighboring colonies, pushing bit by bit into places they were not welcomed, their greed fueled by promises of further wealth all too often carried on the backs of slaves.

Jack's head spun. He was not used to thinking about the world beyond the bulwarks of his schooner. He was not a fool, but he had enjoyed the convenience of autonomy for too long. Now, he realized, he was becoming part of something far larger than himself and the profitable plying of his merchant trade. He no longer lived the simple life of a sailing master, and as he moved along the gently moaning deck he realized that regardless of the future course he charted, it would be a damned dangerous one.

7. A TRAP SPRUNG

THE marines tentatively boarded the gig, most finding it out of their depth as novice boat men to keep a sure footing while at the same time holding onto their firelocks. Once this was effectively if not efficiently accomplished, Jack shook Captain Warren's hand, the two men exchanging wishes of good luck, and climbed down to the boat. After the order was passed to give way, the bowman shoved off with his hook and the boat caught the current, shuttling rapidly shoreward with the help of a few strong pulls by the oarsmen. Grounding a few feet shy of the oozing banks, Jack and his marines waded out of the river and turned to watch the gig crawl back to the schooner. Tossing a wave of farewell to Alan, Jack ordered his men into the bush lest they be discovered lingering by rebel lookouts.

Though the woodland offered dimness, it did nothing to dispel the oppressive afternoon heat. The overarching tree limbs and spindles of hanging vine seemed to capture the humidity and hold it in place, smothering even the faintest promise of a fresh breeze. The ground was rotten with trapped moisture, more like a bog or swamp bottom than a patch of proper woods. The men's feet were slathered with the clutching muck before marching a few hundred yards. In addition to the vegetable nightmare, malevolent clouds of mosquitoes floated in among the marines, alighting to feast on the unsuspecting hosts, raising hard, painful welts on the men's faces, arms, and necks. Progress through the tract was intolerably slow, leading Jack to march the men further inland in the hopes of coming across a section of more firmly packed earth. After a half mile spent seeking better ground in vain, he ordered them back on their original path of advance. With so much time misspent, the marines had a great deal of ground to make up. To do so they proceeded at the double quick, the straps of their gear slapping against the musket stocks, straining their muscles and taxing their lungs. Were they not strong field slaves only a week earlier, the marines' physical limitations may have prevented them from traversing the soft ground in reasonable time given the circumstances. However, it was they who periodically stopped to allow their commander to catch up.

By the time he sighted the rebel earthworks, Jack feared his lungs were about to explode. He chided himself for being so ridiculously out of breath. A damn sorry example to set for a so called officer of marines, he recognized. He told the men to lie still ten yards inside the tree line while he investigated the scene further. Cautiously stepping forward and kneeling at the edge of the woods, he shrugged out of the lanyard that held his telescope diagonally across his back and glassed the area before him. The field of high grass stretched from the riverbank on the left all the way up to a small grouping of hills choked with young pines. Jack guessed the distance from the water to the hill base to be about two and a half cables length, or five hundred yards. Presently, he was about two hundred yards inland. The earthworks itself was built right into the hill base, taking advantage of the topography to guard against flanking attacks. It faced south southwest, situated so as to command the approach to the cannon warehouse wharf, which was roughly four hundred yards due west from the earthwork's perimeter. As far as Jack could tell a good three hundred yards of open rising plain separated his marines from the rebel fortification. He turned his glass on the *Norfolk Gold*, seeing that she had already dropped anchor and was in the process of putting Warren's boat over the side. Good, that meant he had time to move his men closer to the earthworks before Warren made contact with the rebels. Striding over a moss covered log, Jack motioned for the marines to follow him along a game trail that wended up to the hill country.

He sensed reluctance on the part of the men, a perceptible hesitation that did not bode well for any upcoming action. Reminding himself that the men were not proper marines in any official sense, he did not fault them for cowardice. What reason would they have to follow him into a sharp fight, what loyalty would secure their obedience? Jack shook his head. He could hardly pretend that he wouldn't understand if they lit into the wilderness on their own and took their chances among the uncharted territory. That much unaccustomed freedom looming up before them must be a damned difficult temptation, he thought. He turned his head over his shoulder to check their progress. They all remained with him for now, Mister Pliny at their head, plunging through the brush, his musket held tightly across his chest. Jack smiled. Hard to imagine a more natural soldier than that one. A damned sight better suited for it than his current commanding officer.

As they reached the hill country the ground finally began to stiffen beneath their feet, the hard rocks and baked earth allowing a more regular advance. Moving through the pine was trickier than Jack had first imagined, however. The hills had apparently been cleared within the last year or two and the young growth spurting up in its place was a maze of pine quills. The marines were forced to stay together within just a few steps of the man in front of them, lest they lose one another and wander inadvertently into a clearing.

The foliage opened up enough at the crest of the second hill for Jack to glass the area anew. From this vantage point he overlooked the earthworks at just under a hundred yards, and from a semi-flanking position. Also, because of the superior height he was able to see behind the fortifications. At first the redoubt appeared deserted, but by chance he spotted a hand lifted to swat away a bug. Examining the area carefully, Jack was eventually able to discern eight men dressed in the animal skin hunting shirts of the rebel militiamen. They were very good at disguising their presence within the earthworks. No sentinel walked the perimeter, and each of the men Jack could see was lying close to the protecting embankment, peering through small loopholes housing the rebel shirtmen's rifles. This was no band of town fools, but trained woodsmen, more than likely experienced Indian fighters, and not unfamiliar with spilling their fellow man's blood. He looked for signs of cannons but was unable to determine any, though much of the fortification's interior remained concealed from his view. Training his telescope back on the warehouse's wharf he could see that Warren's boat had just tied off and the man himself was going ashore in his dress uniform. Three rebel shirtmen greeted him with what appeared to be benevolence, though something in Jack's guts told him otherwise.

"Anything peculiar, suh?" Mister Pliny was at Jack's shoulder, narrowing his sleepy eyes to see at that great distance.

Jack shook his head and passed the young man the glass. "Not that I can be certain. However, I have seen a number of rebels within the earthworks who are doing their best to remain concealed. If the rebels don't have anything to hide, then why pretend they don't command the river advance?" The question was posed more for Jack's own reflection than a desire to solicit the young man's counsel. Yet Pliny answered in his direct way.

"They mean trouble, Suh. Damned no good rattlesnakes are aiming on mischief. Should I tell the men to get ready?"

Jack smiled at the marine's ardor. "No, Mister Pliny, we are not going to provoke anything if it can be avoided. We will sit here and wait until the rebels prove to us that they mean to break their word. We may be in this place for some time after all. Tell the men to break out rations and try to rest while they have the opportunity."

"Aye, Suh," Pliny said, jerking his head in acknowledgment as he turned toward the obscuring brush.

"And Mister Pliny?"

"Suh?"

"Do you think I might be able to get my telescope back?"

The marine shrank with embarrassment, sheepishly returning Jack's glass, before going to find the men to pass his commander's latest orders. He is a fire eater that one, Jack thought. He made a note to recommend Pliny for an appointment to NCO for the squad as soon as they returned to the schooner. It would do wonders for the marines to see one of their own elevated in stature, even if there was no official recognition from the navy or Lord Dunmore.

As the afternoon wore on Jack watched as the *Norfolk Gold's* boats worked laboriously against the current, low in the water, heavy with their burdens of rice. He wondered how the crew and Warren were bearing the tedium. Complacency was a dangerous enemy to guard against. One moment of not attending fully to the task at hand could have disastrous results. Jack wondered too how well Warren was coping without his regular dose of rum. Jack pulled his watch from the inner pocket of his light pilot jacket. Nearly 7 p.m., the slow decline of the sun now becoming more rapid as it neared the horizon. He did not relish the idea of the men working in the dark to retrieve the cannons. Already the circumstances warranted concern; with the arrival of darkness Jack felt the exchange would demand utmost vigilance.

To his surprise and growing consternation, he noticed activity on the deck of the *Norfolk Gold*, the crew manning the capstan with what appeared to be every intention of weighing anchor. He smothered an oath and searched the wharf looking for signs of Warren. The English officer was there all right, still talking amicably with the rebel delegates, unconcerned with the behavior of the schooner. Jack glassed further for some explanation for this strange turn of events. From the far tree line he caught a glimmer of movement. It was a train of rebel militia dragging the six pounders from where they had cleverly concealed the guns in the woodlands. So, that was it, they had refused to show their part of the bargain until they had secured all of the rice. Warren must have sent word back in one of the boats for MacDonald to sail up to the wharf and moor there so the guns could be brought aboard before nightfall. Warren, despite his cool outer demeanor probably was every bit as eager as Jack to be clear of the rebel position before dark. Still, Jack grimaced, sailing that close to the rebels was putting the schooner in a vulnerable position. He hoped the Englishman knew what he was doing.

The schooner closed the distance under topsails and jibs, ghosting forward with what Jack felt was almost perceptible resistance. If he knew his old friend Alan at all, he knew that he would share Jack's sense of trepidation. Every instinct in his body was bound to be railing at the idea of warping the *Norfolk Gold* alongside a dock unarmed and unable to swiftly escape. Jack set his teeth on edge, gripping the handle of his naval hanger. Something was not right. He watched the rebels towing the cannons by hand. They were making unusually good progress for so few men, far too good in fact to even be possible. As the word "trap" shaped itself in Jack's mind an abrupt thunder confirmed his fears, a plume of acrid smoke rising from the earthworks. From the corner of his eye a black blur caught his attention, drawing his gaze towards the *Norfolk Gold* as the cannon ball crunched into the schooner's bulwarks, propelling a shower of large splinters into the river beyond. Almost immediately the English ensign was struck, Alan having the prudent sense to realize the rebel gun had his range and would have destroyed the schooner in a matter of minutes. Jack urgently searched the wharf for signs of Warren. The Englishman was furious, screaming at the rebel delegates but to no avail. A company of rebel riflemen emerged from the tree line, about fifteen or twenty men in buckskins, trotting across the open ground to take Warren prisoner and board the *Norfolk*

Gold. Jack swore futilely.

Fighting an instinct to attack the earthworks at that moment, Jack considered his next move. Within the hour the sun would go down and the rebels would relax their guard, believing that they had overcome all of their enemies. Surprise alone was to Jack's advantage. Every other tactical superiority fell in favor of the sly rebels. They occupied the earthworks with probably a dozen men. At least another dozen would shortly be aboard the schooner with no certainty that more did not lurk in the shaded woodlands. Jack had only ten ill-trained men as yet unproven in action while the rebels looked to be comprised of seasoned colonial veterans. Hardly odds he would have taken in a serious bet. And yet this was the most serious gamble of all: men's lives. As he was wrapped up with these unfriendly musings, Pliny appeared at his side.

"Looks like action after all, Suh," the marine said eagerly.

"It appears that way. Tell the men I will join them shortly. Looks like we have a busy night ahead of us."

"Aye, Suh!"

***

After reviewing the orders once again with Pliny, Jack selected the two best swimmers from among the marines, two tall lean fellows with the improbable names of Mars and Mercury, and led them along the tree line toward the riverbank. They removed their boots and slung them over their shoulders to mask their movements, lest they happen upon a night sentry walking his rounds. Jack suspected the rebels would not be likely to consider such security necessary. He was, in fact, counting on rebel complacency to give his bold plan of action even a small chance of success. Silently counting off the passing minutes, Jack took long strides across fallen deadwood, wincing every time he or his marines unintentionally stepped on a twig, the cracking carrying across the field with alarming volume. He hurried forward to make sure he and his small party would be able to carry out their half of the coordinated action on time. They had only fifteen minutes, give or take a few seconds of Jack's imperfect estimation, before Mister Pliny with his six marines would launch their assault on the rebel earthworks. To capitalize on the first crucial moment of surprise, he, together with Misters Mercury and Mars, would simultaneously sneak aboard the *Norfolk Gold*, freeing the captive sailors and hopefully overwhelming the rebel forces aboard before the first shot was fired. His main concern presently was whether or not his internal chronology would match the time piece he had entrusted to Mister Pliny. If the coordination was accurate then he had every reason to entertain sanguine hopes for success. If it was not, then he and his marines might be slipping aboard a schooner full of armed and alerted rebels who outnumbered them nearly four to one.

Jack flung his boots down in the mud at the river's edge and turned to give his final instructions to the marines. They gathered close to him to hear his whispered words.

"Remember, once we are up the ladder stay in the shadows. Follow my lead and don't rush the anchor watch unless the rebels have spotted us, understand?"

The two men nodded mutely, clenching their only weapons, their bayonets, between their teeth as they waded into the cool evening water. Jack strode past them, bracing for the cold shock as the water lapped against his loins. He blew out an exclamatory breath and surged into the water until the river covered him to the top of his chest. Because they had to work upstream, expending their energy by beating against the current would tire them needlessly; Jack and his men walked the strand parallel to the river's bank. The footing was soft and often threatened to become quicksand, but fortunately it lasted to within twenty yards of the anchored schooner. Jack paused before swimming out to the channel to see if there was a watch being rowed around the *Norfolk Gold*. He doubted the rebel lubbers

would have known to take such a precaution even if they did
suspect someone might be plotting a cutting out expedition.
Thankfully, there was no apparent watch boat to be seen;
the only likely resistance they would face would come in the
form of a bored and probably drowsy sentinel walking the
deck. Jack hoped no one was posted on the wharf. If there
was, he would have the perfect vantage point to spot the
swimmers moving out to the middle of the river, giving him
an opportunity raise the alarm before the scheme could be
fully sprung. There was no time to avoid that possibility
now. He was going to have to trust in the rebels' conceit and
lack of preparation. Pushing off from the strand, Jack
reached into the churning water with long even strokes,
fluttering his legs to cut across the moderate current.
Because of the hard rains of a couple of days before, the river
gushed formidably, making the swim more than a routine
effort. By the time he had reached the schooner's transom
and worked his way carefully around to the starboard
accommodation ladder, Jack was grateful he need not breast
the current any longer, his muscles twitching with strain.
He shifted to the side and grasped the main chains to give
room at the ladder for Mercury and Mars. Heaving himself
up and over the bulwarks, Jack was first aboard, crouching
with his sword drawn. He glanced quickly at the starboard
side and found the deck unoccupied. Thrusting his head over
the side, he whispered for the two marines to follow him up.
They clambered aboard. The water rolled off of their bodies
and pooled on the deck, rinsing aft as the hull tipped gently
in time with the river's undulations.

The cordage and lashed boats cluttered the deck, not
stowed with the precise order customary for the schooner,
Jack noted. Doubtlessly the slipshod practices of the rebel
landsmen. He eased forward and rose up from behind the
inverted hull of the gig, scanning for signs of a sentry. He
knew his time was running short and Pliny would launch his
attack in a matter of a minute or two. The deck appeared to
be empty, a damn peculiar thing. Feeling a cold uneasiness

close its fingers around his heart, Jack cocked his hanger up in a vertical line as he stepped for the forward hatch to see if there was hope of freeing the Norfolk Golds battened below. Peering down into the dimly lit 'tween decks, he saw a few scuttling, indefinable shapes and heard the raucous sounds of drunken revelry. Turning to ask Mercury for a hand, a bright stab of flame suddenly pierced the gloom from the vicinity of the bowsprit, the murderous report of a rifle cracking a brief instant afterwards. A fierce pain seized Jack in the thigh, literally sweeping his feet out from beneath him. As his body struck flat on the deck with a thud he became aware of a rising panic in his chest which quickly spread to his extremities. The sounds below deck ceased, a palpable moment of strained attentiveness, then came the shouts and screams that a surprise attack was underway. The general alarm was followed by a trundling of boots on the berthing deck as the rebels snatched whatever weapon was at hand as they flew up the companionway. Curiously, the flash of pain in Jack's leg was lost to a general numb, warm stickiness. He stared down at the ugly stripe of dark blood staining the inside of his slop trousers as he tested his weight on the injured leg. It bore the strain. Thank god the ball hadn't nicked bone. Buoyed up by this stroke of good luck, Jack told Mercury and Mars to sneak below to free the crew while he contended with the remainder of the rebel force that was due to arrive momentarily.

His first order of business was to dispatch the cruel fellow on the bowsprit. Springing up onto the prow with his blade extended, Jack raced up after the rebel who was retreating precariously along the long spar as he frantically tried to reload his rifle. Was it not for a misplaced step, the rifleman might have made good on his intention of putting a second round through Jack's chest, but as it was, he crashed head first with a yelp as he struck the water below. However, the immersed adversary was by now the least of Jack's concerns; a file of enraged rebels swarmed up the aft companionway armed variously with rifles, pistols, tomahawks, and cudgels. He ducked behind the foremast as a pair of shirtmen let loose from their rifles, the shots digging small chunks out of the oaken mast. A small man with a shaven head charged directly at Jack, raising a fearful, if somewhat drunken war keening as he brandished a nefarious looking tomahawk. The spirited fellow took a swipe at Jack's head, missing his crown by a fraction of an inch. Flicking his sword down, Jack bit his hanger into the man's red cheek, eliciting a gruesome howl of pain. Before he had a second to enjoy the victory of this encounter, another two rebels fired on Jack, one shot zipping so close to his ear that he could feel the air quiver on his skin as it passed. Sensing that he had soon quit his position or risk losing life and limb, Jack fell back past the forward companionway to seek a safe egress overboard. Just before springing over the side, he heard a new whoop of vengeance rising unseen in the darkness of the deck, and he felt his loins shiver with terror, knowing he was about to be hacked to pieces by some Virginian's lusty tomahawk.

The cries, however, were not formed in the throats of the rebel usurpers, but by the wrathful company of the *Norfolk Gold*. The seamen blasted through the aft companionway, seizing hold of their former captors with merciless violence. Fistfuls of nails which had been converted into crude brass knuckles were shoved into the shocked faces of the enemy. Blood fairly painted the normally pristine deck, leaving a slippery veneer of gore. The rebels not immediately overcome with the initial uprising stumbled forward and gathered amidships in line abreast to regroup. Wasting no time, they quickly began priming and loading their weapons to pay back the Norfolk Golds for the insurgence. Jack knew if he was not able to disrupt the shirtmen's concerted volley that the tide of battle could quickly turn back in the rebel's favor. Rushing at the riflemen and raising a war cry, Jack sprang on the nearest rebel, brining his hanger in a mighty overhand stroke. The swing ceased abruptly with a hard, jarring as the blade cleaved into the man's shoulder. The rebel fell to the deck, wide eyes locked on Jack's with incredulity as he sank to his knees. The surprise of Jack's attack from an unexpected quarter broke the resolve of the remaining riflemen and they dissolved into a headless panic, throwing down their weapons and attempting to jump overboard. A fortunate few made it to the water, swimming for their lives to get to the safety of the far shore. Those who were not so lucky did not live long to regret their capture.

A nearly fatal weariness emptied Jack of his strength as he collapsed to the deck, his vision coming and going in bright giddy lights. He heard the heavy footfalls of men approaching him, thought he heard a familiar voice, though he could not be sure, his mind seemingly lifted free of his body in comforting darkness. He distinctly heard the words, "Lost a right amount of blood," but he wasn't sure who the voice was talking about; he clearly remembered the awful carnage of the fight, so it could have been nearly anyone. For a moment he fancied the schooner was herself a living thing and she might be the object of the voice's concern. It pained Jack to think the *Norfolk Gold* might be slowly bleeding to death, alone without proper attention. He only wished he was well enough to staunch the flow of blood from her seams; he, better than anyone, could nurse her through a difficult time. Finally, overcome with an irresistible desire to sleep, he surrendered his fears to a growing sphere of unconsciousness.

***

Jack awoke to the afternoon sun magnified through the small stern galley windows of the great cabin. He tried to lift his hand, and, as he did so, he discovered a peculiar lethargy in that trustworthy limb, as if instead of blood coursing just beneath the skin, an unfortunate substitute of tar was oozing through his hemp veins. He was able, however, to manage enough strength to turn his head on the pillow. As he did so, he was greeted by the kind, attentive face of his old friend Alan MacDonald.

"And a delayed good morning to you, my bonnie lad. We had near given you up for the gloaming."

Jack grimaced as he tried to sit up, an overwhelming attack of vertigo keeping him firmly in place. After a silent moment of recovery, he thought to ask the state of the schooner and the number of men lost.

"Well, we were right lucky, Jack. No man killed, though we have three roughed up pretty badly by the rebels when they first came aboard. Worst of all is poor young Parkinson. They gave it to him in no small measure."

"Pete? Why in God's name would they take out their rage on a boy?"

Alan smiled with a touch of pride in his recollection. "Wasn't their intentions, but the fire eater just refused to give in when the shirtmen boarded us. He grabbed one of the rebel's tomahawks and tried digging it into their officer's head. May well have done it too if it wasn't for a sharp eyed fellow who swung his rifle butt down on him. The lad lost a mouthful of teeth but he looks like he'll mend in a few days. Right now he's got enough rum in him to sink a Man of War. In truth, Jack, you were the only one we really feared. Lost a damned mess of blood from that bullet wound of yours."

Jack felt his heavily bandaged thigh, remembering for the first time how he had been injured the night before. "What about the earthworks. Have you heard anything from Mister Pliny?"

Alan explained that Pliny had sent one of the marines at first light to say that the marines had been successful in their action, capturing a handful of injured rebel sharpshooters and the nine pound cannon that had fired on the *Norfolk Gold*. He reported one man with a minor bayonet injury, no men killed and no deserters.

"I'll give it to the fellow, he's got pluck enough for this war fighting business," Alan allowed. "If he hadnna secured that cannon we would have had to sail out of here at first light. He must be a damned fine leader to keep those men together."

Jack nodded. He was relieved to hear that Pliny had held the marines in a cohesive unit, a feat he was uncertain he could have achieved himself.

"And your two men, Mercury and Mars, did a fine job once they got below. As it was, we were already planning to try to take over the ship sometime in the middle watch, but when we heard the rifle shot that pierced you, we knew it was time to act. Those stupid shirtmen hadn't seen to clapping us in irons properly. Most of us were left to wander unbound in the hold. Isaac had already found a way up and strangled the guard looking over us. Then we found Mercury and Mars sneaking about near the sail locker, trying to stay hidden from the rebels rushing up to do their worst to you. They let us know you were causing a distraction until they could find us. Mercury was the one who suggested we use the nails on the rebels. Has a damned bloodthirsty imagination, that one," Alan said, giving an involuntary shudder.

"What about the cannons, have they been brought aboard?"

Shaking his head, Alan soberly said, "Luck ain't in it, Jack. What we thought were cannons were wooden dummies, painted up black to pass for great guns from a distance. I suppose we can bring the nine pounder down from the earthworks, but that will hardly go for outfitting the schooner properly. Very damned clever of the rascals to get us to turn over the rice before Captain Warren had a chance to run a close eye over them."

"So we've lost our cargo and haven't got a damned thing in return!" Jack said in a severe voice that belied his physical frailty. "What does Captain Warren propose we do now?"

As soon as he had spoken these words Jack saw a cloud pass over his old friend's face. "Well, the thing of it is, lad, that Captain Warren ain't here to propose much of anything. The rebels took him somewhere inland not long after dark. Dinna say for what purpose, just snatched him up and headed ashore."

"They kidnapped a King's Officer. They're goddamned fools to hold a ship's captain hostage. No one overheard where he was to be taken?"

Alan shook his head. 'Perhaps they have a camp nearby. I will send someone to the earthworks to see if one of the shirtmen Pliny captured has any information. Likely as not, they'll be halfway to Fredericksburg by now. Poor Captain Warren will have to pray for an exchange of prisoners or he'll be seeing this war from the rebel side of the fence."

Yes, if he lived long enough to make it wherever the shirtmen intended holding him prisoner, Jack thought bleakly. From the bald duplicity they had revealed thus far, he doubted the enemy would extend the civil treatment normally accorded to captured officers of disputing nations. These rebel shirtmen were not your common disaffected merchants who joined town militias and shook their fists at English interference in their daily lives. They were experienced killers, outliers, backwoods assassins. They reminded Jack more of a belligerent band of Indians than respectable white men. He could not allow men like that to hold Warren at their whim. He did not feel remorse that the Norfolk Golds had wiped the shirtmen out so brutally. They had earned their final moments of suffering, and he would have happily paid them out himself, down to the last man.

Wincing as he swung himself upright, Jack leaned forward, testing his equilibrium. He remained dizzy but still was able to focus on the immediate surroundings. Over Alan's voluble protests, he carefully stood and shambled up to the quarterdeck, pausing periodically to steady himself. On the main deck, a light, invigorating breeze was blowing out of the west which Jack drank in with grateful lungs. He looked toward the declining sun, gauging approximately two hours before sunset.

"Alan, have Mister Pliny send his prisoners aboard immediately. I would like a word with them."

"Aye, Jack."

"Mister Gavin!"

"Yes, Captain?"

"I would like a hangman's noose tied and slung over the main yard if you please and four men told off to serve as an executioner's party."

"Aye, Captain!" the burly mariner gruffly acknowledged.

Alan paused, searching Jack with a beseeching gaze.

"Don't worry, old friend. I'm not as bloodthirsty as all of that. Just a little healthy persuasion to ensure our captives are motivated to answer my questions truthfully."

Alan made a clipped sound of protest in the back of his throat but uttered nothing intelligible. He would see Jack through on this account, whether he agreed with his methods or not. Such was the difficult position of an executive officer aboard ship during a time of war.

Less than half an hour passed before three bedraggled men bound with rope were roughly escorted aboard by a pair of the black marines. Jack stood on his quarterdeck with his back to the prisoners for several minutes, allowing the tension of the moment to play to his favor. His hands were clammy. He turned to face the rebels, taking stock of their character with a discretionary glimpse. Three hard cases. How they had let themselves be captured was beyond Jack's comprehension. They each had the hard, stolid looks of men accustomed to the very worst of warfare. It would not be a pretty business making them talk, though pretty or not, Jack knew it had to be done.

"Gentlemen, you have been captured as part of a pirate conspiracy. You know what the navy does with pirates, don't you?" Jack's voice was eerily calm. Giving a short nod to Gavin, he had the noose fitted over the head of what he took for the most senior of the three men, a giant of a man with bright orange whiskers. Though the giant remained stoically unmoved by the ceremony, the man at his right spoke out earnestly.

"How you figure us for pirates when we weren't nowhere about the water?" the rebel cried. "You ain't about to hang a man without cause."

"Heave away if you please, Mister Gavin!" Jack said, ignoring the shirtman's objection.

Gavin raised his hand to the team of men at the bitter end of the rope. They tensed, readying their strength. As Gavin's hand dropped, the men pulled steadily in a single, fluid motion, the rope giving from the block and tackle with a hushed moan as the rebel's kicking feet were hoisted free of the deck. Other than these lurid sounds, the deck was silent as Jack gazed on the strangling man with a removed, pensive air.

"Let him down, you blackballing bastards!" the angry rebel shouted. Jack fixed him with a quizzical gaze before nodding to Gavin to lower the giant to the deck. As the man's feet touched the wood he was seized by a paroxysm of painful coughing. Jack casually strode forward, looking on the rebel's gasps for air with a sense of abstract loathing.

"Perhaps I could see the three of you are properly tried before I hang you. Though, I would have to have good reason to keep you alive. Presently, I have no such reason. Mister Gavin, give the man some air!"

The giant was once again seized violently above the deck, his entire body jerking with futile protests against the inescapable pull of gravity. The rebels watching helplessly became more distressed with each passing moment of their comrade's suffering. Finally they pleaded for the hanging man's life with renewed spirit.

"For God sakes, Sir, that man is my brother! I will tell you whatever I know as long as you spare us."

Jack turned his attention to the rebel who had said this, a tall angular youth with fair hair and a handsome face marked with small pox scars. The first sprouts of a beard were upon the boy's chin, but without the coarse wires of mature growth. Jack nodded to Gavin to release the giant; as he did so, the fair haired brother poured out as much as he knew about the whereabouts of his fellow shirtmen.

According to what the youth said, the rebels' main

encampment was no farther than four miles from the tree line behind the cannon warehouse. That was likely where they had taken Captain Warren, though the boy was uncertain whether they would keep them there for long. Jack was startled to hear, however, that the six pound cannons did actually exist and had been removed to this secret encampment a few days earlier. Apparently there were two factions among the rebels, those who wished to exchange the cannons and the rice as agreed, and those who wanted to trick the English and capture their ship. The youth claimed that most of the men had been opposed to the plan, but that their leader, a man called Colonel Higgins, had ultimately insisted they comply with his orders or risk being shot. That was all the boy said he knew, and from the appearance of his unclouded eyes, Jack believed him.

"Do you believe you could serve as a guide to this encampment?"

The youth struggled with the weight of what he was being asked, wrestling with protecting his brother and the stigma of turning traitor.

"Can you guarantee these two won't be hurt?" the boy said, inclining his head in the direction of his fellows.

"I will order them released upon the successful completion of our mission," Jack promised.

"Then I reckon I can take you there right enough, providing we wait until morning. I couldn't get you there before sundown and at night I'm likely to get us lost."

"Very well. Isaac!"

"Yes, Captain?"

"See these men fed and watered and given a pallet in the hold."

"Aye, Captain."

"What is your name, boy?"

"William Dodd, Sir."

"Mister Dodd, I expect you will be faithful in your duties as our guide, or else your brother will pay the consequences. Are we quite clear?"

"Yes, Sir," the boy said, bowing his head.

"Good. I will see you first thing in the morning."

After the prisoners were dismissed, Jack returned to his cabin, secretly grateful that he would be unable to proceed in their pursuit of Captain Warren that evening. His time on deck had unexpectedly sapped him of strength. Perhaps Alan was right by insisting he take it easy until the wound on his leg had further time to mend. Jack would have preferred to cover the distance on horseback, but since there were no animals available, he would have to trudge through the wilderness alongside his men. Undoubtedly, Alan would volunteer to lead the shore party, but wounded or not, Jack could not in good conscience allow the rescue be carried out by anyone else but him. He felt a personal responsibility towards Warren and he knew he could not ease his troubled mind until he had exerted every personal effort to bring the Englishman back alive.

Dressing himself after a night of tossing sleeplessness, Jack went on deck a half hour before the men were to be turned out and volunteered for the rescue attempt. The predawn darkness was thankfully cool, and while the muted band of gray in the east bespoke the coming of the Sun, there was a feeling that the cool weather should hold throughout the day. A necessary respite if the men were to march against the rebels and still have a sufficient store of energy to carry the fight sharply to them. He nodded good morning to Mister Gavin making his rounds as deck watch, a long musket balanced casually on his shoulder, looking more like a gamekeeper than a proper sentinel. Still, a damned fine man to have in times of a scrape, Jack thought, however loose his ideas of military appearance. He dearly hoped Gavin was one of the men who volunteered on the shore going expedition. Alan, of course, would have to stay aboard the *Norfolk Gold*, though he would give Jack no small amount of grief for that decision. Eventually his old friend would have to relent, knowing as well as he that someone would need to remain to command the schooner in case the rescue effort failed. Jack caught his breath at that grim possibility. Damned unfortunate way to start a career in the navy. He continued to pace idly across the moaning deck as these thoughts crowded in on him, suddenly realizing that the musket shot in his thigh had ceased causing him pain. There was still the general soreness, of course, but his humors appeared to be restored. That was a fine piece of luck. Best to be fully mended before trotting off to die, he smiled at his own black wit.

From the corner of his eye, he caught a dim flicker of movement ashore. He immediately froze, concealing himself in the long shadow of the main mast. Now what mischief is this befalling, Jack thought as he drew his pistol from his waistband and clicked the hammer back to the half cock with the palm of his free hand. He bent at the knees, moving ever so cautiously to the bulwarks, catching his breath in a shallow rhythm while he waited for further signs of movement. For what seemed like several minutes there was nothing and he began to wonder if he had not mistaken a robin darting from its roost. By this time Gavin had circled back on his rounds, Jack halting him with an imperious look and a motion towards the shoreline. The thick-chested mariner waddled closer to his captain in slow, gradual increments, quietly resting the long barrel of his musket over the schooner's bulwarks as he looked for signs of ambush. He too had been unable to detect the presence of hostiles and Jack could see that his credulity was beginning to waver.

A snapped tree limb dispelled both men's doubts. Jack slipped his finger inside the trigger guard of his pistol, readying himself for the sound of a boat pushing off. Gavin rose up, laying his cheek to the stock of his weapon, his breath arrested with a barely perceptible jerk. A moment later a hail from the vicinity of the wharf, "Hey there, *Norfolk Gold*, we has volunteers over here! Mightn't you be sending a boat across?"

Jack smiled, recognizing the voice of Mister Pliny. "Indeed

we may, Mister Pliny, and happy to have them."

As Jack answered his marine's request the crew began to appear on the main deck, turning out for their morning duties precisely on time. Jack immediately told off a boat's crew and had the gig lowered over the side to bring the unexpected volunteers aboard. As they swung themselves through the entry port, Jack caught Pliny by the shoulder and gave it a hearty shake of welcome.

"My congratulations, Mister Pliny on the success at the earthworks. A handsome accomplishment by anyone's standards. I should like to hear all about it when we have the time. First, however, I have to ask you how you learned of my need for volunteers. Surely we have not been so imprudent as to let the whole countryside know of our plans."

"No, Suh. But Mercury was aboard when you got them dirty rebels to talk. He managed his way back over the water and let me know late in the evening what had happened and what was being planned for this morning. So I took these four volunteers and lit out so as I could get your permission to come along. There are still six good men at the earthworks, old Mercury included, though he was awful upset I ordered him to stay behind to tend the fort. I think he was every bit as anxious as me to deal it out to them rascals."

Jack smiled, aware that the time was drawing near to when he would have to issue a similar, unwelcome order to Alan. "Well, I am happy to see you, however the news made its way. Get your men some breakfast. We still have an hour before beginning this fool's adventure."

"Aye, aye, Suh."

Jack watched as the marines filed down the forward companionway. Turning, he saw the bright red cusp of the rising Sun split the iron gray envelope at the edge of the earth; he dearly hoped the bloody dawn did not foreshadow the fortunes of the coming day.

8. RECOVERY AND FLIGHT

THE rescue party marched through the shaded woods bearing their various tools of war: muskets, cutlasses, tomahawks, pistols, cudgels, capstan bars, bayonets, handspikes, and any other object of an ugly or frightening aspect. There were about twenty men in all, led by Jack and his reluctant rebel guide, strung out in changing intervals, moving in irregular concert—bunching, stopping, and starting, and bunching again—progressing at the maddeningly slow pace of an expedition of men in unfamiliar country. The volunteers were made up of the best and youngest of the schooner's crew as well as Pliny's hand picked marines. They had been two hours on the trail and, despite the relative coolness of the morning, they were quickly wearying of what seemed to be aimless wandering through the trackless woodland. Some had begun to mutter that the rebel guide was tricking them, leading them into ambuscade, but like it or not they continued following in file, trusting that Captain Cunningham knew what he was doing.

Jack too, was beginning to have doubts. As they forded a muddy creek and came into a stand of mixed hardwood, he carefully watched the rebel cast about anxiously to get his bearings. The boy showed every sign of being lost, regardless of his assertions to the contrary.

"Mister Dodd, you realize I will not abide deception

kindly," Jack warned.

"No, Sir. But these woods are fearful different coming from this direction. I've run the hill country plenty of times, it's just that this low country...ah, here is the old tree," he said, excitedly pointing at a huge oak with limbs spread skyward like the arms of a giant catching pieces of falling sky. "We are close now. Might be better we take just a few men to get a look before tramping the whole mess of us in on camp."

Jack agreed, telling off a party of three men to accompany him: Gavin, Pliny, and his attendant Pete Parkinson. They decided to travel lightly, leaving behind their muskets, carrying only a sword or cutlass on their hips; Pete carried a tomahawk culled off a dead rebel. He smiled up at Jack, the youth's blood encrusted mouth making him look like a fearful goblin. Jack had wanted to leave him aboard the schooner to recover from the beating he had taken at the shirtmen's hands the night before, but his faithful steward had managed to eventually overcome his protests. Despite Pete's youth he had the fighting heart of a skilled campaigner, and Jack could not deprive him of the chance to exercise his natural talents.

Following the rebel guide's lead, they moved cautiously along the most densely forested section of the hardwood stand, the leafy canopy above concealing their progress in deep shade. Their footsteps made a soft mashing of the loose soil underfoot, but could not be heard more than a few yards away. Any posted sentry would be hard pressed to detect their approach. Finally they came to a clearing edged with spirals of thick honeysuckle vine. Dodd squatted and carefully shuffled his feet to get in among the congested brush, leaning forward to peer at the rebel encampment. Jack sidled up beside him.

"Where are the guns?"

Dodd pointed to a long, humped row of canvas covered objects. "There's six in all. The shot and powder should be loaded up in a wagon somewhere abouts. Last time I saw they had a team of horses for pulling it. Don't see a sign of them now though."

That was not good news, Jack realized. Cannons would be no more than dead weight if he couldn't acquire the means of firing them. The guns, however, were not his primary concern. He scanned the clearing, looking for evidence of Captain Warren. What he saw did not bode well. The camp appeared ill tended, the few men still lingering not postured defensively. Jack counted only half a dozen men idling around campfires. It seemed remarkable that they would be so haphazard in their guard, particularly if they were holding an English naval officer prisoner. Was it possible that they had not heard the earthworks had fallen and the schooner been recaptured? Unlikely since those men who had escaped the fighting would surely have informed their comrades of the reversal. In fact, one of the men seated at the closest campfire had a bandage wound around his head, meaning he had recently seen action of some kind. What then could explain this sorry state of the rebel forces, their seeming indifference of holding the cannons? Perhaps it was another rebel trap designed to lure them into attacking the camp only to be surprised by a greater hidden force. But if that were the case then Dodd would have to be a party to the deception, which was impossible since he had had no opportunity to confer with his fellow rebels after being captured. It was a damned peculiar business.

Satisfied with the reconnaissance, Jack and his advanced party quickly returned to the rest of his men. Putting Dodd under the guard of two seamen armed with pistols, Jack led the expedition to a small grassy rise overlooking the rebel encampment from the Southeast. The wind blew the smoke of the shirtmen's campfires in the Norfolk Golds' direction, carrying with it the smell of roasting meat. Jack would wait until the rebels began their midday meal, hoping to catch them as unaware as possible to keep the fight out of them. Better to take them all prisoner and see if he could make sense of their inexplicable behavior.

Jack did not have to wait long. The shirtmen soon began tearing off chunks of the roasted meat and eating it with their hands, rinsing it down with what appeared to be hard spirits of an indeterminate origin. So much the better. Nodding to Gavin, Jack raised up with a blunderbuss tucked underneath his right arm, and dashed for the clearing. On both sides the Norfolk Golds exploded out of the brush with a savage whooping, brandishing their weapons as they sprinted for the unguarded campfires. The feasting rebels staggered back, those who had pistols or knives on their person, divesting themselves of their weapons immediately and throwing their hands up in supplication. Not a single one of the woodsmen offered resistance.

"Who leads this rabble?" Jack demanded as he kicked a burning log off the top of a cooking fire, sending pannikins flying. An elderly man wearing buckskin trousers and a cotton shirt hesitantly stepped forward, his eyes lowered submissively.

"Reckon that would be me, Sir. Sergeant Abraham Swift."

The man was at least sixty and his tall frame could not have carried much more than a hundred and twenty pounds. His chest, revealed through his open collar, was an architecture of brittle skin stretched over bone. His white shock of hair was thin and hung loose over his stooped shoulders. When he lifted his brown eyes and gazed half-apologetically at Jack, there was nothing lurking in them to suggest the workings of a deceptive mind.

Jack looked round at the other gathered rebels, the wounded shirtman with the head injury standing next in line to Swift, seven men in all, all weary and seemingly pleased to be relieved of the burden of fighting.

"Your name, Sir?" Jack addressed the injured woodsman.

"Corporal Higgins, Sir."

"Corporal Higgins? Wouldn't be kin to Colonel Higgins by chance?"

"Yes, Sir. That goddamned whoreson is my own brother, Sir."

This was indeed an unexpected stroke. Unusual that the militia commander would leave his own flesh and blood in the most likely path of a counterattack. What kind of devilish game was the fellow playing? By the looks and behavior of Corporal Higgins, the enmity between the two brothers was genuine, but as he had already well learned from dealing with this band of rebels, looks could easily be misleading. Better to buy any information he was willing to sell with a generous investment of skepticism.

Turning back to Sergeant Swift, Jack directed his intentions. "You understand, Sergeant that you are now my prisoners and any attempts you or your men make to escape will be dealt with most harshly."

Swift nodded, rolling a quid of tobacco inside his gaunt cheek. "We figured on being made as much. That was why we was waiting here with the guns. Reckoned you'd be along to collect them."

"I'm afraid I don't understand. You're saying that you knew we would come to capture the guns and you stayed on regardless?"

The old man nodded sagely. "You see, Sir, there was a right ruckus between us and Colonel Higgins when we found out what he meant to do with the cannons. We've been living off the fruits of the land a powerful long time and we were anxious to get our hands on that rice. Many of us has served with Lord Dunmore out west against the Shawnee and we knew we could trust him to stay true to his word. We had all voted on turning over the guns like we promised. But a couple of days ago the Colonel decided he was going to find a way to get the rice and hold onto the cannons too. That didn't set well with most of us, I can tell you. That's why after what we heard of what happened at the river a group of us said we were staying right here with the guns until you and your men came to claim them. The Colonel, he was meaner than a rattlesnake under a flat rock when he heard what we were going to do, but he only had a couple of men with him so he lit off with that officer of yours late in the night."

"Do you know where he was taking him?" Jack put in quickly.

Sergeant Swift shook his head. "Reckon it could be about anywhere. The Colonel knows a lot of folks all up and down the Tidewater. Could be hiding in any cabin or cove between Norfolk and Baltimore within a day or two. You got any ideas, Corporal Higgins?"

The injured man indicated in so many words that the best place to find his brother was in hell. Other than that, he too was unable to add to the intelligence. Jack felt a growing sense of dread for Captain Warren's welfare. The fact that he was now in the hands of an increasingly desperate man did nothing to dispel this foreboding. Jack balled his hands into tight fists. There was nothing he could do for Warren now but report his capture back to Dunmore. That, and carry out his original orders.

He told the rebels he would authorize their release as long as they aided the Norfolk Golds in towing the cannons back to the warehouse wharf. Swift brightened at the proposal and said he could promise a team of strong laborers, additionally offering to guide them over better ground than the expedition had covered earlier that morning. Jack welcomed the sergeant's superior knowledge of the territory and instructed his men to heed the old man's advice.

Despite the willingness of the rebels to help and the exhausting efforts of his own men to drag the heavy pieces through the woodlands, progress was maddeningly slow. Several times throughout the day the gun trucks became mired in the soft ground and had to be tediously levered free with handspikes or the long trunks of cut trees. Even these obstacles would not have uncommonly disturbed Jack except that he noted an ominous change in the weather. A veritable continent of low slate colored clouds advanced out of the east, the wind freshening and backing in that direction. Each small setback with the cannons, each five minutes lost, caused him increasing worry and gave credence to his desire to be safely away from the shore before the storm arrived.

A few minutes after 6 p.m. the last of the guns was brought aboard the *Norfolk Gold.* Jack shook the hand of Sergeant Swift and thanked him and his men for honoring their word. He then said he released them on parole with the promise that they would take no further part in hostilities against the English navy. Swift simply smiled cunningly, both men recognizing that the formalities of the parole was a farce, and slipping back into the densely forested Virginia countryside, showing a hand of friendly farewell before vanishing into the bush.

Eager to be away from the river mooring as soon as possible, Jack appointed the more recently joined men from the British navy to lash the guns in place, telling them that he expected one hell of a blow and to ensure the breechings were as secure as they could make them. The old Norfolk Golds were simultaneously ordered to fetch up the stoutest storm canvas from the sail locker and bend it to the schooner's poles. The wind had continued to build in intensity throughout the afternoon, already nearing gale force. Even the normally placid river water was stirred up into a steep little chop. Jack checked the glass: it continued to drop faster than he ever remembered seeing. Alan appeared in the midst of the boiling activity, his gray coat tails whipping out behind him like grimy little wings.

"Captain, everything below has been secured. I've said no galley fires are to be lighted under any circumstances, though I couldn't imagine why they would do that at this time of day unless it was to boil coffee. I've looked the cannons over and the breechings look stout as towlines. I don't think we'll have any problems there."

"Very good, Alan. I am grateful for your vigilance. Let us hope the *Norfolk Gold* is up for this test."

"Why, Captain," Alan was all incredulity, "I'm ashamed to hear such doubts uttered against this bonny schooner. She's a fine as the day she was laid down, and hadn't shown the first sign of giving up her ghost."

Jack smiled at Alan's romantic notions, but he was keenly aware that the *Norfolk Gold*, though still eminently serviceable, was not the weatherly coaster she had once been. She was getting tired deep down in her timbers, beginning to show soft, though the decline was still limited to only the closest scrutiny. She required loving attention. This coming storm was not likely to be kind to her and only by careful tending could she be brought safely back to Norfolk.

The anchor was hove short and weighed by 7 p.m. Jack watched the sky restlessly, wishing he could coax as much speed from the *Norfolk Gold*'s canvas as he dared in the narrow river channel. However, he was forced to remain satisfied with the six knots the schooner was presently making. Anything more than that would be leaving Isaac with far too slender a margin for error when rounding the hidden mud banks.

Clearing the river's mouth as the remains of twilight melted into darkness, Jack ordered the schooner on a northeast course to try to gain as much distance off shore as possible before the full fury of the storm struck. The seas bucked truculently under the bows, flinging spray in a deluge, the high octave winds driving the airborne water into the seaman's faces like needles. As much as Jack tried to muster faith in the schooner's abilities in raw weather, he was genuinely worried the spars would be unable to bear the strain without snapping. He wrestled with whether he would risk sending men aloft to take in a second reef on the topsails. The decision was made for him when the steady hum of the drawing sails was shattered by the snapping thunder of a sail blown foot loose. The foretop sail had been blown out of its middle and upper bowline cringles on the weather side and was beating a frantic tattoo above the roar of the seas. If it was not secured immediately, the sail would unzip itself in a matter of seconds, leaving the *Norfolk Gold* with precious little canvas to maintain steerage on the helm. Jack quickly ordered Isaac to fall off from the wind, bringing the heavy seas nearly on the schooner's beam. While this maneuver reduced the strain on the canvas and bought time to send a team of men aloft, it robbed the *Norfolk Gold* of her powerful thrust, causing her to wallow drunkenly in the cascading range of waves. Jack would never have risked the course change if he did not have an expert man at the wheel. Isaac knew the schooner every bit as well as her captain, and he would trim her to the seas to her best advantage. What Isaac could not prevent, however, was the violent swing of the masts. The ascent up the rigging would be nothing short of perilous. The crisis of the moment forced Jack to compress his deliberations into a few brief moments as he cast about to select the right men for the job.

Gavin, Edwards, and two of the more experienced transfers from the Men-of-War under Dunmore's command, cautiously clambered up the spray soaked shrouds. The livid flicker of lightening appeared to freeze the upward motion of their bodies in tableau, as if the burst of light had pressed them into that single moment eternally. Yet the illusion departed with the next salvo of electricity that flashed across the sky, illuminating the men further up, almost to the main yard. Slowly, they were successful in their treacherous climb. Jack put his hand to his face, vainly trying to swat away the blinding rush of water, unable to determine what degree of success the men aloft were having. The rabble of the loose sail spoke of the challenging task assigned to them. If they were normal men he would have never asked so much. Perhaps even now he was pressing them beyond the limits of reasonable endurance. Jack knew, however, that being reasonable would not be enough to save his ship.

The cross seas battered the schooner, the larger waves breaking over the bulwarks and flooding the main deck. The *Norfolk Gold* was unaccustomed to such prolonged punishment and she was beginning to roll heavily in the troughs, taking water aboard more quickly than she could drain from the scuppers. Isaac cried out to Jack over the crash of the quaking seas, his words unintelligible. Cunningham did not need to hear to ascertain his meaning: the experienced helmsman was unable to keep the schooner on her present course without allowing the ship to swamp and broach to, a death warrant for all hands aboard. Jack nodded his understanding and motioned for Isaac to bear up into the wind, knowing that if he did not do so soon he would risk losing what control over the schooner the helm still managed. Reluctantly, the *Norfolk Gold* swung across the contrary sea, bringing the wind once again close hauled. As she settled back on her original point of sailing, the deck regained its steadily reassuring pitch fore and aft. Only a few seconds later, a massive tearing sounded above; the white blotch of the topsail ripped free from the yard, carrying over the schooner's larboard quarter like an enormous bird in flight, vanishing into the murky dark. Jack grimaced but knew there was nothing to do for it now. He studied the bared poles above, watching the men cautiously work their way down to the deck on the wind vibrating back stays. At least they had all made it. To have lost a good man would have made it much harder to bear.

"I'm sorry, Cap'n Cunningham! There was nothing we could do for it. The wind was too strong. It kicked like a thing alive!" Gavin shouted at Jack, his normally cheerful face contorted with exhaustion.

"No worries, Mister Gavin. We shall weather it, I'll warrant. Get below and pour some rum down your throat. God knows you've earned a tot."

"Aye, Sir," the seaman answered miserably, slouching for the aft scuttle.

The water rushed down on the schooner's lifting bows, a constantly rolling barrage. However, even the threat of violent death can grow tedious when repeated often enough, and after half an hour of near disasters with veering wind and rogue waves, Jack had to guard against boredom. His orders came as a matter of course, dreamlike, the words he uttered seeming strange even to his own ears, as if spoken by someone else. He moved across the deck with a sure, even stride, pressing the arms of men who appeared to be faltering, passing a kind word of encouragement. He felt natural, at one with this watery element and his tried crew, comfortable with the particular demands and pressures of command. The storm became not a terrifying enemy, but a challenge of leadership, something outside of mortal fear.

Twice more in the night Jack sent men aloft in an effort to bend on sail when the wind appeared to slacken, but both times the brave attempts met with failure. Pushed beyond all limits of exhaustion, Jack finally turned the con over to Alan at two bells in the morning watch, stumbling down to his cabin. Dropping his wet clothes to the deck, Jack toweled off and pulled a nightshirt over his head before fairly falling into his cot. Though weary and sapped of physical strength, Jack was unable to immediately give himself over to sound sleep. He was no longer preoccupied with the handling of the ship; Alan would see her through well. What lingered in the back of his mind were misgivings about Captain Warren. Had he done everything possible to try to rescue the poor man? Should he not have tried to track his abductors beyond the rebel encampment? Yet Jack knew that neither he nor any of his sailors had the woods skills necessary to successfully conduct such an endeavor. He realized that he had developed an uncommon liking for the Englishman, perhaps because he reminded Jack so much of his brother. Jonathan too was a kind, generous man, but like Warren, suffered from terrible attacks when deprived of spirits. Regardless of why Jack had felt a bond of friendship with Warren, he keenly sensed that he had failed him in some respect, and his conscience would not rest easy until he had liberated him from the ruffian Colonel Higgins. Eventually, however, even this piece of Jack's troubled thoughts dissipated in the greater ocean of sleep, his body succumbing despite his mind's disquiet.

His eyes snapped open some hours later, the profundity of his unconsciousness destroying any sense of the time that had passed. Sitting bolt upright, he immediately felt an odd change. The deck was still, the howling winds quieted. He leapt from the cot and put on his wet clothes as quickly as he could manage. Wasting no time with his boots, he strode up the aft companionway, leaving a trail of slimy water dripping behind as he stepped onto the quarterdeck in bare feet. Looking around he saw the schooner surrounded by a heavy swirl of gloominess, the circling fury of the leaden clouds arrested, hanging, ready to dash its full force against the frail little ship. The eye of the storm, Jack breathed out a muted exclamation. Knowing the slackened weather would not abide for long, Jack ordered men into the crosstrees to bend on the fore topsail as quickly as possible. As they swarmed up the shrouds, Jack took in rough bearings by a careful examination of the shoreline. The little inlet roughly three miles due West was the small fishing village of Robin's Point, about two miles north of the mouth of the York River. Jack was able to breathe somewhat easier with the knowledge the *Norfolk Gold* had been able to make as much easting as she had during the blow. For the moment they were safe; once they had the sail sheeted into place, he felt confident she could survive whatever malice the storm had left to deliver.

"Captain Cunningham, sail to leeward!" the lookout cried.

Jack slogged over to the binnacle box and pulled his telescope from the rack. Striding over to the main shrouds, he rested the glass on the ratlines as he studied the stranger. She was a sloop with a green hull and low bulwarks, sailing southwards, dangerously close to the shoal water. She carried her jib but no mainsail. Jack thought it particularly odd to fly that plan of canvas; without the counter balance of the square mainsail, the triangular headsail would leave the sloop vulnerable to a wind on her beam, stealing the vessel's steerage with the first strong crosswind. So close to the shore, it meant likely disaster when the first serious assault of weather struck. His curiosity whetted, Jack scanned the vessel for some further signs of explanation. Straining to make out the most of the details the glass revealed, Jack gradually became convinced that the sloop was in dire circumstances. He could see men frantically working in the rigging, apparently trying to strengthen the main mast by bracing smaller spars against it. That was the problem, he realized. The sloop must have taken on serious damage to her single mast sometime during the night and her captain did not want to risk raising the massive spread of her mainsail unless it was absolutely necessary. She was probably trying to make into the mouth of the York and drop anchor at the first inlet she could find, reckoning her chances of weathering the hurricane better at anchor. Jack could see, however, that the run would be desperate and likely fall short, the spiraling arms of the storm already beginning to unfurl great blasts of wind and rain within a few hundred yards.

Something too about the sloop seemed curiously familiar. Her low slung lines and raked mast, her bowsprit so highly angled...the *Shrike*! It was Daniel Greene's ship, his infamous smuggling cutter. The damn fool must have been making a run before the weather was due in and been caught with a hold full of some kind of contraband. That must be why the sloop was so low in the water. He was still intending to deliver his cargo as soon as the storm was past. For a man who claimed to be so devoted to the preservation of his own physical safety, he certainly was taking liberties with prudent behavior. Jack bit the inside of his cheek, hating what he knew he had to do. He clasped the telescope shut and came round to the helmsman, looking out at the monster behind the gray clouds, beginning to crouch, readying for its final spring. From above the men cheered as the sail was finally sheeted in place, ready to bear the wind.

How he would have liked to share their moment of simple joy. Instead, he reluctantly gave the order to come about and bring the wind on the starboard quarter. He was not blind to the looks of horror and dejection that followed, as well as the muttered oaths and insults. He had just ordered them into the inner chambers of the beast; he only prayed that it did not prove a den of slaughter.

9. BOUND AGAINST THE WATERS

THE green sloop swam defiantly along the bordering shoal water, her white taut jib caught in a fit of wind, pressing her inexorably towards the shore. Eventually she wore back around, though the movement was labored and sluggish. Another such bad turn of luck would likely gut her on a hidden rock. Jack ordered the *Norfolk Gold* to jibe and turn on a course parallel to the vessel in distress. Isaac handled the wheel gingerly, careful not to bring the wind over one quarter to another too suddenly, lest the sudden shift in wind direction shred the schooner's rigging. Only a hundred yards separated the two ships from bulwark to bulwark before Captain Greene recognized his rescuer.

"Ahoy, Cap'n Cunningham!" he cried through his speaking trumpet. "I would admire a tow line if you can spare it."

Jack nodded, telling off a boat's crew of his strongest oarsmen. The eye of the storm suddenly closed over the two small ships, the contraction of violent weather striking the men on deck with the savagery of a lash. The water below and the rain above seemed to merge into a massive avalanche, gripping the schooner's frame to toss it cruelly on the rushing void of the sea. If it were not for the safeguards of the lifelines, several good men would have been lost overboard. Stumbling past a line of sailors clinging to whatever stray piece of rigging that happened to be at hand,

Jack called for the help of two men to help him loop and tie off a hawse laid cable around the base of the main mast. The heavy coils of the cable he had carried to the bulwarks and tossed in the bottom of the boat as it was being lowered over the side. There wasn't more than fifty yards of line to spare; he would have to bring the *Norfolk Gold* even closer to Greene's *Shrike.*

"Bear away swiftly, lads! I don't want to leave you in this witch's bucket any longer that I have to."

The boat's crew dropped like shot over the side into the rising boat. Not wasting the time to watch them push off, Jack quickly returned to the helm, guiding Isaac to steer closer to the *Shrike,* the keening wind now raising a fearful din that drowned out everything but the captain's shouting voice. Jack measured the distance between the schooner and the sloop, the boatload of men caught between, the long tether of the tow line unwinding as the boatmen rowed against the bounding seas. He felt damned uncomfortable about the situation. One powerful blast of wind could slam the two ships together with the gig's crew caught between. Yet he had to steer closer by degrees, shrinking the distance between in order to get the line across. He nearly wrung his hand off as he helplessly watched.

The gig's crew shipped her oars a moment before crashing into the *Shrike's* bulwarks at the fore chains. The splintering sound carried across even to the deck of the *Norfolk Gold* where the men watched anxiously as their shipmates scrambled up out of the boat with the heavy coiled tow line. The gig, damaged by the abrupt blow, broke in half a second after the last man had evacuated it, disappearing beneath the waves. With no time to lament their departed vessel, the boat's crew swiftly looped the tow line around the *Shrike's* capstan and made it fast. The boat commander, Mister Gavin, waved his hand enthusiastically to Jack to confirm that the job was done.

"Isaac, bring us close hauled, if you please!"

"Close hauled, aye, aye, Cap'n!" the bosun cried.

At first the schooner answered well, turning strongly away from the breakwater. However, as soon as the slack tow line caught the full burden of the wallowing *Shrike*, the *Norfolk Gold* began to fall off from the wind, making more southing than Jack would have liked, running dangerously close to Gwynn's Island. While Isaac was diverted with this problem, Jack laid aft to the rail with the speaking trumpet and asked Captain Greene if there was anything in his hold that he might jettison to lighten the load. Greene indicated there was and soon had all available hands tossing weighted crates over the side. He will make a note of where it is sunk, no doubt, Jack thought as he watched the anonymous cargo vanish swiftly over the sloop's side. Only Greene and the Devil knew how much profit the smuggler was storing in Davy Jones' locker for the time being. After the smuggled goods had been dumped, the *Shrike* lightened considerably, enabling the Norfolk Gold to hold her course as close to the wind as she could sail.

While Jack could breathe easier in terms of their proximity to the shoal water, he was in no way pleased with the growing ferocity of the storm. Certainly he had not expected respite, but neither would he have imagined the hurricane was saving its intensity for its most brutal attack. The tearing force on the water had become a snarling thing, pawing the schooner under tons of water, bellowing irascibly when the hull's buoyancy thrust her over the sucking surface. The blank granite sky seemed to drop onto the sea at a distance not too far, as if the end of the earth was only a cable length or two ahead. Crying timbers underfoot and in the rigging above sang a strange dirge, one that Jack hoped was premature.

The battle continued throughout the afternoon and into the early evening. The weather remained so violent that though Jack took pains to see that the men were given a chance to eat their meals at the normal hour, few chose to eat; those who did quickly regretted their decision, emptying their confused guts over the rail in a matter of minutes.

Still, many insisted on following their meals with a liberal draught of rum, an indulgence Jack would never have considered staunching given the circumstances. Shortly before midnight the rain turned to a light sprinkle and the wind backed in the north; the truculent swell diminished on the outgoing tide. Jack felt comfortable turning the watch over to MacDonald and slept soundly until daybreak.

Rising at the sound of four bells in the morning watch, Jack changed into dry slops and sea boots. As he gained the main deck he was pleased to see that the pink shell of the new morning was clearing the eastern horizon, untroubled by the sable curtains of the storm's cloud banks; those hanging ministers of fear had long departed. To the West the hurricane's lingering remnants had all but disappeared over the land's horizon, torn apart like a massive veil over the rich Virginia Tidewater. MacDonald had risen the mainsail sometime in his watch in the increasingly moderate winds, the throat and peak halyards drawn tight, spreading the sail by the gaff to capture the force of the wind, driving the schooner ahead with a refreshing, lively air. Jack walked both the starboard and larboard side of the deck, pleased to see that sheets and tacks were precisely coiled in a fitting seamanlike fashion. A reassuring sense of order had been restored to the *Norfolk Gold*. He congratulated Alan for his initiative and sent him below to catch a few hours of sleep.

Jack did not have to wait long to espy activity aboard the *Shrike*. Greene had her yards manned and her bellying mainsail sheeted home as soon as she cast off the towline. As the sloop drew alongside the *Norfolk Gold*'s beam, Jack shouted across an invitation for breakfast. Greene swept his hat off with a dramatic flourish and said he would be honored to welcome his rescuer aboard for a handsome spread. Knowing the table of a smuggler was likely to be more richly equipped than he could ever manage, Jack accepted the counter invitation, leaving the deck in the capable hands of Isaac and calling for the jolly boat to be lowered away.

Greeted fondly by the boat crew he had sent over to the sloop the day before, there were warm handshakes all around, Jack conveying his sincere gratitude for the brave duty they had carried out. Gavin smiled hugely and said that it was a fine ride over and that the late gig was a scuffed up piece of driftwood at any rate. The others laughed, perhaps more to bury their feelings than acknowledge Gavin's stab at humor. Jack knew it had been a terrifying few minutes in the swamping boat; only his best could have survived it, yet they had all weathered the trial with good spirits. A damned fine set. He sent them across to the schooner in the jolly boat with orders to return in an hour, promising a double tot of rum and hot coffee for breakfast. Though he did not doubt their loyalty, Jack noticed a certain reluctance to return aboard the *Norfolk Gold.* Strange, he thought, surely they could not prefer staying aboard Greene's tight fitting little sloop. Granted, it was a snug little vessel, well suited for its short lived runs in the bay, but it lacked the trim dignity of the *Gold,* the weatherliness, the character. As he entered Greene's cramped cabin, however, he understood immediately the pained looks of the men. Daniel Greene sat behind a long dining table heaped with the choicest jams, bacon, syrups, and soft bread that Jack remembered seeing outside an ambassador's mansion. Looking round, he saw that several empty chairs had been set to receive the boat crew for the breakfast. No doubt they had learned of Greene's plans to reward their rescue efforts and been put in a rather bad way when Jack had ordered them back to the schooner. Probably the first time any of them had ever been disappointed to be given a double tot, Jack thought, smiling. They knew as well as he that Greene lived on only the finest vittles to be found in the Chesapeake, a far cry from salt horse and gruel.

"Good morning, Jack, a damned rough day, eh?" Greene said, shooting up from his chair and pressing Jack's shoulder. The smuggler's bright eyes fairly shot beams of merriment from his normally somber face. "I heard you sent your brave boatmen away. Bad luck for them, but I'm sure you'll reward their services handsomely enough. Now sit down and stuff this fine meal down your gullet. There's enough for a crew, I'll warrant, but if you need something more give a shout and I'll have my man fetch it."

"I'm sure this will do. I hadn't credited you with so fine a sense of gratitude. I thought you moonrakers were supposed to be stingy with your goods."

Greene smiled. "Come now, Jack, I won't be insulted on account of my chosen profession. All of this would likely be sitting on the bottom if it wasn't for your help, so you may as well enjoy it."

Jack settled in and spared no corner of his appetite on the luxurious breakfast. After they had finished they adjourned to the ship's quarterdeck with a fresh pot of coffee, sharing a mutual affection for the lines of the *Norfolk Gold* as they watched her tear alongside the sloop a cable's length off the larboard beam. Jack was pleased to hear Greene's high regard for his vessel, his praise for her weatherly handling during the hurricane. Not all he had to say was so affirming, however.

"A damn shame what you have in mind for her, Jack. She's not fit for the job of running after Virginians. Why don't you take her out of the Chesapeake and back to Portsmouth? It's only a matter of time before you run afoul some rebel skipper who can outgun you. Cut your losses while you still can, I say."

Jack expelled a sigh. "Afraid it's too late for that. At least until I can find out what has happened to Thomas Warren."

"The English officer?"

Jack nodded, sipping gently from the small china cup.

"Do you have any information about the men who abducted him?"

"Only a name. A man in the rebel militia who calls himself Colonel Higgins."

"Samuel Higgins?"

"Yes, I believe that is the name his brother gave. You know him?"

Greene nodded soberly, the accustomed gauntness returning almost immediately to his expression. "He is no proper colonel, I can tell you that. He's a goddamned cutthroat, not trusted even among us moonrakers. I've met him a few times, mostly in different smuggling coves. He lived out in the western territory until he turned up on the Potomac a couple of years ago. He has a reputation for offering free traders a handsome sum for some particular good; after the cargo is delivered these same free traders have a tendency to disappear without an explanation. I know half a dozen ships' captains who refuse to even talk to the man for fear of getting too intimately involved with his schemes. I can tell you this; if he is fighting with the rebels it's not for any sense of liberty. That man is the worst kind of sort you're likely to find in the Tidewater. It's a pity he has your friend. Doesn't bode well."

"Nevertheless, I have an obligation to the man," Jack declared. "If you gain intelligence about the whereabouts of this rascal Higgins, I would admire anything you could pass along."

"Whatever you ask, Jack. Though you may well wish I hadn't."

***

Reaching Hampton Roads shortly after noon, the *Norfolk Gold* and the *Shrike* parted company, the schooner dropping anchor alongside Lord Dunmore's fleet while Daniel Greene's sloop continued on for Norfolk Harbor. Almost immediately Lord Dunmore's ship the sloop of war *King's Fisher* signaled for Jack to report aboard as soon as possible. While MacDonald struggled with the signal flags to acknowledge, Jack went quickly below to change into more suitable attire than his working slops and called away his jolly boat. When he returned topside a few minutes later he was pleasantly surprised to find that his boat's crew had already piled in and were wearing their cleanest ducks. Isaac smiled at his captain.

"I reckoned how it might make a better impression if it was all spit and polish, us being part of the navy now, Cap'n."

"Thank you very much, Isaac. It should make all the difference indeed. Alan, please see that a fresh pitch is laid along the deck seams. God knows how many seams might have opened up yesterday. Also, I have no idea how long I might be away, so I trust you will take any measures needed to get us back up to trim."

"Aye, aye, Captain," Alan said touching his hat.

Jack settled into the boat's stern sheets and passed the word for the oarsmen to give way. The boat sprang to life beneath him as the men dug in lively at the stroke, propelled over the slight slapping wavelets of the warm current. As he watched the high, imposing ships of the English fleet gradually near, Jack felt a growing sense of trepidation. His first report to Lord Dunmore would not at answer well, no matter how he tried to present it. An officer was missing and likely in peril with no one left to claim accountability but Jack himself. He grimaced. How in the devil anyone would have expected success from the mission eluded him. Even as a merchant skipper who was not supposed to know a whit about naval affairs, he had sensed the hazardous nature of the undertaking. It had not taken a prodigious degree of insight to see that the gun seizure was doomed to failure from the beginning.

As he stepped aboard the *King's Fisher*, however, he quickly realized that the news of Warren's capture would be of little consequence amidst the general chaos attending the fleet. The main deck was in pandemonium, officers carrying dispatches from various ships thronging the area amidships. So many blue coats were fluttering about that Jack fancied he had stepped on a nest of jay birds. He overheard brief snippets of information from the knots of gathered officers.

It seemed that two ships had been stranded in the hurricane, perhaps one lost entirely, though there was a great deal of confusion surrounding the specifics. Jack was looked on as suspect by the navy men and they did not take him into their confidence, so he had to glean what he could. After half an hour of kicking his heels on deck, a tall severe man of about sixty wearing a Lieutenant's uniform, approached Jack and asked him to please follow him to meet with Lord Dunmore. The naval officers watched aghast as this mere civilian leapfrogged past them in his attendance on the Royal Governor, muttering coarse suggestions as to Jack's ethical and moral character.

Though Jack had been welcomed into larger cabins than that of the *King's Fisher*, he had never been invited to one so opulent. Whether the furnishings and small amenities were indicative of her captain's taste or additions since the time Lord Dunmore had occupied the sloop of war, he was uncertain. He did, however, have a rich appreciation for the silver serving tray, the fine burgundy settee, the elegant oil paintings depicting two frigates locked broadside to broadside, the damask table covering...

"I have already heard news of Warren," a middle aged man with rheumy round eyes and a broad outdoor face said quietly from behind his mahogany desk, the soft music of Scotland just perceptible in his voice. "It is a bad turn to have lost him, wouldn't you agree Mister Cunningham?"

"It is indeed, my Lord," Jack answered softly. It had been easy to believe the popular rumor that Dunmore was an incompetent fool when he had not had to face the man himself. Standing before the veteran Indian fighter was a different matter altogether. Whatever his mistakes in regional diplomacy, Jack could not deny the governor's imposing figure, his commanding dash.

"I understand you were still able to secure the cannons for your schooner, is that right?"

"Yes, my Lord. We shipped six six pounders as well as a long nine to serve as a bow chaser. There was no powder or shot available. The rebel commander apparently hid it somewhere before we had time to discover his encampment." Jack wondered how Dunmore had come so quickly by the information, realizing the only possible way he could have heard of Warren's capture was by courier overland. And that could have only come from the lips of some rebel informer...

"I regret Mister Warren's disappearance. Unfortunately, the situation dictates that we not tarry too long in our mourning, do you understand?" the words came with unexpected force, almost like a physical blow. "We are in a very bad way as a result of the hurricane. Both the *Otter* and her tender the *Liberty* ran aground. Eventually we should be able to tow the *Otter* off. However, the *Liberty* and her crew of ten men fell into rebel hands. They are being held somewhere in the woods near Hampton according to the best intelligence reports I have been able to gather. These same reports place Captain Warren among these prisoners."

Jack's bewilderment met Dunmore's steady gaze. There was something peremptory in Dunmore's eyes, a touch of the savage. For some reason he could not readily explain, Jack felt cold fingers close around his heart.

"Have there been any conditions for release?"

Dunmore shook his head. "I'm not sure if they have any intention of releasing the poor fellows. These damn rascals lack the moral courage of proper gentlemen. With the fleet in such a state of disrepair I'm afraid there isn't much chance we will be able to mount a rescue attempt, officially that is..." Dunmore trailed off, his round fingers interlaced on the solid desk before him.

"But you mean to suggest something unofficial," Jack finished for him.

"Indeed. There is a possibility that a local ship like the *Norfolk Gold* might be able to work in closer to the land without arousing suspicion. She could then land a small party, perhaps even a single person, to reconnoiter the area to locate the prisoners. Once that was done she could bring forward a party of marines to liberate the sailors, presumably with no lives lost on either side, if the thing went as planned."

"And if it did not?"

The governor shrugged. "That of course is the risk that is part of this profession, Captain Cunningham. We each have to decide if the risk involved is worth the possible reward."

The cabin was silent for a long minute as Jack lingered over the details of the plan.

"My marines are not capable of such a mission. They did well enough at the cannon warehouse, but they are not professional soldiers. Leading them into something like this would be a fool's death."

Dunmore bent his head forward, momentarily resting the burden of his thoughts on clasped hands. "I may be able to do something for you. There is a marine officer, a Lieutenant Porter, late of the cutter *Boxer* currently commanding a small garrison of men in Norfolk. I believe he is there recovering from injuries he received during the fight last week with the rebel privateer schooner you helped defeat. I may be able to spare him and a handful of his detachment for a few days. I will have orders drawn up that you can deliver to him yourself, if you please."

"Yes, my Lord."

"Also, I will have a lieutenant's commission drawn up immediately, placing you in temporary command of the *Norfolk Gold*, to make everything square up with navy regulations, you understand. It will make you senior to Porter so there aren't any questions about who is in command. Navy officers always hold seniority over marines of the same grade as I understand it. Otherwise, having two chiefs can run into a damned difficult business."

"Very good, my Lord."

Dunmore scraped his chair back and circled round to lay a hand on Jack's shoulder. "I wish you the best, Captain Cunningham. Already you have proven yourself an admirable asset to His Majesty's forces here in the

Chesapeake. I feel certain this is but the beginning of a consummately invaluable service."

Jack smiled with the diffidence of the uncertain, bowing as he took his leave. After a few minutes waiting on the main deck, Dunmore's clerk delivered the official papers appointing Jack as Lieutenant in the Royal Navy and entrusting a platoon of marines in his charge. He folded the papers and tucked them inside his coat, pressed warmly against his breast.

He could not, however, escape the idea that he had just signed a pact with the Devil.

10. A CIRCLE OF TRAITORS

NO sooner had the *Norfolk Gold* made fast her moorings than a black coach drawn by a pair of matched bays rattled to a stop at the end of the rain slick wharf. The driver was a short bareheaded man with a mud spattered frock coat who looked like he, rather than the horses, had been beaten within an inch of mortality to make the best possible speed. As soon as the coach door opened and the occupant tumbled out, Jack sympathized with the poor man's plight. Charlotte Fraser, all in a thunder, shot the driver a dirty look, saying something about handling the horses like a nasty puritan, pinched a few coins from her purse, and told him to wait for her at her pleasure. The man went to tip his hat in acknowledgement, whereupon he realized that sometime in his mad dash to the waterfront his head covering had been plucked from his head. A pained expression followed, then a resigned one.

"Trouble coming aboard," Alan said quietly.

Jack nodded. "Indeed. Please let our 'guest' know that she can find me in the cabin."

"Aye, Jack," Alan smiled, scratching a stay for his friend's luck.

Cunningham had not had time to find his seat before the cabin door was thrown open with a flourish and followed by a juggernaut of rustling skirts and curls.

"Miss Fraser, so good to see you again."

"Don't start that way with me, Jack, you holy fool! I

should sit you down and box your ears for what you've done," she chided, her effort at *hauteur* undermined by a fiery color rising to her cheeks.

"I fear you have me by the hip, my Dear. What is it exactly that you think that I have done?"

Her lit eyes were not quick to cool. Leveling her gaze as best as she could manage, Charlotte forced herself to sit and catch her breath before continuing. "It is true, is it not, that you have hired your ship out to this villain Dunmore?"

"At your father's suggestion, yes, I have."

The young woman's incredulity was matched only by her returning passion. Three times she made an attempt to rejoin, but each time was overcome with an excess of feeling. Jack placed a long stemmed glass of claret in her hand to quiet her nerves. After a minute, she spoke in a trembling voice that strived to contain her excited state. "I would expect such folly from my father. I had, however, credited you with a finer sense of judgment. It appears I was wrong. I thought you were planning to leave Norfolk, go home to your wife."

Jack shrugged. "As your father would say, it appears I am bent on adventuring. Surely you aren't worried for my safety, my dear Charlotte. I would not have imagined you cared so much," he said with a hint of amusement.

She cleared her throat, ignoring his irony. "You misjudge yourself and more importantly me, Captain Cunningham. My concerns are for the cause, not your personal well-being. Individuals are not noteworthy in the larger tomes of history."

"What in the devil do you mean? How have I done ill to the cause? Surely serving the governor should please your patriotic fancy," Jack's words came with unaccustomed acerbity, the strain of the past few days no longer concealed behind a veil of banter.

"Again, Jack, you misjudge me. Do you really believe that though I have lived in Virginia since the time I was a babe that I would ally myself with men who would invade my home, keep it in thrall to a government on the other side of the world?" she paused with a short, mirthless laugh. "I am not my father's daughter when it comes to politics."

Or perhaps at all, Jack thought briefly. He was not really surprised to learn of Charlotte's sympathy with the Virginians. It was, after all, far easier for a young woman to romanticize the extravagances of a few raucous frontiersmen than celebrate the virtues of conservative loyalty. He doubted, however, how deeply she was able to penetrate the depth of the decision she was making. The lofty words of radicals might sound well enough and stir the hearts of the people, but the glib charisma of men like Patrick Henry and his ilk left Jack feeling decidedly cold. To now hear these very same arguments from the mouth of Charlotte Fraser not only failed to move him, it called up his disgust. The empty phrasing, the practiced deductions, it all smacked of blind folly. At least he could respect Daniel Greene's reasons for allying himself with the Virginians; his cause was naked and unwavering: self-interest. This girl's opinions, however, lacked all real conviction, and were the words of others.

"I am so very sorry, Charlotte, but I have an appointment that I cannot miss. You understand, of course?" Jack said, suddenly coming to his feet, his tone peremptory.

"I certainly do not!" she fired back quickly. "What do you mean by walking out while I'm speaking with you? I will have my say with you or God damn your eyes, Jack Cunningham!"

"And your tongue, my Dear. Really, I don't have the time for these histrionics. If you would like to air your radical opinions, I would advise you to do it somewhere other than aboard a King's ship. Perhaps a public house might be more to your liking. From my experience, I know you to be uncommonly vocal in that setting."

If Charlotte's visage had been inflamed before, it now turned absolutely volcanic. Her words failed her entirely, though Jack thought the hostility in her gaze more than compensated for her lack of reply. Gathering her skirts with a murderous air, she quitted the cabin with no further declamation, slamming the door sharply behind her. Jack gave vent to a sigh as he fastened on his naval hanger. He suddenly felt very low about the abuse he had heaped on the poor young woman. She was simply ardent, a quality he could have admired were he in less of a dull humor. In many respects he envied Charlotte. Her enthusiasm would have been impossible if there was not some powerful belief behind it. At least she could claim allegiance to a higher ideal, a motive, unlike his own dubious alignment with a governor and a government he neither honored nor trusted. The rope's bitter end of circumstance, he thought, grimacing. Checking his military appearance briefly in the mirror, he left to meet with the marine officer Lieutenant Porter.

The pleasant early evening sounds of banter and light occupation turned out in the streets, a soft harmony of honest labor and well earned fatigue. The long day of repairing storm damage had given way to the respite of drinking, visiting, and gossip. As Jack found himself amid the social phenomenon, he marveled at the seemingly unconcerned faces of the men, women, and children he passed. There was not a whiff of discontent in the salt air, not a single harsh word. In the wake of the hurricane there was a sense of muted relief, a steady pride in having survived the violence nature had visited upon the harbor. It would have been wrong to describe it as serene; rather, the mood was one of hardy endurance. Was it not for his own vivid memories, Jack would never have suspected he was walking through a city on the brink of war.

The marines were billeted in a large mansion some ten minutes hard walk from the center of town. As Jack neared the front door of the edifice he was struck by its imposing architecture. Before serving as the temporary barracks for a detachment of the St. Augustine reinforcements, the classical home had housed the Morganton family, one of the oldest names in Virginia, its wealth reaching back to the beginning of the colony's founding. Now the severe white pediment and colonnades were lent a touch of martial color, two uniformed marines standing rigidly at attention at either side of the massive front door, their scarlet regimentals and clay piped cross belts starkly modern against the Grecian backdrop. Jack passed through the entryway and came into a large, high ceiling foyer commanded at its far end by an elderly sergeant behind a simple field desk heaped with correspondence. The sergeant rolled suspicious eyes in Jack's direction and dryly asked his business. Before he could give a reply, raucous laughter boomed from behind the closed doors of the adjacent drawing room. A second later the door was thrown open by a jolly looking man in the scarlet coat of an officer of marines. This first impression of prime manhood was so strong that it came as something of a shock for Jack to see that one of the coat's sleeves was empty and pinned to the man's chest.

"What is this, Sergeant Caskill, a gentleman kept waiting? Why wasn't I told there was a man here to see me?" the rubicund lieutenant demanded, though not unkindly.

The old man blinked before he spoke, thinly veiling his aversion for his young blooded superior. "The gentleman has just arrived, Sir. I was about to gather his purpose just as you stepped in. He has not as yet said whether he is here to see you or someone else."

"Tosh! That's all stuff Caskill, and you well know it. Who else in this infernal company should he want to see? Well, let's ask the man himself instead of prattling on like school children. Speak up man, what can we do for you? I pray you aren't another of these Virginian fellows that have come here petitioning our choice of quartering. God knows I've had a fill of that nonsense."

Jack smiled, drawing his papers from his breast pocket. "If you are Lieutenant Porter then I can safely say that you are indeed the man I'm looking for, and no, I won't take issue with your quartering, for the present at least."

Porter looked over the papers quickly, his excited spirits growing more so as he took in the full meaning of the orders.

"I thought you had a familiar face. Is this right, I'm to gather a group of men for service aboard your ship?"

Jack nodded. "Only for a few days, but yes, we are expecting some action. Lord Dunmore saw fit to send you and a few of the reinforcements along. I hope you don't bear any harsh feelings on being volunteered."

"To the contrary, Sir, I am only too happy to quit these quarters if it means we have a real chance of fighting. Particularly considering your brave conduct the night the *Boxer* was attacked. I had very much wanted to express my gratitude but was unable to attend," his eyes cut momentarily to his empty sleeve. "I was the man you shouted across to to have the marines take cover before your men served their swivel guns."

Jack remembered Porter's incredulous face the night of the action, strained and haggard, quite different from his drawing room jocularity.

"Pardon my manners, Captain Cunningham. Please let's sit down in private and discuss the particulars of our mission. We wouldn't want all manner of gossip to spread by laying our plans within earshot of the men." Porter shot Sergeant Caskill a purposeful look. The old man simply harrumphed and shuffled a stack of requisitioning papers.

Jack and the marine lieutenant adjourned to the drawing room, shutting the double doors behind them. Like the rest of the mansion, the room was large and spacious, painted light ochre and furnished in an elegantly restrained manner. Family portraits hung in gilded frames along the front wall. Apparently the marines had been quite respectful in their occupation of the house, not disturbing the private property of the Morganton family in any sense that Jack could see. In a settee situated before the empty fireplace, a tall, ungainly looking man in civilian clothes reclined with the latest copy of the *Virginia Gazette* spread out on the short legged table before him. Porter introduced him as Peter Morganton, the eldest son and current proprietor of the mansion. The man inclined his head civilly but offered no further overture of warmth.

"Don't pay attention to him; he's just chewing his insides because I bested him at backgammon three matches in a row. You don't play do you, Captain Cunningham?"

"Ah, no, I'm afraid not," Jack answered, catching a piratical gleam in the marine officer's eye.

"A pity. Mister Morganton, may we ask you for a few moments of privacy? We have official business to discuss."

Morganton narrowed his eyes severely; after a moment of abstract study, he neatly creased the newspaper over his knee and left the room without a word.

"Sorry about that. He's an eccentric fellow. Usually makes for adequate company, though he's a damn sore loser when it comes to a friendly gentleman's game. Now what is it that you can tell me about the mission exactly, if I may press you, Sir. Any details you feel like sharing could help me decide on how to prepare the men."

Jack understood Porter's curiosity, but as he gave a fairly detailed accounting of the proposed rescue attempt, he kept one thing to himself: the possibility that Thomas Warren might also be held captive along with the seamen. That was the real reason he had agreed to take on the task, to try to satisfy a debt that would have been hard to explain to someone else. Dunmore had apparently been aware of it and turned Jack's loyalty against itself, a clever if somewhat cynical move. How Dunmore could have seen that deeply into Jack's character was a mystery, but men who rose to power could sometimes have uncanny insights into their fellow men. Jack had already decided to resign his acting commission as soon as the seamen and Warren were freed; he was not capable of carrying war to the people of Virginia, regardless of the money or lieutenancy the governor had offered. Daniel Greene and Charlotte Fraser had helped him realize that, each in their own way. He had spent too many years in the Tidewater, developed too many important relationships to think of these people he knew so well as rebels or traitors. He may have been born a Scot, but fate seemed determined to have her way: Jack Cunningham, whether he liked it or not, *was* a Virginian. However, he was also a man who honored his friends, and he would not let Thomas Warren languish while being held by a band of criminals. Porter could help him, and for the moment at least, he was an ally.

After Jack had given the marine officer as many specifics as he dared, the two men sat down to a late supper of steamed cabbage in a hearty beef stock, chicken in cream sauce, and a glass of marsala, followed afterwards with cigars and Scottish whiskey. Both men found one another easy conversationalists, and before either of them rightly knew what time had passed, the grandfather clock thumped sonorously that 9 p.m. had arrived. Jack gazed through the front window at the dim evening and the faint specks of the street lamps twisting and guttering in their glass cages. Extending his gratitude for the hospitality, Jack excused himself, explaining that he needed to get back to the *Norfolk Gold* to make sure everything was in order for their departure the following afternoon. Porter led him to the front door and promised to have his detachment aboard and ready to sail by the middle of the morrow's forenoon.

As Jack turned the corner from the Morganton mansion he realized the heady effects the evening of liberal drink had taken. The dark roadway momentarily stretched out confusingly in a number of directions, causing such dizziness that he paused for a moment at the edge of a park, leaning against an oak tree to regain his bearings. The cooler night air slowly revived him; after a few minutes he set back on his way. There were few people still in the streets. Most had apparently decided to make an early evening of it, perhaps too tired from repairing what they could to the storm beaten buildings of Norfolk. A few whores loitered in the lower quarters; one strawberry headed girl who could not have been more than fourteen had half-heartedly offered herself to him. She was wan and desperate and the hollowness of her face had made Jack inadvertently gasp. So terribly sad and young. The poor lives of women without consequence was as bad here as in the slums of London. Another lasting import from the Old World, he thought glumly. Pinching into his purse, he dropped a few coins in her hand and continued on his way.

He decided to take a quick turn through the town square, lingering for a moment to gaze up at the evening sky. Instantly he was lost in a geometric patterning of the stellar positions, working out a navigational formula from force of habit. He became so caught up with the star gazing that he failed to notice the approach of a group of unfamiliar men dressed in threadbare clothes. At first they remained on the square's periphery, speaking in low, guttural tones, not venturing too close, as if they feared coming directly into the street lamp's illumination. Jack's instincts for danger immediately alerted him to their presence. He quietly damned himself for allowing them to slip up on him to such disadvantage. The weakness of drink, he had to admit. Now was no time to chide himself for something he could no longer help. He crushed the heavy headedness to the corners of his mind. The men were still casting about and grumbling at one another as if they had not quite made up their minds of what to do. Hoping to capitalize on this reluctance, Jack resumed his walk towards the waterfront.

Turning down the deserted market street, he thought for a moment that he had lost them. Before long, however, their humped shapes appeared in silhouette, marching in a clumsy line abreast, their shoes scuffing on the cobbled street. Jack felt his heart leap within his chest and a surge of blood slam against his temples; his nostrils dilated with fear. He had counted at least six of them. If these blackguards meant to do real harm there was no way of fending them off. As he continued at a brisk pace, he briefly turned his head over his shoulder to see how much distance the strangers had closed. Their pace quickened, their footfalls echoing against the facades of empty buildings. Ducking into a side alley, Jack broke into a trot, his legs suddenly feeling light, panic lending him an unnatural nimbleness. The initial suspicion that the men meant to harm him gave way to certainty, and he felt his nerves translate into a readiness for action, sharpening his senses and purpose. A shout rang after him, but he did not dare look back or slow his pace. He was hunted and any delay now would make him easy prey.

Weaving behind a row of empty hawker's carts, Jack discovered a deeply shaded alcove at the rear entrance to the central market. He edged into the concealing shadows as far as he could manage, careful not to upset any objects hidden in the darkness that might betray his presence. He caught his breath in shallow rasps, waiting for his pursuers to pass. What could they possibly intend? Were they simply idle criminals looking for a rich pocket to pluck or were their designs more malignant? He heard them slow as they came nearer, petty arguments breaking out as each of the men believed he knew how best to proceed. Jack edged forward to see if he could make out any familiar faces among the band of ruffians. A wan band of moonlight fell across the alleyway between a gap in the tightly crammed buildings. The men paused, trying to reorder their plans; Jack studied each of the figures minutely. They were a pack of generally strong looking youths with the stiff gaits of landsmen. Their clothing was made from animal skins in the main, though a few wore broadcloth jackets and linen shirts. Jack could not see any weapons in their hands, but he was convinced that they were rebels.

Eventually they moved on out of earshot, allowing Jack to slip out of his alcove and retrace his steps. He hurried for fear that the rebel thugs might have become wise to his ruse and decided to reverse their course. His head swam with a number of questions and uncertainties. Why would these men have been following him? Did it have something to do with his plan to liberate the trapped seamen at Hampton? He became so caught up in these worries that he failed to notice a shadow fall from the corner he approached. A second later a dark figure emerged from the shadows and whipped a thin, weighted cane at Jack's head. Before he could step away the polished wood cracked across his left temple, the world going bright with pink flashes as his legs sank beneath him.

Jack's mind reeled under the force of the blow, his thoughts confused and random. His first returning sensation was the feel of the clammy stones of the alley beneath his body. Shortly thereafter, a shout and the sound of running footsteps. He opened his eyes to see who had assaulted him, but the colored lights continued to dance a few feet in front of his eyes, masking the culprit's face with shifting smears. He felt hands tugging at him, raising him to his feet, but for some reason he was let go and dropped back to the ground. A searing pain slowly grew more intense as the momentary shock began to wear off. He lightly touched the corner of his brow, probing the circumference around the hard knot with his fingertips. The contusion was the size of a musket ball and seemingly just as hard.

The men babbled in confusion over him. At first Jack was unable to follow the tenor of their conversation, his head still pounding from the injury. Gradually, however, he began to make sense of their words. They were arguing over what to do with him. Apparently some wanted to kill him on the spot while others were interested in taking him prisoner. Jack cast a few surreptitious glances about him, looking for the first opportunity to bolt. As he did, his vision began to clear and he turned his gaze on the man with the cane.

The white haired gentlemen!

The pale wings of his unbound hair caught the moonlight like a silver sail, lining his countenance with a spectral quality. His face, however, was not that of an elderly man. His skin was taut with youth, struck with an uncanny perfection, almost like marble. His eyes were a fierce light color, perhaps blue or green, though it was impossible to discern in the darkness. Seeing Jack's renewed awareness, he smiled and leaned close to him, not further than a few inches from his staring eyes.

"Getting a good look are we, Captain Cunningham? I hope you have seen enough to satisfy your curiosity. I'm afraid, however, I will have to let the rest of the riddle remain unsolved." He drew a small pistol from his waistband, thumbing back the hammer.

Jack's eyes slammed shut as he waited for the blast of finality. The delay seemed without end, his pulse thumping in his ears with the ferocity of a tide-rip. Yet for some reason the shot did not come. Jack opened his eyes, two slim crescents looking up to see what hand had arrested fate. Someone laid a slender, grey, gloved hand on the white haired gentleman's sleeve and drew him away in conference. The henchmen stared at Jack curiously, as if they were trying to decide whether he was worth the effort to kill. He dearly hoped they found him wanting. He was comforted to find that they did not seem particularly bloodthirsty, but rather reluctant about this business of murder. They were shifting uncomfortably, casting furtive glances up and down the intersection. Jack tried to see around the men to the person who had called the white haired gentleman away, but they were gathered too closely, their rough shins blocking his view.

The white haired gentleman returned, still holding his pistol. He kneeled and narrowed his eyes, taking stock of Jack once again.

"Looks like you've earned a reprieve, Captain."

The gentleman deftly flipped the pistol in his hand so that he held it by the barrel; he swept it sharply down in one single motion against Jack's uninjured temple. Unconsciousness overtook him before he had time to register a whit of pain.

Waking some time later, however, pain was the first undeniable presence in Jack's mind: staggering, blinding pain radiating across his forehead and face. He stumbled to his feet, bracing himself against the building corner, his balance a precarious, frail thing. Softly touching the sides of his face, he felt the rough texture of dried blood. At least he was still alive, he thought. He traversed his head slowly, scrutinizing the dark to see if anyone was lurking about. There was nothing. He ventured forward, deserting the temporary crutch of the building in the hopes that his legs would not buckle under independent power. In five minutes he had made it back to the waterfront.

He slumped against the wharf bollards to rest, his exertions having brought on a disorienting dizziness. A ship's bell sounded somewhere in the inner harbor, 3 a.m. It had been hours since the white haired gentleman had accosted and then curiously released him. A damned puzzling gift horse, but one he would never have dreamed calling toothless. Better now to try to put the strange business out of mind. He had much to do and several difficult decisions to make before sailing on tomorrow's evening tide.

He just prayed there would be no further surprises wielding canes.

11. A PLOT DISCOVERED

JACK ignored the many soliciting looks he received as he came onto the quarterdeck after breakfast. The two neat contusions had continued to swell overnight and presently looked like a pair of hard black marbles sewn into fleshy pockets just beneath the skin. Ordinarily Jack would not have minded explaining to Alan how he had earned the bruises, but on this morning he lacked the mental strength to withstand polite interrogation. It was already taxing enough that he must explain the details of their mission and the added complication of Porter and his detachment of marines coming aboard. To add to that the idle speculation revolving around the white haired gentleman would utterly sap him. Admittedly it was a queer business, and damned well meant something that needed figuring out. However, until he had a clearer idea of how pertinently it affected the current mission, Jack would not indulge his friend's suspicion.

He had already seen the smirks and smothered guffaws among the crew. Rumor probably had it that the captain had been too far gone in his cups and been beaten out of some doxy's bedroom by an enraged cuckold. Jack afforded himself a slight smile. Perhaps there were worse things the men could think of him.

Staying true to his word, Lieutenant Porter and his detachment of a dozen marines reported aboard in the middle of the forenoon watch. Jack detected a slight aversion on the part of the marines, as if they held themselves in higher esteem than service aboard a mere hired vessel. While this did not appear to be encouraged by Porter, it was nonetheless real, and noted by the general crew of the schooner. A quiet air of mutual hostility immediately ensued; Jack recognized how fortunate it was that the professional soldiers would only be aboard for a short duration. Anything longer than a few days could all too easily erupt into a small crisis.

The most egregious example of the tense relations was between Porter's marines and Jack's own platoon of black soldiers. A minor scuffle was narrowly averted shortly after the noon meal when Mister Pliny had assembled the *Gold's* marines amidships to practice their manual of arms. As the men devoted themselves to a precise and proper execution of the drill, Porter's marines congregated a few feet away. They pretended to speak to the side, though their talk was deliberately clear and meant to be heard by anyone on deck.

"Sloppy darkeys, eh Bob?"

"Never seen such in my drillin' life, there Tom."

Mister Pliny stiffened at the criticism, spinning sharply on his heel to face the hecklers. This gesture added fuel to the marines' derisive fire, drawing out other men who had heretofore remained silent but were not willing to abide a black man's acid stare. Jack was occupied on the quarterdeck with Isaac over a discussion about the schooner's spare canvas supplies when his attention was suddenly diverted by the sounds of fisticuffs. Moving brusquely forward, he saw the two groups of men squared off against one another, both sides waving their muskets threateningly. One of Porter's marines had just risen from the deck, his hand pressed to the side of his clouted cheek; the English marine had the burning vision of hatred in his round, jellied eyes, the look of a man bent on reprisal.

"Mister Pliny!" Jack cried. "You will immediately dismiss your men below."

Pliny stifled a scowl and faced the black marines.

"Platoon, dismissed!"

The rows dissolved into a random flow of mutters and harsh words. Jack anxiously watched as they left, sensing that time was working against him if he was to prevent an unrestrained brawl. As soon as the last dark head ducked into the forward scuttle, Jack passed the word for Lieutenant Porter. It took several minutes for anyone to determine the marine officer's whereabouts until one of the men said he had seen him on the way to the officer's head. In the time it took to send a runner to fetch him Jack's slowly building anger had set like a hard jewel embedded in soft flesh. Despite Porter's rather absurdly perspiring and flushed face from his late physical exertions, Jack poured out an invective in barely whispered language.

"For God's sake, don't you have any control over these men? Are you trying to encourage a mutiny? I promise you I will land your marines on the first inconvenient island I come across if they so much as blink impolitely at me or my crew. Do you understand?"

Porter nodded mutely, his eyes fastened to the deck.

"I do not offer excuses, Captain Cunningham, only apologies. I will see to it."

Jack could see that Porter was not accustomed to censure. He was after all the same man who had sacrificed his limb in defense of his ship. His composed expression had the appearance of strong self-assurance, the determination and passion of a strong leader. The broad forehead and handsome, strong features suggested a real depth of character, capable of withstanding the challenges of command.

"What is the matter with them, Mister Porter? I have never seen marines so...unlike marines."

Porter sighed as he gazed at his detachment, a perceptible sense of weariness pulling at the corners of his frowning mouth.

"They are not properly 'my' marines, Captain Cunningham. They are reinforcements shipped up from the fort at Saint Augustine. There are sixty at all, spread thinly around the fleet. I fear I inherited the King's hard bargains. I suppose the powers-that-be figured a one armed Lieutenant only rated a half-hearted command."

Both men smiled at Porter's attempt at wry humor.

"I understand it must be hard keeping them in line. Just see that they don't cause a mutiny, won't you?"

"Aye, aye, Sir."

Much of the remainder of the day did not allow time for idle conflict. The men labored under the scorching late summer Sun, splicing frayed cordage, tarring the fresh rigging, and laying the adze to any rough edges. Jack walked the deck continuously to ensure the men kept diligently to their duties, showing a pronounced desire to be under way as soon as possible. The close attention kept the crew on schedule and when the evening tide rolled seaward the *Norfolk Gold* had her anchor catted as she raised her full suit of sails.

The early evening weather was graciously mild with a moderate breeze out of the northwest, just enough to dapple white flecks over the black forest of the bay waters. It would have been a pleasant hour to be on the sea, Jack realized, if his business there had not been so dire. He could face shell and storm well enough; it was the thought of failing his comrades-in-arms that troubled Jack the most. Perhaps that was the true test of a man's character. To be bothered by some abstract failure was easy enough for anyone, but to lament the weakness between human bonds, surely that was a noble thing.

After the lookout sighted the Hampton headland at twilight, Jack summoned Lieutenant Porter and Alan to his cabin to share his plans for the night landing. He ceremonially poured them both a glass of wine, remembering how only a few days earlier he had paid a visit to this very same cabin to hear Thomas Warren spell out his carefully laid plans. The memory disconcerted him for a moment, but acting the professional, he pushed it to the corner of his mind as best he could.

"Gentlemen, we should have a busy night of it in the next few hours, so I will not keep you here with unnecessary prattling. However, I believe it is important that we understand each other clearly before the wheels of this machine begin turning. First, I want you both to understand that you are not to come ashore unless you have been signaled to do so by me."

"But, pardon me, Sir," Lieutenant Porter broke in. "I had expected the marines would land from the start, even if only in a small reconnoitering force in order to provide some measure of protection."

"And I don't see why you should be going ashore at all, Captain," Alan added. "Unless I'm mistaken about navy customs, it's the first officer that normally commands the men in a cutting out. If you're thinking I'm too old, then you could at least send Isaac. He's as sharp as any man sitting in this cabin, and just as likely to get those seamen away from the rebels."

"He is also a Negro, and damned likely to arouse suspicion if he goes lurking about by himself. No, I will not expose anyone to unnecessary risks. As for the marines, I want them to be held in reserve and used only as a last resort. I will go ashore alone before dawn. After I have reached land's end the gig will return to the *Gold* and, Mister MacDonald, you will stand off out of sight during daylight hours. It simply will not do for the schooner to be suspiciously beating back and forth on the lookout for land signals. Besides, it's not impossible that the rebels have mounted some kind of shore defenses by now. What's more likely is that they have coast guardsmen looking for any strange shipping. Any premature discovery of our plans could put the whole business in the balance. Now, at two bells in the morning watch you will bring the *Gold* within sight of the land. If I need the gig sent in I will be at the landing area and I will signal you with three long flashes from a shielded lantern. If I want the marines to come out it will be four long flashes. I will make the signal three times in intervals of two minutes. If there are no signals before daybreak you must be in the offing by the time anyone on the shore can see you. Is that perfectly understood?"

"It's understood alright, lad, but why are you insisting on going in alone. Surely at least taking another man along will serve you better. Another pair of eyes to do the scouting." Alan offered.

"I have to agree, Captain Cunningham," Porter interjected. "Surely you can see the need of having an escort ashore. Why don't you allow me to come along in civilian clothes? It would put my anxieties a bit more at rest."

"Thank you, Lieutenant Porter, but I must have you stay here with your dreadful marines. I'm afraid I simply don't trust them unless you are here to enforce discipline. But I will take your concerns into account. I will take young Parkinson along to help serve as my eyes and ears. He is young and likely won't cause any suspicion among the rebels."

"Are you certain taking your cabin boy is all that wise, laddie?"

"A boy!" Porter gasped. "Surely, Sir, you can't be serious. He may well not cause suspicion, but how in God's name can you expect him to fend off these rebel blackguards if it comes to a serious scrape?"

"You might be surprised on that account," Jack answered, smiling mysteriously. "In any event, you should both be satisfied with the compromise. I have agreed to take a bodyguard ashore. Who it is remains entirely to my discretion. Thank you gentlemen, I don't believe I have anything else for you this evening. I am going to turn in early this evening and get some sleep before the landing. Somehow I suspect it will be the last chance at rest I get for some time."

The marine officer reluctantly accepted his dismissal; Alan lingered a few minutes to confer with Jack about the makeup of the gig's crew that was to take him ashore. After the business was satisfactorily settled in both their minds, Alan tried to leave his friend to his privacy, but for some reason, he was unable to cross the threshold.

"What is it, Old Man?" Jack asked.

Alan turned his spray damp hat in his hands and sunk in the rocking chair, the straw back ticking with his weight.

"Jack, I have something to tell you that I think you should know before committing yourself to this landing."

"Go on."

"The thing of it is, I don't see why you're doing it. None of the men do. When I took issue with your decision to lend aid to the *Boxer* it was more than because I was afraid our cargo might be damaged in action. I knew there was slim likelihood of that. What troubled me was that you were willing to help the English at the expense of rebels' lives."

"Pirates' lives," Jack corrected.

"Virginians' lives," Alan's face was somber. "I think we may be on the wrong side of this war, Jack. I've heard much of the same from the crew. They don't understand why we should serve the likes of Dunmore, Amis, and Porter. That's why they hate these new marines aboard, they're English. What does a crew of Scotsmen and Negroes have in common with a passel of jolly jacks? I'm afraid if you go through with this rescue attempt you may be putting yourself in a position where you will have to kill more Virginians. For what? To save English sailors who think less of you than they would a homeless cur?"

"If these were your feelings, why did you agree to stay on board when I gave everyone the chance to leave? I never put an ultimatum to you."

Alan smiled wearily. "I stayed the same reason every other man stayed, Jack. Because you're a good captain and a friend. I would rather sail with you against the legions of God's own fleet than serve aboard another man's ship just because his politics happened to agree with mine. But, lad, we're not Englishmen, and to ask us to keep doing the Englishman's bidding is too much by half. We know these people we've worked with for years; they're good people, Virginia people. If we have any loyalty that means anything it should be to our friends, not a King on the other side of the world."

"Damn your eyes, Alan! Do you believe I'm doing this for England? Do you really think that I believe a word Dunmore has said? He knows this so called commission he has granted me is no more valuable than the paper it is written on." His voice dropped sharply. "I am going to find Thomas Warren, not a boatload of English tars. He may be English, but he's a good man. The same idea is true of this villain Higgins. He may be a Virginian, but by all accounts, he's nothing short of a butcher. I can't abandon a good man and I won't be allied with an evil one. Look here, I mean to find Warren and bring him safely back aboard. Once that is done we can return Porter and his marines back to Norfolk with our conscience clear. Then I will put anyone ashore who wishes to remain under Lord Dunmore's authority. I promise that after this is done, the *Gold* will never sail under an English ensign again."

***

The fog was thin in the predawn darkness, a wispy curtain drawn across the jutting promontory of the Hampton headland. It brought with it an uncommon chill, the first indication that summer had given way to autumn. Jack drew his boat cloak tightly around his shoulders and breathed down into the dome of his open collar to let the heat of his breath warm him. He had not expected the abrupt change in temperature, though he was thankful the seas had not stirred up with the new weather front, forcing him to put the landing off until the next evening. He realized that Thomas Warren might not have very much time left and any further delays might well cost him his life.

He gave Pete Parkinson the once over before watching him drop over the side into the waiting boat. He looked ready, less frightened than many, though that may well have been out of ignorance. His smashed mouth was smiling, the boy all caught up in the moment of excitement. Jack hoped he was not making a terrible mistake by inviting the boy along. He would know soon enough.

The bowman, Gavin, pushed smartly off and a mixed crew of old and new Norfolk Golds laid to their oars with a fine, spirited stroke, the muffled oarlocks preserving the boat's secrecy. The sea was running smoothly; ten minutes of easy traveling put the boat on a small beach at the base of a grassy rise. Jack and Pete splashed over the side into knee deep water that sucked and gurgled as it lapped incrementally up the tide flat.

"Good luck, Cap'n," Gavin said, smiling hugely. "And to you too, nipper," he said clapping Pete affectionately on the shoulder. "Here, take these." He handed them both a small parcel tied tightly with a bight of string. "A bit of salt horse and a nip of whiskey to get you through. Won't be enough for more than two meals, but I figure you can scrounge if needs be." His face was unusually kind, almost as if he was bracing himself for a longer goodbye than these perfunctory words would allow. Hope he isn't burying us prematurely, Jack thought.

"Thank you, Mister Gavin."

"Aye, aye, Sir. We'll be looking for your signal Cap'n."

Jack nodded. The boat's crew had the gig turned around and ready to return to the *Norfolk Gold*; Gavin hopped into the stern sheets to man the tiller as the men bent to the oars and began to give way. Jack and Pete watched them as they gradually crawled out of sight, merging into the outspread gloom of the bay. Both were struck silent by the profound loneliness of that moment hanging over the nameless beach. They turned and moved inland without exchanging a single word, as if guided by some dark, half-known instinct.

Jack remembered to stow the signaling lantern in a concealed but well-marked place so he could find it even in the dimmest hours of the night. Beating the tall grass in the half-light revealed a small embankment that concaved in the hill forming a protected but hidden ledge. He carefully swaddled the lantern to protect it from the elements and placed it as far back in the indentation as he could and then covered the long grass back over the opening to disguise its location. Satisfied that he had left no evidence betraying the lantern's whereabouts, he motioned for Pete to follow him up the rise and into the woodlands.

The false dawn came sooner than Jack had expected. Consequently, a pallor spread in the East that lit the way far more distinctly than he would have liked. Certainly it made tramping through the vine choked woods more convenient, but it also made it far easier for any potential sentries to espy their movement. Deciding it was deucedly more suspicious to be seen beating through the bush in the dark hours of the early morning, Jack had Pete hole up with him under a leafy hardwood bough and catnap until the Sun had risen.

A few hours later the pair rose groggily from the copse. Though neither was familiar with the immediate countryside, they proceeded inland with a fair degree of certainty that they were headed in the right direction. After a half hour of hard walking they came to a rutted turnpike and followed it south until it led them to the Hampton outskirts. The village was unusually active despite the early morning hour. An open air weaver's market was doing brisk business in front of the low-slung store fronts. Widows and their children manned the various stands. Jack lingered for a moment, fingering several different bolts of cloth as he listened to the women's talk, hopeful for some casual slip of gossip that might aid him in his mission. This morning, however, seemed to be more concerned with boxing the ears of mischievous sons rather than discussing the fortunes of war. Buying a few of the less expensive pieces, Jack handed the cloth to Pete for safekeeping and moved on.

After an hour of touring the streets and markets, Jack became convinced that the prisoners were not being held within the town limits. There were too few unoccupied spaces, and those that were would not have afforded sufficient secrecy or protection. The rebels would have had to establish a base of operations in some outlying camp or cabin. The question was how far away.

At the southern end of town Jack and Pete shifted off to the side of the road and untied the parcel of food and whiskey Mister Gavin had so kindly given them at the beach landing. As Jack ate the standard fare, he realized his appetite had been suppressed by the excitement of the mission, but now whetted, he ate nearly his entire ration and downed half the flask of spirits. Standing, he felt the warming effects of the liquor spread pleasantly to his vitals. Pete likewise had partaken and the heady effects were plain even to a casual observer. Already following in the delinquent footsteps of his predecessor Mister Yeoman, Jack smiled to himself.

Walking the roadway cleared Jack's head, and soon he was fairly cantering along at a pace that would have normally collapsed a lung. Pete pumped his shorter legs to keep abreast, looking rather like a miniature longshoreman in his round hat and pea jacket. By noon they had covered nearly five miles and still were no wiser in their intelligence gathering efforts.

Coming to a steep bend in the road, Jack paused, peering ahead and then casting a long glance back. "Well, Pete, what's to do? Where are they keeping the poor lads?"

Pete shrugged. "Maybe we should find some horses. Be easier than hoofing it along as we are."

Jack agreed and they sat down together on a fallen tree limb to await a passing vehicle. They were not kept in suspense for fifteen minutes before an old carriage driven by a surly looking man with ginger colored sideburns and prodigious shuddering jowls ordered his team of nags to halt. The man rolled a large protuberance of chewing tobacco from one side of his cheek to the other and spat a long, dirty stream from his crooked mouth. For a full minute he studied Jack and Pete without uttering the first word, scrutinizing.

"Where you going?" he finally asked.

"South for about ten miles or so. Supposed to find this lad's mother and bring her back home."

"She run from you?"

Jack bent his head, intent on playing his part as convincingly as possible. "Something of that description. I can pay you out well enough for your troubles."

The ginger haired man slowly shook his head. "I don't take advantage of a Christian in need. Make a place up here for you and the lad. Ain't room in the carriage."

Jack lifted Pete up and swung himself onto the outboard side of the driver's bench. He barely had time to settle himself before the driver put the horses back into their plodding motion, lurching in a controlled fit down the rutted track. At least they were on the move again, Jack thought. He felt sure that he was moving closer, that the rebels would have chosen to muster to the south, nearer to the calm water inlets on the innermost face of the peninsula. That would have been the most likely place to have put in after capturing the stranded seamen. It seemed odd that Dunmore's intelligence reports could be so specific in some respects and yet so general in others. If the governor knew Warren had been transferred to the same camp that held the captured seamen, why wasn't he able to give a more exact location? What was the source, and how faithfully could it be trusted?

As the carriage ferried them further south Jack's worries became more pronounced. He began to doubt that his decision to make contact with the rebels would answer to his advantage. An instinctive wariness had possessed him and it seemed to grow with each turn of the carriage's squeaking wheels. A little over an hour later the ginger haired man turned off the road onto a small patch of bare earth. At the end of a narrow trail hunched a small log cabin beneath a lush bower of shade trees.

"This is my home," the man said perfunctorily. "I can offer you a place to eat and rest if you mean to go further in the morning."

Jack thanked him and accepted his invitation, grateful to find a comfortable bed freely offered rather than having to spend the dark hours beating the bush in search of a straw pallet. Pete was more than willing to conclude his adventures for the day. Jack realized he had pushed the boy's physical limits, though to Pete's credit there had not been a single word of complaint.

The ginger haired man let them off at the entrance to the cabin and called for his wife. A stoop shouldered woman with coal black hair bound tightly on top of her head shambled onto the porch, turning a severe, perhaps even hostile, gaze on her guests. Her skin was stretched so tightly that the bone structure beneath her face dominated her hard expression with a stark, angular architecture, almost as if she was made out of bars of iron rather than bone. She did not welcome them, merely turning and vanishing back inside the dim recesses of the house. Laying his hand protectively on Pete's shoulder, he led the way in.

The woman sat in the corner knitting by the light of the single window. Jack and Pete sat down on a settee made from split pine trees cut so recently that they still reeked of pitch. The sharp smell seemingly penetrated everything in the house, reminding Jack in many respects of living aboard ship, though the fetid smells of so much humanity crammed together were thankfully absent. The company, however, fell considerably short of that aboard the *Gold*. After nearly half an hour of tomb like silence the ginger haired man swung the door open and clumped his muddy boots across the bare floor and flung himself into a rocking chair across from his wife. She immediately set her knitting on the small table before her, retreated to the kitchen and laid a cooking fire in the flat topped stove.

"That, you may be witness, Sir, is a good wife. Perhaps you may remember what one looks like when you find your own," the ginger haired man said purposefully, reaching for a pipe from a rectangular personals box and stuffing the bowl with tobacco.

Dinner was a simple affair of pan seared beef conspicuously devoid of salt and a small round loaf of bread. The meal time was as cold as the previous entertainment. Jack could not imagine daily life in such a cheerless household. After eating they were shown to a hay pile in the small barn to the rear of the cabin. It was still only 8 p.m. by Jack's watch, but neither he nor Pete protested taking their leave to private quarters at an early hour. Better to sleep among indifferent beasts than in the home of a stern host.

The ginger haired man lent them a single lantern and led them to their lodgings. Jack again thanked him for his kindness and was answered with a curt grunt and the turning of his back. Closing the large swinging door behind him, Jack settled the shivering lantern on a narrow board and cast himself onto the nearest pile of hay. Pete likewise made well with his vegetable mattress, sprawling out and yawning, even the pungent smell of horse manure failing to dampen his enjoyment of so much free space; the extra room was a luxury he had learned to value by sleeping aboard the *Gold*. A hammock was fine, but nothing compared to a proper bed.

"How do you fare, Pete? Not too sapped to keep going in the morning, I hope," Jack said, his tone teasing.

"Not if you aren't, Cap'n!" the boy returned brightly.

His enthusiasm was so keen that Jack could not bring himself to chide Pete for referring to him by rank, lest it betray the charade. He turned the lantern down and almost immediately fell into a profound sleep. The kaleidoscope of shifting darkness seemed to propel him to a separate dimension of unconsciousness. His dreams were light, airy things, a step removed and subordinate to a greater gravity of unbeing. His mind wandered freely, setting upon various images of pleasure: the long curve of Charlotte's waist, the *Gold*'s full suit of sails straining with a fresh quartering wind, the fine conversations with close friends he's held in his great cabin. Each passing memory seemed to resonate with a harmony beyond hearing, the inheritance of a completed quieted mind...

Rough hands stabbed out of the blackness and seized him by the lapels of his coat. Opening his eyes, Jack saw only strange hulking forms wrested out of the dark surroundings. Before he could open his mouth to cry out an alarm for Pete's sake, a wadded handkerchief was shoved in his mouth and a bight of rope swiftly clamped over it and made fast. The pain shot through his face, touching on the deeper injuries to his already bruised temples. Jack's entire body rioted in rebellion, but the hands that seized him were too many and too determined. They began to push and guide him somewhere outside, sending him reeling. He could not see what had become of Pete; though he was so dazed he might well have stared him in the face and not registered it.

Someone kicked him hard; another kidnapper brought him roughly to his feet only to clout him with the butt of his pistol. Jack stumbled on, mumbling desperate prayers, driven savagely through the empty and blind country.

12. THE FACE OF THE ENEMY

JACK did not know how long they had been on the march
before the Sun met the tree tops, but when it did he was
finally spared a moment to rest. He collapsed onto a tree
stump and tried to relax his bound hands. The place on his
wrists where the cord pinioned them had rubbed raw,
drawing a fine trickle of dark blood. Thankfully the gag had
been removed, though his throat still felt like dry cotton.
One of the kidnappers came around and offered a ladle of
water. It was just enough to buoy his flagging spirits before
resuming the forced march.

Pete trudged along in front of him under single guard. He
was saddened to see that the boy had also been captured in
the middle of the night but relieved to know that he was still
alive. The kidnappers seemed less interested in Pete at any
rate. The majority of their spite had been delivered
unremittingly on Jack. There were periodic beatings and
profane verbal abuse, heaped on with malice. For many
hours he had failed to make anything of the men's
appearance; they simply had the looks of rough-hewn
woodsman. But as his addled brains eventually resumed
their normal bearings, Jack realized that two of the men
were the same ones that had appeared in Norfolk in
company with the white haired gentleman. Who is this
damned fellow, and why is he intent on my demise, Jack
wondered.

Regardless of the game was being played, Jack knew that

he should have been more cautious about the ginger haired man and his wife. Their unusual behavior coupled with a willingness to host him overnight should have given him more concern than it did. He had been a fool to write the quiet hostility off as mere eccentricity. The rebels apparently had far more influence on the peninsula than Jack had credited. With so many supporters living in the Tidewater the Virginians had a far more effective system of surveillance than Lord Dunmore had claimed. Jack cursed that devil for perhaps the hundredth time in the last few hours, though he knew that he could find fault with his own stubbornness just as easily. He was a fool to have been tricked into this dangerous contest, and he made a promise to himself that if he survived he would never again find himself trapped on the wrong side of this war.

Shortly before noon the troupe halted at the edge of a haphazard encampment. Pete was led to an open tent past a file of shirtmen who ambled away from tending their cooking fires to stare at the new arrivals. They wore long, dirty beards and buckskin trousers. Many were stripped to the waist to cool themselves in the midday heat. A few women were among them carrying buckets of water balanced on shoulder yokes; the women were the only ones who went on about their chores with almost mechanical regularity, ignoring the prisoners as an irrelevant interruption to their plodding routine. Jack watched the open tent fly fall shut after Pete had entered, concealing him from view. He hoped that he would be all right.

Two men took him under the arms and fairly dragged him to another field tent at the head of the camp. It was much larger than the others and had a pair of sentinels standing guard with muskets. One of Jack's escorts nodded to the guards and poked his head inside, muttering something inaudible. A moment later he withdrew and turned to Jack.

"You can go in on your own. They're expecting you," he said shortly, cutting his bounds with a small clasp knife.

As he rubbed the chaffed line on his wrists he ducked

inside the tent. He saw precisely who he had expected: the white haired gentleman. Now, however, the man was not dressed in his customary black frock. Instead he wore the seemingly ubiquitous buckskins with moccasins that reached to his knee. His prematurely white hair was pulled back tightly in a queue intensifying his strong, handsome features. He smiled thinly.

"Do join us, Captain Cunningham. We have been expecting you for the past hour or more."

Jack smothered a nearly uncontrollable desire to strike the man's smug face, forcing himself stiffly onto a short camp stool. The other man present circled around his field desk and handed Jack a large tin cup of brandy. He was likewise dressed in tanned skins, but his bearing seemed superior to any of the men Jack had encountered so far. He had a round, benevolent face with dark side whiskers just beginning to gray.

"Forgive Lieutenant Fisk's light manner, Captain," the man said evenly. "I had not wanted to resort to the methods of kidnapping if it could have been helped. As it was, however, I'm afraid it was simply too dangerous to allow you to roam freely about my territory."

"Your territory?" Jack said, half-amused. "That's erring on the side of assumption, isn't it?"

The man smiled. "Perhaps. Though I'm sure time will tell. My name is Colonel Alexander Selby, commander of this hereto unnamed and unnumbered regiment of Virginia militiamen. I believe we have a friend in common, if I'm not mistaken. Daniel Greene, captain of the free trading sloop *Shrike*. He and I have made many mutually profitable exchanges over the years. He had mentioned you as an uncommonly loyal friend. That is an admirable though all too rare quality in an acquaintance I find. But all this aside, I have to ask what you're looking for on the peninsula. You must know that this is a dangerous time for a Tory to bluster about the woods."

"I credit that you already know. I've come for the

Britishers your men took prisoner when the tender *Liberty* ran aground during the hurricane. It has upset Lord Dunmore most grievously."

Selby laughed, laying a hand on Jack's shoulder. "I'm sure it has, my man, I'm sure it has. But you needn't worry about them. We're simply playing with the fool to show him to be more careful where he sends his sailors. The seamen are being treated perfectly well. We can go see them if you like. I think we will release them in another day or two. Hard enough as it is to outfit and provision my own men without having to feed the enemy's as well."

"Is Captain Thomas Warren among them?"

Selby glanced in Fisk's direction. The militia lieutenant blandly shook his head.

"Not to our knowledge, Captain Cunningham. A midshipman was taken. Other than that they were all common sailors. I have never heard of a Captain Warren. Is he a friend of yours? If so I can assure you I would have been the first to offer parole to an enemy officer. Despite our rustic attire you can be assured that I expect only civilized and professional behavior in my men."

Jack stared accusingly at Fisk, though something told him that Selby was genuine in his sentiments. Turning his attention back to the colonel, he continued. "Warren was formerly in command of my schooner before he was kidnapped by shirtmen on the Rappahannock. I had heard that he was being held here by a Colonel Higgins."

Fisk and Selby braced at the sound of the name, as if a secret shame had been unexpectedly exhumed. Jack was surprised to see the effect of his words. What on earth could it mean?

"Is that Samuel Higgins you mean?" Fisk asked.

"That is the name that has been given to me. Do you know him?"

Prior to answering, Fisk searched the face of his commanding officer, apparently seeking his permission to communicate privileged information. Before he could begin,

Colonel Selby answered the question for him.

"He is not a proper colonel in any sense, Captain Cunningham. His men are not interested in fighting for the safety of Virginia. They are a vicious band of outliers that have no place in a dignified man's army. I fought with Higgins in the same company against the Shawnee. Even then he was known for avarice and brutality. I can assure you that if he were to step into this camp he would not be welcomed and you may also be assured that I certainly would not allow him to hold his prisoners here. He is more of a bandit than a colonel."

Selby seemed to be a man of some conviction, as well as someone that commanded the trust of a great number of men. Jack decided that the colonel was sincere in his dislike for Higgins and felt there might be the first stirrings of a possible alliance with the Virginians. Even Fisk, a man who had in no way disguised his animosity for Jack, seemed to share abhorrence for the blackguard Higgins. After Jack finished his whiskey he was led away to a small lean-to where he was closely watched by a pair of rifle toting shirtmen. He suspected he had been removed to give Fisk and Selby time to discuss what they should do about him, whether he was to be released with the other British prisoners or ransomed off.

Given the chance to take a closer account of things, Jack reviewed what he knew about the strange man Fisk. He was more mystified by him than ever. If Selby was to be believed then he had no reason to closely track Jack's every movement. That would mean that Fisk had singled him out for some reason of his own. But what could possibly have been the motivation for such personal interests? He never remembered seeing the man before the prior week. Surely he would have been able to recall such a lasting offense? He wracked his brains fruitlessly, finally giving up and turning his mind to a close observation of the camp.

Jack was surprised that the rebels were so well organized. Though there were undoubtedly some rough edges, Selby had assembled a creditable force. The men had come on foot, bringing supplies to sustain them through the season on the humped backs of mules and horses. Their weapons were simple but effective: tomahawks, rifles, clasp knives. No man would have dreamed placing them rank and file against well drilled British regulars, but only a fool that would have chased them into the dark coves of the Virginia back country. They each had the mien of seasoned woodsmen. Their bushwhacker methods could be exactly the style of warfare to upset King George's expectations of an easy victory, Jack realized.

A slender shadow fell across Jack's view as a visitor entered the confined space of the lean to. He expected it to be one of Selby's messengers. However, the light step was a whit too airy, the manner suggestively familiar.

"I should have known you were too much a fool to stay away," Charlotte reproached as she gathered her skirts and settled on top of a bale across from him, fixing him sternly in her narrow eyes.

If Jack had not been exhausted, he may have managed an exclamation. As it was, however, he merely lifted his head, nodded, and turned his eyes earthward again.

"You turn up like a bad penny, my Dear," he said, amusing himself.

"I see your manners have not improved as a result of your captivity. That is a shame. I had hoped you would have been humbled enough to at least muster an apology."

"I do hate to disappoint you, Charlotte. But you should know me well enough to know that I don't conform well to ill treatment. I lack the constitution for unjust punishment. There are those of us who dislike that sort of thing, you know."

"Don't be so damned difficult, Jack! We have more important things to talk about now. Surely even you can appreciate that."

Jack looked at her and smiled. In a way, he was grateful to see Charlotte here, unexpected as her visit might be. He wondered if she understood how dangerous a game she had involved herself in by aiding the rebels. He knew Dunmore was not above hanging a woman for spying. It was one thing to thrive on the excitement of intrigues but quite another to suffer a stretched neck from the hangman's noose. "I must admit, you are the last person I expected to see here. What has drawn you out?"

Charlotte glanced away, uncomfortable under the frankness of Jack's gaze. Her fingers played at the hems of her skirts, making a dimpled ridge in the fabric, a place to hide her hands. "You will not be pleased to hear the answer, I'm afraid," she said in an uncharacteristically apologetic tone.

Jack was surprised to find her so reluctant. Surely this was not the mark of the intemperate young woman he had hereto known her to be?

"Despite my love of country, I am not here strictly on my own account, Jack. There is a more complicated reason for the things we allow ourselves to do and I..."

"For God's sake girl, be straight about it!"

She composed herself with a sudden jerk of the head.

"Lieutenant Fisk and I are engaged," her admission came in a quick, breathless rasp. "He has been seeing me these past six months. Just last week he made his offer and I accepted. I hope this doesn't hurt your feelings too very much, Jack."

He roared with laughter. "My Dear, this is absolutely rich! You've been made into an honest woman."

"Keep your voice down, you villain! Do you not have a sense of decorum?"

"Quite right. I apologize. But do tell your fiancé to no longer bear me such ill will. I have no intention of obstructing your matrimony and I should damn well prefer not getting chased about and knocked on the head so regularly."

"I have already warned him about that. He is very passionate about me, you know. He gets carried away in these jealous fits and becomes some thing that absolutely needs to be tamed."

"I am certain you are the woman for the job," Jack said, smiling.

She simpered, but wisely ventured no further rejoinder. From across the small clearing Lieutenant Fisk emerged from the command tent and strode briskly across. He bowed gallantly to Charlotte, smiling faintly, before turning rigidly towards Jack.

"Captain Cunningham, Colonel Selby sends his compliments and would like a word with you. I am also charged with telling you that he intends to offer you parole in exchange for your word as a gentleman that you will not attempt an escape."

"You have it, Lieutenant Fisk."

He nodded stiffly. "Very well, please come with me."

He followed warily, healthily suspicious of Fisk's new found cooperation. As he entered the tent he was met quickly by Selby.

"Ah, good, Captain Cunningham. Please have a seat. I have been speaking with Lieutenant Fisk here and I've reached a decision regarding you. Another drink?"

Jack declined, preferring to keep his head as clear as possible for whatever mischief the colonel might be cooking.

"I'm afraid I wasn't entirely truthful about Colonel Higgins earlier. He did come through here late yesterday evening with a man who may be this Captain Warren you are looking for. I had no idea at the time that it was a King's officer because he was in such shabby shape. Very beaten about the head and bedraggled I'm afraid. Higgins and his men apparently are making public spectacle of him wherever they go. I refused to allow them to camp here but I suspect I know where they were going. There is a small fishing village about fifteen miles along the inside curve of the peninsula by the name of Elder's Cove. Not more than ten or twelve families from what I can remember, all fierce partisans when it comes to Virginia, but good people on the whole. Higgins may be staying there to provision and gather recruits. Now, I'm not willing to allow you to return to your ship and bring a troupe of marines against men that are supposed to be my allies. However, I will give you a horse and a guide so that you might have a chance of liberating your friend. Lieutenant Fisk here is my best soldier and the most experienced woodsman in this part of the peninsula. He will ride with you and give you any assistance that he can. Of course, it simply will not do for him to be seen in action against Higgins' men, so I expect that any activities you require of him will be as discretionary as possible. I hope this will meet with your satisfaction?"

Jack hardly knew how to reply. He had counted Selby as an honest man but would have never hoped for such support. The addition of Fisk— well, he could learn to manage that.

"You must understand, Captain Cunningham, that I will need certain assurances if I do this for you. I still hold your parole. Once you have found your friend you may return to your ship. However, you cannot take further part on the Britishers' side in this rebellion and still claim yourself an honest gentlemen. I'm afraid I simply can't spare a valuable prisoner like you for Lord Dunmore's cause."

"You hardly need worry along those lines, Colonel. My reason for doing this has nothing to do with the rebellion. I owe the good governor nothing."

Selby smiled. "I'm glad to hear it. Of course, you should know that I would not be opposed to releasing you if you were to take a different view of your loyalties. I hear that over in Williamsburg the Virginia Committee of Safety has been signing letters of marque for Colonial patriots. If one were to petition them for recognition, I'm quite sure one would be most welcomed."

Jack returned the colonel's smirk.

"I will take it under advisement, Sir."

"Very good. I suppose you are eager to be away. Lieutenant Fisk here will take you around to the horses. We will look after your boy here, make sure he is fed and what not. If I gather your intentions, I imagine it will be a damn sight too dangerous for that youth to be around."

"You might be surprised at his resourcefulness, but I agree; it is best that he stay here."

"Good thing. Captain Cunningham, I wish you the best luck and hope to see you and your friend here by tomorrow morning."

"Thank you, Sir. Good bye."

***

They rode at a slow canter along the hoof-pocked mud, the trail more heavily trafficked than Jack had expected. Fisk rode ahead, occasionally checking over his shoulder to ensure Jack stayed with him, but content to show his back for most of the ride. *Doubt if he's very happy about running errands for the enemy,* he thought. *Damn fine horseman though, no doubt about that.* After a few miles they turned off into the woods to better conceal their movement. Fisk handled his mount with technical precision, weaving in and out of overhanging limbs, jumping felled tree trunks and dry creek beds. Jack struggled to mimic his moves as best as his limited experience would allow; to his surprise, he came through with considerable credit. *At least he wasn't thrown,* he was congratulating himself when Fisk abruptly reined up.

Jack walked his horse alongside his guide to ask the reason for the delay when he caught a nauseating stench with the shifting wind. His horse shied under him, the beast recognizing as well as the men the unmistakable reek of death. He could not tell where the smell was coming from, but he suspected it was very near. Fisk pointed to the distant line of large hardwoods. Hanging from a long tether like a lump of tainted meat was the body of a man.

Jack drove his heels into the horse's flanks, plunging ahead. He clumsily halted at the edge of the small clearing and tripped out of the stirrups, staring up at the remains of Thomas Warren. He was naked and the skin on his thighs and stomach had been peeled away. His swollen purple tongue protruded from his lipless mouth.

Jack immediately cut Warren down and wordlessly turned to digging a grave with a small spade from his saddlebag. Fisk looked on without saying anything for a few minutes before joining in. In less than an hour, Warren was covered under his shallow grave and the men who had buried him drank a tin of whiskey. The early evening had come on and Fisk began cinching down his belongings for the ride back. Jack remained, gazing moodily over the grave.

"We need to leave now, Cunningham. It's best to go now while we still have some daylight. Easy to get lost out here once the Sun is down."

"I'm not going back tonight," Jack answered tensely. He poured a second tin of whiskey. He could feel the effects working smoothly now, allowing him to focus. "Your friend Higgins tortured that man to death. Cut him up like a piece of beef."

"He isn't my friend, Cunningham," Fisk answered tersely. "I'm sorry we were too late, but there is nothing to do for it now."

"How far to the village?"

"Not more than a mile." Fisk studied Jack closely. "You intend to kill Higgins?"

Jack nodded as he stood and shoved his pistol in his waistband. "You mean to stop me, Lieutenant Fisk?"

"No, I have no reason to want to stop you. Higgins is a liability. His behavior only makes Virginia militia look like a band of savages. If you kill him then we are rid of a significant problem. If, on the other hand, he kills you, then I don't have to worry about your intentions with Charlotte."

Jack laughed sardonically. "You are a pragmatist, Fisk; I won't deny you that. But you're an honest man too. Thank you for getting me this far. I wish you and your lass the best."

Jack turned and strode for the outskirts of the village. Pattering footsteps caught up with him a minute later. Fisk had retrieved his blunderbuss and now slanted it rakishly from his shoulder as he came abreast.

"Surely you will require some support in this venture?"

"I thought you weren't to be seen fighting your allies?"

Fisk shrugged. "I'm simply taking a walk through the woods on the lookout for wild predators. One can hardly fault me for taking precautions."

Jack found it difficult to repress a liking for his bold companion. If it were not for the Byzantine complication of Charlotte, Jack could easily see the two of them becoming friends. As it was, he was content to know that he was no longer bent on putting a sword through his heart.

As they entered the village the wide expanse of the bay suddenly opened up. The small fishing community was built on a sandy promontory that shot out from the interior woodlands. Below a forty foot drop a snug harbor of small fishing schooners bobbed at their moorings, grinding softly as they rose with the evening tide. The village itself ran along the rim of the bluffs: small driftwood shacks mostly with tile roofs, primitive looking yet entirely sufficient. A stray cur dashed about, yipping at a loose rooster on his way to tend an open hen house. At the end of the row was a larger public house that seemed to be the center of the evening activity. A man and two women loitered about the entrance, apparently sharing idle gossip, though they were too far away to be heard.

"He'll be at the tavern," Fisk said. "He's not a man known for restraint."

"Are his men loyal?"

"Hard to say. My guess is that they're loyal when they're afraid. Other than that, I don't believe they give a fiddler's damn whether he's alive or dead."

"So much the better."

Fisk dropped the blunderbuss into a straight line with his legs, trying not to alarm the villagers prematurely. The sand hissed beneath their boots as they walked the line of shacks and passed the talking villagers. As they stepped into the smoked filled tavern Jack opened his clasp knife and held it by his side. He waited for Fisk to identify him. The moments were spinning in long, concentric circles, seemingly endless. Jack noticed only patches of things: the clinging smoke, the quiet table of fishermen playing whist, the mottled wormwood walls.

"He's there, alone."

Jack saw the man Fisk indicated. He was shorter than he expected with a fair, pox marked face. He wore a tailored blue frock and ridiculous satin breeches. He was sunken in a drunken stupor, his bleary eyes barely open. Jack kept his eyes on that stupid sodden face as he crossed the low ceiling room and stood over him. Higgins' half-conscious face stared up at Jack without recognition.

"Samuel Higgins?" Jack said, his voice trembling.

The drunken man did not move his head but gaped his mouth unintelligibly. It was like looking into the face of a helpless idiot, Jack thought.

"It's him, Cunningham," Fisk said at his shoulder.

Jack leaned over the man, seizing him firmly by the coat lapels to steady his own hands, as he said, "For Thomas Warren."

He sank the blade four inches deep into Higgins' throat. The blood shot darkly across the table as Higgins lurched against his death with an animal's simple reflex. His eyes fixed finally on Jack with an expression similar to relief before clouding completely over. Fisk pried Jack's fingers from the dead man's coat and hustled him outside past the staring crowd. Then somehow they were running, the woods and sounds around them whirling into a fantastic blur as the night pressed in.

And yet no matter how far Jack ran, a vision of death hurried after him.

13. THE BROKEN SWORD

"I must protest this action, Captain Cunningham. You are committing an act of insubordination and treachery!" Lieutenant Porter roared as his men were driven into the gig at bayonet point.

Jack was in no mood to entertain his protests, legitimate though they might be. He turned to Isaac and asked him to bring the wrapped parcel from his cabin. Turning back to Porter, he invited him to walk the quarterdeck while the rest of the marines and their gear (with the exception of their weapons) were put into the boat.

"I am sorry we have to part on these terms, Lieutenant Porter. You must understand, however, that the nature of this conflict has a way of dividing a man's allegiance in certain ways. I respect your own decision, of course. Unfortunately, at this time our purposes are not in agreement, so I think it is best that you proceed independent of the *Gold*."

"Captain Cunningham, I beg you, please listen to reason! Surely you must understand that marooning marines of his King's navy is a serious offense, one that is not easily overlooked."

"Lieutenant Porter, I know exactly how serious the offense is. It is not as severe as throwing you and your men overboard, however. Besides, I will provide you with a compass and provisions to raise Norfolk. If for some reason this fails you, simply follow the shoreline south. You are a fine officer and I am confident you will be able to achieve your destination without much difficultly; I have no desire to maroon you. There is a package and a message I would like you to pass on to Lord Dunmore."

Isaac returned and handed Jack a narrow bundle of canvas approximately two feet long. Balancing it across the binnacle, Jack gently unwound the protective cloth to reveal his fencing rapier broken in two equal halves.

"I would like you to convey this to the Governor with the message that it signifies the end of our arrangement. Make him understand that it is not presented in terms of surrender but rather as an understanding of disagreement between he and I. One that I fear cannot be reconciled. I trust he will gather my meaning from this."

Porter received the sword, tucking it neatly under his arm. "You mean to turn rebel, then?"

Jack smiled but offered no reply. "It appears your boat is ready, Lieutenant Porter. I wish you a safe and speedy passage. A pleasure to have briefly served with you."

The marine officer reluctantly shook his hand and lowered himself into the waiting gig. The English marine bowman shoved off and the oarsmen gave way, beetling across the bay. Jack watched until they had made half a cable's length distance then passed the word to have the anchor hove to the short peak. As the crew made preparations for getting underway Jack strolled forward, past the mainmast and capstan, past the foremast, to the butt of the bowsprit. He gazed out along the powerful stroke of the beam's up thrust line, pointing skyward, as if in accusation to some invisible deity. He placed his hand there on the strong white oak, his shaking hand still marked with the stains of dried blood.

"Anchor's hove short, Jack," Alan cried. "What's her heading?"

Jack wrapped his hands behind his back and leaned into a stride for the quarterdeck.

"Away from here, helm. That will do for now."

The breeze rose and met the hard curve of the *Gold*'s sails as the schooner dug fiercely in, propelling her like a javelin into the heart of the Tidewater. There was life down in her, from the digging keel, up through the bowed futtocks, passing the rank crew compartments, and finishing somewhere high in the rigging above. Yes, it was still there, feverish and unremitting. He felt it.

He paced to windward, not saying a word to betray his rising emotion, though he could feel his heart beating against its fleshy cage. Homeward bound or be damned, Jack thought, homeward bound to Virginia!

NAVAL GLOSSARY

Amidships: The middle of a ship between the bow and the stern; also known as the "waist."

Beam: The maximum width of the hull.

Bilge: The lowest part of the hull where water collects.

Block: A pulley.

Boom: The spar extending at the bottom of a gaff rigged sail.

Close-Hauled: Sailing as close to the wind as possible. Also known as "hauling wind."

Cutter: A single masted vessel with a large main mast and bowsprit that can sail well either close to or before the wind, often used as revenue inspection ships. Also, a small boat carried on board a large Man of War.

Give Way: Command to start rowing.

Gunwale: The top edge of the hull of a boat or ship.

Halyard: A rope used to raise a flag or a sail.

Handsomely: To move steadily and smoothly.

Heel: The tilt of a boat to one side.

Keel: The lengthwise fin under a ship's hull.

Lee: The direction or side towards which the wind is blowing.

Leech: The leeward edge of the sail.

Port: The side of a boat or ship that is to your left when facing the bow. Also known as larboard.

Reef: To reduce the area of sail by tying up reef points.

Schooner: A two masted vessel rigged fore and aft; superior point of sailing close to the wind.

Sheet: A line controlling the position of a sail.

Spar: Any lumber used in rigging sails on a ship.

Starboard: The side of a boat or ship that is to your right when facing the bow.

Stays: Lines to support a mast, running from near the top of the mast to the bow and to both sides of the hull.

Sternsheets: The place in the stern of a boat with seating.

Strake: A hull plank.

Tacking: To sail in the direction of the wind by making alternate tacks as close to the wind as is possible.

Tiller: The lever used to control the rudder.

Transom: The panel forming the after end of a ship's hull.

Warp: a dock line for a ship.

Windward: The side or direction from which the wind is blowing.

Yard: The spar at the top of a sail.

Charles White is an avid outdoorsman and student of history, particularly concerning the beginnings of the American Navy and Marine Corps. He served in the Marines as an M1A1 Tank Crewman before attending college on the Montgomery GI Bill. Since then he has earned a BA and MA in English. He currently teaches English at Western Carolina University and Southwestern Community College. He is at work on the next book in the Jack Cunningham series, *Men of War.*

www.ingramcontent.com/pod-product-compliance
Lightning Source LLC
Chambersburg PA
CBHW051823020726
47502CB00005B/1607